Sabal Palms

and the

Stormy Past

By Terry Overton

Middle Grade Books:

Charlotte McMaster and the Messenger Angel

The Newton Chronicles series

The *Oddball Ornaments* series

The Messiah Brigade series

Adult Books:

Both Sides of the Border

The *Sabal Palms* series

Terry Overton

Sabal Palms
and the
Stormy Past

Ambassador International
GREENVILLE, SOUTH CAROLINA & BELFAST, NORTHERN IRELAND

www.ambassador-international.com

Sabal Palms and the Stormy Past

©2025 by Terry Overton
All rights reserved

ISBN: 978-1-64960-404-0
eISBN: 978-1-64960-453-8

Cover design by Hannah Linder Designs
Interior typesetting by Dentelle Design
Edited by Katie Cruice Smith and Lindsey Jones

Scripture taken from the Holy Bible, New International Version®, NIV® Copyright ©1973, 1978, 1984, 2011 by Biblica, Inc.® Used by permission. All rights reserved worldwide

AMBASSADOR INTERNATIONAL
Emerald House
411 University Ridge, Suite B14
Greenville, SC 29601
United States
www.ambassador-international.com

AMBASSADOR BOOKS
The Mount
2 Woodstock Link
Belfast, BT6 8DD
Northern Ireland, United Kingdom
www.ambassadormedia.co.uk

The colophon is a trademark of Ambassador, a Christian publishing company.

Prologue

The town of Sabal Palms has had its share of excitement in the last two years. Jada, a major hurricane, all but destroyed the tiny Texas coastal town. Most of the town's buildings and homes suffered damage that required repairs or complete rebuilding. Elaine's cottage was nearly leveled, and Bonnie's beach cottage was completely gone. Mary's house had part of the roof taken off. Adriana's house was the least damaged of the four homes. But the hurricane also brought people together. Elaine Smith's writing talent was discovered and served as the instrument of Divine intervention to reunite families and change lives from Texas to New York. A new partnership was formed between Elaine and an emerging country singer, Billy Wrangle, that continues to this day. Elaine was content to remain behind the scenes writing lyrics for Billy's music. She now used the pen name of Terry Overton, a fact known only by her closest friends.

Not long after the hurricane damage was repaired, a threat of a different sort arrived in Sabal Palms. A financial development company, Evergreen Recreation and Conservation Industries, attempted an unfriendly takeover of the little town. Coupled with the proposed financial takeover were other unwelcomed guests: followers of a new age religion group who attempted to change the little Christian Church on the Shore. But again, Divine intervention made His presence known. This time, a pop-up thunderstorm, common along the Texas coast, caused a plane crash; and pilot Trent Fortune, the Evergreen investment company mogul, changed his heart and became a born-again Christian. Along with the people in the community of Sabal Palms, Trent fended off the believers of the New Age religion and the proposed financial takeover.

And last Christmas, Elaine and her friends had a new Christmas adventure riding in the Christmas boat parade. Elaine then assisted a new young man, Chris, a widower, to find his way back to God.

Now that things had settled down in Sabal Palms, the town was busy planning activities to welcome the change of seasons along the coast. In truth, the seasons didn't change much from summer to fall on the southern coast of Texas. Both seasons could be hot and humid and had their share of unpredictable storms. But the lack of noticeable change between seasons never stopped the town and the nearby island from celebrating the arrival of fall with sandcastle competitions, monarch butterfly migration parties, and shrimp cookoffs. But this year, Elaine, Bonnie, Mary, and Adriana make a discovery that could change everything for Sabal Palms or place them in imminent danger. And added commotion erupts in the tiny town when a dubious stranger shows up and the history of ancient storms becomes important once again to Sabal Palms.

Chapter One

The large drops of cool rain spattered Elaine, Bonnie, and Bella, Elaine's dog. The rain had not been predicted before they took their routine morning walk along the shore. They were now mid-route and caught with no umbrellas or rain gear. It was not enough to be measured in the rain gage, just enough to drench through the walking clothes worn by Elaine and Bonnie. The tide was low, and the typical southerly sea breeze had yet to appear. The brief rain was not sufficient for the semi-tropical foliage, but it added to the oppressive humidity. Elaine believed the only thing worse than humidity when wearing wet clothing was swarming mosquitos.

Bonnie's hair was now sticking in strands to her forehead along with one smashed mosquito. She swatted the annoying insects, never successfully landing a single blow. "These things sound like helicopters when they whiz by. I just want to clobber them!"

Elaine swiped at the pesky bugs with equal effort. "Don't remember swarms of mosquitos being this thick in a long time. I haven't smashed even one."

Bonnie chuckled. "Me either. And I don't recall them being monstrous. And these blood-sucking rascals are quick." Bonnie stopped ambling and waving her hands in mad circles, stopped in her tracks, and faced Elaine. "Mary and Adriana meeting us at the coffee shop?"

Elaine gingerly stepped around the small jellyfish that had washed ashore and glanced at her watch. "Yes, in about an hour. And Trent said he'd pop in if he could. We should go back."

They turned along the warm, wet sand and approached Bonnie's beach cottage. Slapping at yet another buzzing pest, Bonnie said, "Okay, I'll dress quickly and be right over."

"You need to run any more errands while we're in town?"

Elaine waited for Bonnie's response and hesitated, thinking about her own plans for the rest of the day, which nearly always included cooking.

Placing her finger to her forehead, Bonnie replied, "Come to think of it, I might need to pick up a few items from the farmer's market."

"Sounds like a good idea. See you in a few minutes."

Elaine and Bella walked beyond Bonnie's beach cottage and up the slightly weathered, wet, wooden steps to Elaine's aqua and white cottage. "Come on, girl. Let's get you some breakfast."

Bella wagged her nub of a fuzzy tail and shook off the sand and raindrops from her fur. Having a miniature schnauzer on the beach meant frequent visits to the dog groomer and lots of brushing to remove the sand from the dog's gray and white furry coat. Elaine didn't mind, though. She couldn't help but fall in love with the tiny bundle of a dog abandoned after Hurricane Jada. Now, she just couldn't imagine her life without the little pooch following her everywhere in the house, those two dark eyes staring at every move. No matter where Elaine went, the two perfectly round black eyes fixated on each move whether on the deck, in the house, or on the beach.

Elaine set the small dog dish filled with dog chow next to the counter on the kitchen floor. "Here you go. Breakfast fit for my princess pooch."

Bella's munching brought a smile to Elaine's face every time she heard the little dog crunching her meal.

"All set, little one? I'd better get dressed." Talking to the dog was another habit quickly established after the puppy adoption. Bonnie and Mary teased her about the one-sided conversations Elaine had with her fur baby. But to Elaine, Bella was a family member; and the pup needed to stay informed of the comings and goings in Sabal Palms. She recalled the last time Mary questioned her about conversations with Bella.

"We all know you do it," Mary blurted out too loudly one day in the café on Main Street.

Elaine's face turned red as a tomato. "I don't know what you are talking about."

Bonnie chimed in, "Elaine, you know *exactly* what Mary is talking about. You talk to that mutt twenty-four seven."

"Well, Bella doesn't mind it one bit. In fact, she understands every word I say. She never talks back like some humans I know," she said glancing at Bonnie. "And," Elaine said with a laugh, "she never repeats anything."

Mary chuckled. "Seriously? You do know that animals don't really understand humans, right?"

Elaine ignored the rhetorical question. She knew perfectly well that Bella understood every word.

Back to reality, she thought. *I need to hurry. Don't want to be late.*

After a quick shower, Elaine donned a fresh set of capris, a Hawaiian floral print top, and dressy flip flops. Saying her goodbyes to Bella, she peered out the bay window and saw Bonnie shuffling along the beach toward Elaine's cottage. She grabbed her car keys, patted Bella once more, and locked up the cottage.

"Perfect timing," Bonnie yelled, waving a piece of paper containing her grocery items.

"Oh! Wait a second. Forgot my list on the fridge." Elaine ran back inside. Her return confused Bella, who assumed Elaine was back at home for the day. Bella wagged her tail and jumped around in a circle as if Elaine had been gone for hours. "Sorry, girl. You're going to stay. But I won't be gone too long." She patted Bella again, who turned her tiny head and looked up with sad eyes. "I promise."

Bonnie waited at Elaine's car until Elaine returned with her list. Elaine pushed the remote and unlocked the car. Bonnie huffed and plopped down in the front seat. The women were soon on their way.

Bonnie glanced at Elaine's lengthy list. "Wow. Are you planning on feeding an army?"

"Oh, no, just us girls and Trent—and maybe Billy if he is in town. I figured we would want to eat together this evening and continue planning for our own fall festivities."

"Who am I to turn down a meal?" Bonnie laughed.

"And a healthy meal, at that," Elaine added.

Ever since Bonnie's doctor broke the news that Bonnie was borderline diabetic, Elaine had taken extra steps to prepare food that would not spike Bonnie's sugar. All the women in the group were on board and offered food to promote good health. The women exchanged recipes, announced new discoveries of healthy treats, and shared healthy posts they found online. All the food was sugar-free and low carb whenever possible. In the process, all the women in the group were healthier and dropped a few pounds. No one wanted Bonnie to ever need medicine or insulin to control her sugar. In truth, the women were more like sisters since their husbands had passed away.

Elaine maneuvered the car out on to the main road toward town and turned on the Christian radio station.

"Hey, Elaine, remember after Jada? All we saw were blue tarps on rooftops all the way into town?"

Elaine nodded. "Yes, a solid line of blue-topped roofs down the road and more in town."

Bonnie continued, "Now there is not even one. Repairs completed."

"It's nice to see our town has been completely restored. It has the same quaint beachside charm it has always had."

Bonnie added, "And can you imagine what the town would be like today if Trent's plane hadn't crashed and God turned his heart and mind in a different direction? I mean, Sabal Palms a resort town? Horsefeathers! How crazy would that be?"

"It would be different. People would be crowding everywhere—packed shops, traffic, horns honking—oh my, it would have been a mess."

"Yes, and to think Adriana wanted a silly, old mall here."

Elaine smiled. "She now realizes she likes our little town just the way it is—palm trees lining the streets, beautiful homes with impeccable landscapes in town, and beach cottages on the shore. The feel of the local artists, shell collectors, and beach crafts in the shops."

"And of course, Billy Wrangle's music CDs and your devotionals are stocked on the shelves in the bookstore and gift shops—if only people knew your real name! I don't know why you don't want people to know who you are, Elaine!"

"Can you imagine, Bonnie? We would never have any peace and quiet."

"You mean the paparazzi would surround you?"

"Don't know about that, Bonnie. But I would probably stay inside my own beach house rather than get out very much."

Bonnie rolled her eyes. "Oh, I suppose."

Elaine turned the car into the small parking lot. "Here we are. I don't see Mary's or Adriana's cars here. It's unusual for Mary to be late."

Bonnie looked puzzled. "Is this a first? She is usually early. She's almost always the first to arrive! If she is on time, she says she's late."

Elaine added, "We know Adriana rushes in at the last minute. But you're right—Mary ranges from early to promptly on time."

The women entered the coffee shop and heard the familiar jingling of the bell on the door and the greeting, "Welcome to Sabal Palms Coffee" from Alexa, the barista, behind the counter.

"Good morning, Alexa," Elaine said.

"Hello, Elaine, Bonnie. What can I get started for you today?"

Bonnie replied, "Coffee with room for cream."

"Same," Elaine added. "Alexa, did you hear from Mary this morning?"

Alexa turned her back to Elaine and Bonnie as she tended to the coffee pot. "Haven't seen her."

Elaine and Bonnie took their steamy coffee cups to their usual table in the back of the charming shop beside the window overlooking the little town of Sabal Palms. The women could see everyone coming or going down Main Street.

Bonnie scanned across the café. Her eyes stopped at a table across the shop, and she frowned. "Look." She nodded toward a couple sitting at a small table. "There they are. The same couple we have seen before. She yammers on and on at him, and he looks at his computer and ignores her."

"Now, Bonnie, I am sure they prefer their regular routine."

"Routine? Routine of not speaking to his wife while she chatters away? What *is* he looking at on that computer, anyway? It must be something he doesn't want her to see."

"Why would you say that?"

"He always turns the screen away from her; and if she stands up and moves toward him, he shuts the laptop. Don't you wonder what he looks at all the time? Look at that smile. He must be up to no good. There is something he is hiding from his wife on that computer screen. I'd bet money on it."

"Maybe he is buying her a present online."

"Horsefeathers!"

Elaine swallowed her coffee and glanced at the other table. "What could he possibly be looking at that is bad?"

Bonnie laughed, "Oh, I don't know—a dating site? Or worse. Maybe it is one of those what they call adult sites."

"Bonnie, you have no earthly idea what he is doing," Elaine protested. "Maybe he is trying to surprise his wife by arranging for a trip together."

"Surprise her! Oh baloney! I'll bet if she saw that screen, she *would* be surprised!"

"Shhh!"

"Anyway, Elaine, you are always looking on the bright side," Bonnie said.

Elaine shook her head. "Bonnie, seriously."

"Pollyanna," Bonnie mumbled under her breath.

The jingle of the door quieted Bonnie momentarily. Gesturing to the door, she said, "Oh, look who is coming through the door. About time."

Mary, carrying a small shopping bag and decked in her green Save the Manatee t-shirt, blue shorts, and flip flops, arrived and placed her order at the counter. She waved at Bonnie and Elaine.

"I can't wait to hear what took her so long to get here," Bonnie said.

"I'm sure she will tell us if she wants us to know."

"Wants us to know? Hogwash! I'm going to ask her first thing when she sits down."

One thing was certain about Bonnie and Mary: they both had to know every tiny detail about each other. People who didn't know them might think they didn't like each other one little bit. But the truth was, they were best friends. Bantering and bickering was their quirky way of showing each other how much they enjoyed their relationship.

Mary brought her latte and sat down with Bonnie and Elaine. "Sorry I'm late girls."

Bonnie tried to hold her lips shut but she was about to burst. She couldn't hold back. "Spill it! Where were you all morning?"

"All morning? I'm ten minutes late."

The bell ringing on the coffee shop door distracted Bonnie's attention. "And here is the other tardy one."

Adriana's bling bracelets were heard jangling as soon as the door opened. The clinking of her fashionable bling reverberated from the front door and on through the coffee shop. Her bracelets made more noise than the steamer frothing the milk for Adriana's specialty drink. As always, her overbearing floral perfume arrived at the table a full two minutes before she did. Walking to the table, caramel latte with heavy whip in hand, heels clicking on the tile floor, Adriana loudly greeted the other three women. "Ladies, good morning. Do tell, what did I miss?"

"Other than being on time, nothing," Bonnie chuckled. "Now, Mary, back to your story. Why were you late?"

"Well—"

Adriana gasped. "Late? You of all people? This *must* be good." She gestured for Mary to hurry. "Come on. Talk already."

"Trying to. As I was about to say, I went over to the t-shirt shop to pick up the latest design. Made it up myself. Want to see?"

The paper shopping bag crinkled as Mary placed it on the table. She pulled the colorful shirt from the bag and proudly held up a bright orange, yellow, and black t-shirt with several large monarch butterflies strategically placed across the front and tiny ones scattered along the edge of the hem. In bold letters, the words "Monarch Migration Festival" adorned the front of the shirt.

With raised hands and jangling bracelets traveling up and down her arms, Adriana exclaimed, "That is exquisite! Amazing! I kid you not! Oh! Girl! Mary, you just outdid yourself on this design! It's marvelous!"

Bonnie rolled her eyes at Adriana's exaggerated response, then added, "It is certainly colorful."

Mary sighed and asked, "Did I overdo it?"

Elaine patted Mary's arm. "It is lovely. I think this shirt will be a hit this year as a fundraiser. What will be the price?"

Mary hesitated and replied, "Um . . . I think I am going to ask $15.95. Too much?"

Bonnie was the first to answer. "I'd pay it."

Adriana added, "I'll take two. A girl can't have too many t-shirts, after all."

"Great! I'll keep that price point. My cost is only $6.99, which means a good chunk of the sale of each shirt will go to the Wildlife Refuge."

A clinking on the coffee shop door brought another regular customer inside. A striking woman, at least thirty years younger than Elaine, entered the shop, bookbag on her shoulder and toddler in tow.

"Look," Mary said, "It's Kristy and her foster child."

"She is so sweet. There is a special place waiting for her in Heaven. She's a saint doing all that fostering," Elaine said.

"Foster?" Bonnie said, "I heard she and her family adopted the little blond-headed boy. Her own teenage kids love that little guy. I read in the paper that she and two other good friends adopted three boys, all brothers! The women are good friends, and they planned it so the three boys could see each other often and be together but live with each of their families."

"What a blessing for those three youngsters!" Elaine said. She examined the butterfly t-shirt. "By the way, that brings to mind another consideration. Mary, are you having child-sized t-shirts made for the festival?"

"I haven't ordered the sizes yet; but now that you mention it, it's a great idea. You know there will be plenty of parents and grandparents bringing their kids to see the butterflies."

Sitting at a table near the four women, Kristy sat the toddler in a chair; talked calmly to him; gave him his milk, fruit cup, and cupcake; and opened her backpack. She placed her computer on the table. "Now, let Mommy study for a while. Here are your cars."

"Isn't it wonderful women continuing their education?" Elaine asked. "And I love the new families with little children moving to the coast."

"As long as we don't have too many people moving here. Sabal Palms would lose its charm if it turned into a big city," Mary said. "And any additional new construction of developments of rows of houses would take away more wildlife habitats."

Bonnie grumbled, "Oh, you and your animals! I remember when we moved to Sabal Palms. My family was young. What a time we had on the beach. We didn't even think about animals and habitats. Just sun, sand, and the water."

Mary blurted out, "Speaking of animals and such, what is with these mosquitos this morning? I thought they were going to pick me up and carry me away! Why are they so big and so many?"

"Big as buzzards. But you're the wildlife specialist," Bonnie quipped. "You tell us why."

"No clue, but the fact that there was no breeze today—and by no breeze, I mean not even a smidgen of breeze—the pesky critters are flying around in swarms. We need more Blue Martins, bats, and dragonflies to eat the mosquitos."

"Bats! Ugh!" Adriana bellowed. "It took me forever to get rid of the one that hid behind the clock outside by the pool."

"You got rid of him? What does that mean? Bats are good for the environment!" Mary scorned.

"I just took the outside clock down off the wall for a few weeks. He didn't come back."

Mary breathed a sigh of relief. "Oh, I thought you killed him."

"Oh, I could never!" Adriana whispered and waved her hand dismissively. "Besides, he was creepy. I was afraid he would bite me."

Mary snickered. "He wouldn't have. They eat bugs."

Elaine thought now was a good time to refocus the women to the task at hand. "So, ladies, what was the purpose of our meeting this morning?"

"Oh," Mary said, "to plan our fall parties? Celebrate the fall equinox? Oh, and I heard another event will be happening, too."

"Do tell. What is that?" Bonnie asked.

"They are going to finally light the old lighthouse again!"

Adriana's mouth flew open.

Bonnie's eyes widened in disbelief. "Mary, you wouldn't tell me that unless it was the truth, right?"

Mary continued, "It is the truth."

Elaine thought for a moment but couldn't come up with the date. "Mary, when was the last time it was lit?"

"It has been over a hundred years ago. I read it was taken out of service in 1905."

"Wow!" Adriana exclaimed. "That is a long time ago!"

"We can add that to the list of our activities this fall," Elaine said.

"It is scheduled for December, I think. Anyway, no need to worry about that event just yet. But we do need to plan our other parties for fall."

"As if we even have a real fall," Bonnie laughed. "It is just as warm in the fall as it is in the summer. And the mosquitos are just as bad!"

Elaine felt she had to correct Bonnie on this issue. "Bonnie, the temperatures do cool off a bit in the fall. It is one of my favorite seasons here."

Bonnie nodded. "Good point. We can be outdoors more after the summer heat of August and early September."

Mary cleared her throat. "According to the calendar this year, the fall equinox will be on September 22," Mary clarified. "But at our latitude, 260° 6' 3" N, we don't see the twelve hours of sun and twelve hours of darkness until around September 27. Even if we don't get cooler weather that day, at our longitude and latitude, we will begin to notice a little less sunlight each day."

Bonnie rolled her eyes. "Seriously, a science lesson before I finish my cup of coffee? But that does sound about right—end of September, like you said. The temperatures are better."

"Fall equinox—that sounds like a good enough reason for a party to me," Adriana said.

Bonnie nodded, "Me, too. Any reason is okay with me. Oh! I can have a big party on my deck the day before the Monarch Migration Celebration Festival. Mary, you can reveal the t-shirts you will sell at the festival. When is the festival this year?"

"It will be the last Saturday in October. The butterflies come along the intercoastal water and on down to Mexico for the winter."

"That means your party would be the last Friday in October?" Bonnie asked.

"Yes."

"And of course, I'll have a pool party," Adriana gushed. "How about if we do that on the night of the equinox? That's when we had it last year, and it was a hit."

Elaine nodded and replied, "That's perfect. The night of September 22 will be the pool party. Temperatures will still be plenty warm in the evenings."

Another jingle of the door found all four sets of eyeballs turning to see an unfamiliar man entering the coffee shop.

Adriana gasped. "Well, well, well, hello! Who is that?"

Mary tapped Adriana's hand. "Get your eyes back over here now and behave."

Adriana turned to Mary. "What? What did I do? I was just noticing he is new in town."

The stranger, who was probably in his late fifties or early sixties, was amazingly fit for his age with salt and pepper hair and wore an expensive Hawaiian silk shirt, khaki shorts, and leather flip flops. He turned and nodded at the women.

Adriana's next gasp was so loud, Elaine feared the man heard her. "Adriana," Elaine whispered.

Adriana turned her crimson face back toward Elaine and said, "Girl, have you ever seen anything that looked *that* good at that age?"

Bonnie had had enough. "Honestly, Adriana, I think Antony is looking down and frowning at you this very minute! Besides, he is probably younger than you are."

"Oh, poor Antony," followed by Adriana's ritual of making the cross on her chest. "God rest his soul."

Once the women finally stopped gazing at the visitor ordering his coffee, the conversation returned to the nights of the coming fall festivals and how the women wanted to celebrate. But every few minutes, Adriana glanced back in the direction of the stranger in town.

"Want to have a party before the shrimp cookoff?" Elaine asked. "I'll be happy to host. I can see if Billy wants to entertain."

Adriana turned back to Elaine and bobbled her head in agreement. "Oh! We must! We had a party last year the night before the cookout. It was such a success! First Saturday in November, so yours would be the first Friday night in November?"

At that moment, the coffee shop door opened once more. Elaine gestured. "There's Trent."

Trent Fortune ordered his coffee, then shook the hand of the man who was waiting for his order.

Adriana watched every move of the man talking to Trent. "I wouldn't be surprised if Trent knows him. Maybe he invited him to visit Sabal Palms?"

Elaine replied, "Maybe. Trent knows many people through his investment business. I'm sure Trent will tell us."

Trent and the stranger talked for a while, and the women took in every minute. It seemed as if they knew each other. Once the conversation ended, Trent joined the women at the table.

"Good morning, ladies."

"Good morning," they chimed as heads nodded simultaneously.

Anxious to know about the stranger, Adriana asked, "Is that man a friend of yours?"

"Oh, that guy? No. I just met him. He introduced himself to me, said his name was Teddy. He wanted to know all about Sabal Palms. I explained I had only moved here myself last year, but it is a wonderful place."

Adriana quickly reacted to this comment. "Did he say why he wanted to know?"

"No. Sounded like a wayward tourist who wandered down the road from the island. He said he was in town sightseeing."

"Interesting," Mary said.

"Hmph," Bonnie snorted. "Tourists."

Trent sipped his coffee and then asked, "Did you ladies make some plans for the fall festivities?"

Since the celebration of the fall season was Elaine's idea, she led the discussion. "So far, we talked about a pool party at Adriana's house the night of the equinox in September, a party on Bonnie's deck before the monarch butterfly festivities in October, and a cookout at my place in November before the shrimp cookoff."

"All sounds great. Let me add one more idea. How about a party on the island at my townhouse?"

Enthusiasm spurted from Adriana's mouth. "Oh! That would be grand! Fantastic!"

Bonnie shook her head in disbelief. "I always forget you still have your place over there. Ever since you bought your house here, it seems like you hardly go over the causeway."

"Yeah. I think it is a good idea to keep the townhouse, too. It is a great investment, and my out-of-town business folks want to stay over there."

Elaine nodded. "Makes sense. And it is a wonderful place to entertain."

"When do you ladies recommend I schedule my party?" Trent asked.

Elaine replied, "Any time you would like will be wonderful."

Trent turned the planning back to the women. "What day do you suggest?"

For the first time that morning, all four women were silent.

Trent volunteered, "You know what we could do? Instead of coming to the townhouse, what if I host a gathering, just us and a couple of our other friends, and charter a sunset dinner cruise? You know, on the catamaran that stays right here in the laguna during the cruise? Oh, and no cooking required."

Elaine believed this was the best idea yet. "That is a splendid idea. I haven't been on a dinner cruise in . . . "

"Years," Bonnie finished the sentence.

"Yes."

Mary agreed. "Me either. I think maybe ten or twelve years since we all went on one like that?"

Although Adriana had been on boats from time to time and even went on a boat for the Christmas boat parade, she was still a little hesitant about boarding boats since her husband had died on a deep-sea fishing trip. With a sheepish look, she quietly replied, "Oh, I don't know . . . another boat?"

Trent looked directly into Adriana's eyes and said, "Don't worry, Adriana. The sailboat stays right here in the harbor, just like when we all went on the boat for the Christmas boat parade. Nothing out in the open water. You can see land the whole time we are out there."

Elaine patted Adriana's hand. "It will be a wonderful night, Adriana. There will be music, food, and a sunset over the water. A great way to see God's handiwork."

Adriana tapped her bejeweled and perfectly manicured fingers on the table and at last said, "That's it! Let's do it!"

"I was thinking it would be our final gathering before we start the Christmas activities."

Elaine nodded. "That would be a great time to schedule it."

Trent took his phone out and wrote the event on his calendar. "I'll make the arrangements, ladies. Hopefully, Billy can join us if he is in town."

Chapter Two

Teddy, the striking stranger who had entered the coffee shop, made his way around to each table introducing himself. He sat down, uninvited, and initiated his conversations with whoever would participate. His first stop was to zoom in on Kristy, the youngest woman in the coffee shop. She appeared to be in the middle of doing her homework on her laptop for graduate school. She politely let Teddy know she couldn't talk long. Her young, blond-haired son ran a miniature dump truck up and down Teddy's arm and Teddy smiled, abruptly pardoned himself, and went to another table.

Teddy then made his way across the coffee shop to the table where the husband with the laptop and the talkative wife sat. Once Teddy joined them, the man closed the laptop and visited. Elaine couldn't remember seeing the man and woman participating in a conversation together. Somehow, this new customer in the coffee shop managed to get them both into a lengthy and enthusiastic discussion. The three were still visiting when Trent, Elaine, and the other women finished their coffee, stood up, and cleaned off their table.

Elaine stopped, trash in hand, and asked, "How about we meet at my house for dinner later to iron out more details about our festivities?"

"You know me, Elaine. I'm always up for a meal," Bonnie affirmed.

Adriana clinking her bracelets as her arms waved around enthusiastically, added, "I'll be there! I wouldn't miss it for anything!"

Mary nodded in agreement.

They walked toward the front door, where Adriana glanced back at Teddy and then spotted a flyer on the bulletin board. "Look! It's the community garage sale. It is always terrific."

Trent took one of the brochures from a stand beneath the bulletin board. "This is clever. The whole community participates?"

"Yes," Adriana replied.

Trent opened the brochure. "Oh, I see. Inside there is a map with the route of the sale. Just follow the map, and it takes you to all these places. This is wonderful. A stop to raise money for the different churches, a stop for a fundraiser for the animal rescue center, the turtle rescue center, and the wildlife preserve fund raiser."

"Yes, some of the people are selling things they want to get rid of, like trying to clean their house. But others sell craft items and such to raise money." Elaine pointed to the brochure. "On the back are all the donation sites in case you want to donate money or goods to sell for these places here."

"Neat idea," Trent said. "Do you all go?"

Mary replied, "Usually do. Want to go with us?"

Bonnie returned from discarding her coffee cup in the trash bin and joined the conversation. "What's going on? Where are we going?"

"The community garage sale," Mary replied, "on Saturday."

"Such fun shopping! Only a couple of days away! I can't wait," Andriana said.

They walked closer to the door, and Teddy abruptly left the couple at the table. He walked rapidly to the front of the shop and intercepted Adriana.

"Hi, I'm Teddy, Teddy Carter." He extended his hand to Adriana.

"Hello, Adriana Manale—and it is pronounced with the 'e' at the end, Ma-nal-e. Italian, you know," she gushed, then blushed, and a girlish laugh trickled from her mouth. She swiped her perfectly salon-colored dark hair from the side of her face, jangling her bracelets and causing her dangling silver earrings to swing back and forth.

Bonnie and Mary rolled their eyes at each other.

"Nice to meet you," Teddy said.

Mary positioned herself beside Adriana and blurted, "And I'm Mary; this is Bonnie and Elaine."

"Hello, ladies."

While Teddy focused on Adriana, Trent continued toward the door and waved. "Ladies, I will talk to you this evening."

They waved back as Trent exited.

"Say," Teddy asked the four women, "what can you young ladies tell me about the beach?"

A faint giggle emerged from Adriana as she fluttered her eyelashes.

Bonnie gave Adriana a look then responded, "What would you like to know?"

"I am curious about the history of this place. It is very quaint. It's such a nice small town right along the coast. I am thinking of inviting some of my friends to join me here for a few days. I would like to know what to tell them about your beach here and anything interesting that has happened in the last few years. I understand there was a pretty rough hurricane here not long ago."

Adriana fixed her eyes in Teddy's direction and replied, "Why yes." Adriana, working full court press to gain Teddy's attention, continued, "We all experienced hurricane Jada."

Teddy nodded. "Anything change?"

"How do you mean?" Mary asked.

"I mean, sometimes, there are geographical changes—land erodes away, and so on, after one of these storms."

Elaine replied, "There was some beach erosion. But the sand trucks brought more sand out, and the town replanted many of the trees and grasses to hold the sand on the beach. It is a standard procedure here when the beaches erode. The sand is replenished."

"And once the misplaced alligators were placed back in their resacas and in Alligator Lake at the refuge and the land crabs were able to find new holes in the ground, all the animals were back in their natural habitats," Mary added. "Well, except for the few crabs that were run over in the road the day after the hurricane."

"You have alligators here? Interesting. No other noteworthy changes?"

Adriana again interjected, "No. The rest of the town was put back together and restored just as before the storm."

"I see. Well, thank you ladies for your time. Maybe I'll run into you all later." A wink purposely aimed in Adriana's direction appeared along with a smile on his handsomely chiseled face as he left the coffee shop.

Adriana's face and neck were now on fire, and it was obvious to the other three women that she was smitten by this stranger in less than five minutes' time.

Frantically fanning her face with her hands as if to lower her own internal thermostat, Adriana said, "My, my, ladies. Is it hot in here, or is it me?"

The other three simultaneously responded, "It's you."

"Oh my. He is so handsome." Adriana continued fanning herself.

"Adriana, Antony is still watching you!" Mary scolded.

"Oh, horsefeathers!" Bonnie said. "Antony has been gone for . . . how long now? Anyway, it's been a lot of years, and he might want Adriana to have a friend."

Mary piped up, "Oh, Adriana, that guy is probably married, anyway."

"No ring," Adriana protested.

"Probably doesn't wear one at the beach," Mary quipped. "A lot of men who like water sports don't wear their wedding rings in the water."

"Or if they are . . . up to no good," Bonnie added.

The red color disappeared from Adriana's face. "You're probably right. Oh, but, girls, he sure was easy on the eyes. Mama mia."

"I'm sure his wife would agree with you." Mary frowned.

Elaine was ready to change the subject and get going. "Bonnie, let's get to the farmer's market. Mary, Adriana, see you at my place around 5:30?"

The farmer's market, just on the edge of town, was a short ride away. The produce stands were filled with Rio Grande Valley oranges, lemons, limes, grapefruit, avocados, jalapenos, tomatoes, papayas, onions, dried chilis, red and green peppers, and small bananas. Jars of orange blossom honey were lined up on one of the tables. Pickles, salsas, and pan dulce, otherwise known as Mexican sweet bread, covered another table.

Bonnie turned to Elaine and gestured toward the display of produce. "Every time I come here, I want to go right home, cook up a storm, and eat like a pig."

"Me, too! And we'll have a robust dinner tonight with all these goodies."

Elaine and Bonnie examined each section of the produce stand, then got to work picking out the best items.

Gazing at the citrus stand, Bonnie sighed. "Wish I could eat more of this delicious-looking fruit. Never knew how much sugar was in an orange!"

Elaine patted Bonnie's hand. "I will make a sugar free lemon pound cake for dessert, and we will top it with strawberries."

"That would be great. I'll bring over some sugar-free whipped cream to top it off."

"Got that part of the meal planned." Elaine laughed. "Dessert first. Funny, it seems like we always manage to get that part of the meal planned right away." "I am thinking about grilling shrimp kabobs. We haven't had them in a while, and there are plenty of peppers here to choose from. I can use these and some mushrooms."

"Lovely. I'll make some coleslaw to go with it."

Elaine smiled. "Deal."

Elaine and Bonnie returned to the car. Elaine hit the remote to unlock the doors and placed the bags of produce in the back seat. As she closed the back door, a silver convertible whizzed into the parking lot of the market.

Bonnie gasped. "Will you look at that."

Teddy, driving an ultra-shiny convertible, music blaring, parked his flashy car next to Elaine's. Wearing designer sunglasses and smiling a bright white smile, he nodded and stepped out of the car. "Hello, Elaine, and . . . Bonnie, is it?"

Bonnie nodded. "Yes. Hi."

"Thought I would drive around the outskirts of town for a bit and take a look."

"Well, good to see you." Elaine opened her car door. "Enjoy your day."

"Bye now," Bonnie added.

Teddy waved as Elaine and Bonnie got into the car. Elaine steered out of the parking lot and turned toward the beach.

"What is with that guy?" Bonnie asked. "Why in the world does he want to go to our farmers' market, anyway?"

"Certainly is interesting."

"Interesting, my foot. Did he follow us? Is he stalking us? Is he looking for Adriana?"

"I don't think so. He said he was just driving around."

Bonnie grunted. "You are too gullible. I don't trust him. Something about him. I can't put my finger on it, but he is . . . I don't know . . . what's the word?"

"New? Attractive? Curious?"

"No. I was thinking more like . . . slimy."

"What on earth do you mean? Slimy?"

"Or maybe slithery. You know, like a snake. Up to no good. Like when the snake talked Eve into eating the apple."

"What is this? *You* are making a Bible reference? Good for you."

"I knew you'd understand what I meant if put it in your language, you know, referring to the Bible. Speaking of that, are you working on anything? A book perhaps? Or songs for Billy?"

"I am writing a novel—or trying to. And I'm still writing devotionals, but—"

"Elaine, you don't have enough faith in yourself. Look what your writing has done for other people."

"Who is this person in my car? Could this be the same woman who told me to give up Christian writing and write trashy novels to make money?"

Bonnie laughed. "It is true. You could make *real* money if you wrote that smutty garbage. I mean, those trashy things are on the best-sellers lists!"

Elaine laughed.

"But, Elaine, after all, you are working with Billy Wrangle. I mean, he is becoming well-known. That's cool and all. But I guess that kind of writing doesn't pay well either."

"Guess not." Elaine smiled. No one knew how much money Elaine made each month on royalties for Billy's songs. She kept all that quiet. Elaine had suddenly, almost overnight, made enough money to buy Adriana's whole street on the uppity side of town. But she preferred to keep the amount of her royalties to herself. She anonymously donated each week to the Church on the Shore. The rest of the money she deposited in a savings account thinking someday her earnings might dwindle or that some unforeseen circumstance would happen, and she might want to help others. It might rain on her finances one day; and she would need money to fall back on to get out of some kind of storm, catastrophe, or disaster.

"Bonnie, I'll drive you to your cottage, so you won't have to carry your bags of produce across the sand."

"Thank you. I'd appreciate it."

Elaine turned onto the long driveway from the main road to Bonnie's beach cottage.

"Thanks again," Bonnie said. "See you this evening."

"Okay."

Back at her own cottage, Elaine let Bella outside and put the produce on the countertop. Bella scampered down the steps quickly, found her little grassy patch in the back of the yard, did what she needed to do, then scampered back and scratched on the door.

"That's a good girl," Elaine said. "Now, Miss Bella, I need to get to work on prepping for dinner tonight and spend a little time writing before company arrives. Trent and the girls are coming over. I think I'll text Billy, too, and see if he is in town and wants to join us."

Bella turned her head slightly and wagged her little tail.

"See? I knew you understand every syllable when I talk to you—no matter what anyone says."

Elaine sent a text to Billy inviting him to dinner, and he responded right away. "Can't make it today. In the studio in Nashville. Be back on the island in a day or two. Get together in a few days?"

She texted back. "Sure thing."

"Well, Bella, that answers that question. Now, let me get the produce washed and put away."

After preparing for the dinner party, Elaine had only an hour left to write. She hammered out a few words, read them, then ripped the paper up. "I just can't think. But I know that wasn't right. Now, let me try again."

She placed another page of paper in the old typewriter and looked down at Bella who was looking at her. "I know girl. We will go for a walk this evening when our company is here."

Elaine stared at the white page. Her mind jumped from her page to earlier that day at the farmers market shopping and then to the strange man who appeared in Sabal Palms at the coffee shop. Bonnie was right. There was just something about him that seemed . . . off.

Something that felt . . . untrustworthy. Or maybe Bonnie planted that feeling into Elaine's mind.

She whispered, "*Judge not, that you be not judged*," Matthew 7:1. Bella, I need to remember that. Judge not." She looked at the paper once again, attempting to concentrate.

"What's the use? I can't think of how to start the sentence." Bella wagged her tail. "The well is dry, girl, and I'm distracted. Come on, Bella, let's go check everything once again in the kitchen to be sure we are ready."

Elaine opened the fridge, turned the kabobs over on the tray, and gave them one more swipe of marinade. She placed cherry tomatoes and different types of olives and small chunks of cheese on a tray to have as an extra side dish. At five o'clock, everything was ready. The lemon pound cake cooled on the counter, and the kabobs were skewered and marinating in the fridge. Paper plates and matching napkins and cups were ready to go. A large pitcher of brewed tea and sliced lemons and a pitcher of fresh lemonade finished off the preparations.

"Bella, how about your dinner? You hungry? I'll get you fixed up. Then I'm off to change my clothes."

Every day when Elaine dressed, she appreciated the joys of beach life and most notably the standard attire of beach dinner parties. Shorts, simple cotton shirts, and flip flops, and one could attend any dinner party along the shore or on the island. If one really needed to dress up, capris or a Hawaiian sundress worked.

A knock on her door interrupted her thoughts. "Coming."

Elaine opened the door to see a large bowl of coleslaw and a container of whipped cream teetering on Bonnie's arms and blocking the view of Bonnie's face. Elaine laughed and opened the door wider. "You look like you have more than you can handle there. Come in."

"Thanks." Bonnie entered, the large bowl of coleslaw bobbling from side to side. "I was afraid I would drop this slaw in the sand! And I couldn't swat a single mosquito all the way over, so I am covered with bites. Look at me! I look like I have the measles!"

"Oh dear! You should have called. I would have come over to pick you up. Wait, I have some mosquito bite ointment somewhere in this house that will stop your itching, and you will be good as new."

"That would help," Bonnie replied.

"But, first, let's get these put away. And then can you help me? I think I should put that big fan out on the porch when we eat to blow those buzzing critters off the deck."

Bonnie agreed. "Good idea or else we will have to move indoors."

Bonnie helped Elaine place the large fan outside and moved the table and chairs around to catch the manmade breeze.

Mary soon arrived, followed by Trent. As usual, Adriana was the last to arrive.

"Elaine, the big fan outside was a terrific idea. The mosquitos are brutal today," Trent said.

Adriana took one look at Bonnie and announced, "Girl! You look like you have a skin condition! My word! What are all these splotches? Oh dear! Are you sick?"

"Mosquitoes got me on the way over, and I couldn't swat them away because my hands were full of food! Flocks of mosquitoes. Do they fly in flocks? Anyway, now, I am about to scratch myself silly."

"Oh! Bonnie, I got distracted and forgot," Elaine apologized. "Let me get the ointment for you."

"As long as you aren't getting slippage!"

"Bite your tongue!" Elaine laughed, knowing that the secret meaning of "slippage" was when one's memory starts to fade away. Under no circumstances did anyone want to be referred to as the person with "slippage."

"I'll help you out," Mary said. She assisted Bonnie in slathering on the mosquito bite ointment. "There, I think I got you covered."

Bonnie looked down at her arms. "Covered! I'll say! This is a fine how-do-you-do! I'm covered with red splotches and a thick coat of white paste on top of each one." She rolled her eyes at Mary.

"That is quite a unique look." Adriana laughed. "But you feel better, right?

Mary huffed. "Well, I did what you asked and what needed to be done, Bonnie. Now, you should no longer be itchy—and don't scratch any of those bites!"

"Well, ladies, you will be glad to hear the town will be spraying for mosquitoes on Friday. I guess they want to decrease the number of the little beasts before the community garage sale," Adriana said.

Bonnie smirked. "About time. That doesn't help too much out here on the beach. Wish they would spray out here, too."

Elaine scurried around placing all the food and fixings out for the small gathering.

"Elaine," Trent said, "would you like me to fire up the grill?"

"Thank you. Anyone want a glass of tea or lemonade while we get dinner together?"

"Tea for me," Mary said. The others agreed.

Elaine poured the plastic beach glasses full of tea and passed them around. "And here are some slices of lemon for those who want lemon."

The group relocated from the kitchen to the chairs around the table outdoors. Trent adjusted the fan just enough to blow the bugs away from the table. He gestured toward the shore. "Should be a great sunset tonight. Just a few clouds. Something about having clouds over the water-always makes for a great sunset."

"I agree. And this little strip of beach we have here, it's the best view on the shore," Bonnie said. "Except for my deck, of course."

Trent laughed. "Indeed. Your view is amazing also."

The kabobs didn't take long. Within a few minutes, they were grilled to perfection. The colorful platter of grilled shrimp and peppers; a small tray of olives, tomatoes, and cheese; and the coleslaw were placed on the table, and the eating commenced.

"Oh! Elaine!" Adriana gushed. "These peppers! And these tomatoes have so much flavor! Get these at the market today?"

"Yes. All fresh today."

"The kabobs are as wonderful as last time! Fresh produce and fresh shrimp make all the difference," Mary said.

"And wait till you see what we are having for dessert," Bonnie said. "But speaking of the market, guess who we saw out there today?"

Mary blurted, "I give up."

"Teddy!" Bonnie said.

Adriana smiled, tried not to choke on her last bite of shrimp, and gasped, "Really? What was he doing there?" Her face turned bright red.

Bonnie continued, "Calm down, Missy. No clue. He just said he wanted to see the outskirts of town."

Mary looked puzzled. "I can't put a finger on it, but he seems . . . "

"Handsome?" Adriana suggested. "Dreamy?"

"My!" Trent said. "Adriana, you interested?"

"Oh, I don't know about being interested. I mean, you know Antony is always in my heart. But Teddy is handsome," she replied.

Elaine was never a fan of gossip. She wanted to change the subject before Adriana's thoughts triggered another hot flash. "Okay, to get going on our plans, we should plan out the details for the parties."

Bonnie swatted another mosquito. "Could we please not invite the mosquitoes to our fall events?"

Trent laughed. "I heard the forecast for tomorrow. Sounds like we'll get some relief from these bugs. That's the good news."

"Oh? What's the bad news?" Bonnie asked.

"Gale force winds tonight but decreasing in the morning. You might want to pull your outside furniture inside tonight. In fact, it is supposed to be stronger than gale force. But at least the bugs will be blown away or have to hunker down and won't bother us for a while."

Bonnie smiled, "My furniture is already in my storage compartment on the side of the cottage. But I'll take the southern gale force winds any day if it gets the bugs out of the way for a few days."

Elaine cleared the food from the table and brought out a tablet and pencil. "Anyone want to volunteer what you want to bring to the parties? Should we keep it consistent across all the gatherings?"

Adriana nodded. "That would make it easier to host these gatherings. I'll get my caterer to take care of all the appetizers, and I can add some fall décor for the tables."

"Oh flibbertigibbet! You know good and well I want to bring the desserts," Mary said. "And I can bring a side dish or two."

Elaine took down notes as each one spoke. "Okay, Bonnie, should we split the duties for main courses and each bring a side dish?"

"Sounds good to me."

Elaine stopped writing and looked up. "Wait, what about asking Ramon and Maria to provide some of their homemade salsas, chips, and tamales?"

"Yes!" Mary said.

Elaine wrote more notes about who was bringing what and the schedule of parties and festivities.

Trent smiled as if a new idea had come to mind. "How about if I arrange for the entertainment. I know if Billy is in town, he can entertain if he is interested. If not, I can get one of the small bands on the island to come over and play some tropical, Caribbean, country, or Tejano music. And, once we have the invitation lists made up, I'll arrange for the print shop to make the invitations. I can mail them out or hand deliver."

"Okay, appetizers, main course and side dishes, desserts, décor, invitations, entertainment, I think that sums it up," Elaine said. "Do we want to have different themes for each one? Or just stick with general fall equinox themes like last year?"

Adriana waved her bejeweled arms and said, "Either way works for me. I love shopping for the fall décor if we want to switch themes around. I can come up with a million ways to decorate, and I will shop in McAllen, Harlingen, all over."

"Adriana, you love shopping more than anyone I have ever known! You'll be shopping on your way to your own funeral," Mary said.

"Well, I would want to be dressed appropriately for that! That would be my last appearance after all. Anyway, a girl has to shop!" Adriana laughed so loud her earrings wiggled.

"I have an idea," Mary said. "How about if we ask Deb to make some of our wreaths for these events? She made the most wonderful one for me last Christmas. And she likes to make wreaths for all seasons. What do you think?"

Elaine nodded. "I like it. She lives on your street, Adriana?"

"Yes, two blocks down from me."

The planning and conversations continued along with the joking around and talk of town and church events to come. The sunset was one to remember with the pink, lacy clouds gradually replaced with orange and purple colors. Darkness took over the orange sunset; and soon, the bright moon crept upward into the sky and cast shadows along the shore. The group took Bella on a short walk and watched her chase the ghost crabs back into their holes in the sand. The dinner party finally came to an end; and Mary, Adriana, and Trent cleared off the table while Bonnie assisted Elaine in the kitchen.

When everything was cleared from the table, Trent suggested, "How about we help you get this furniture stowed away?"

"That would be appreciated," Elaine said. "Would like to have it secured before the wind picks up tonight. The chairs and tables are probably okay outside but not the cushions—better to be safe than have to search for them later."

Adriana stopped in the middle of lifting a chair. "Ladies, feeling like a morning walk tomorrow after all this food. I'd rather walk here than go to the fitness center."

"If it isn't too windy in the morning, then it sounds good to me," Elaine said. "You know Bonnie and I will be here. Mary, care to join us?"

"Okay. Haven't come out here for a morning walk in a couple of weeks."

"We noticed." Bonnie laughed.

In no time, the chairs and table were put away into the storage area on the side of the cottage. Trent, Adriana, and Mary then said their goodbyes. Bonnie stayed to finish the cleanup duties.

Bonnie paused for a moment after finishing up the dishes and gazed out on the water. "Don't we live in the best place ever?" she asked.

"Yes, indeed. We are so blessed," Elaine said. "Oh . . . the moon reflecting on the waves. I never get tired of looking out over the water and hearing the calming waves. It's like . . . God whispering."

"I like that—God whispering. Maybe you should be a writer." She laughed. "I don't think I will ever tire of looking out over the water, either. Look." Bonnie pointed down to the beach. "Is someone walking along the beach? It's usually abandoned by this time of night, unless it's tourist season."

The silhouette seemed familiar yet unknown.

"That's strange," Elaine said. "With an unknown person walking around at night, I'll drive you home after we get the rest of these dishes put away."

"Thanks. Better safe than sorry."

Elaine patted Bella and explained she would soon return. She drove to Bonnie's cottage and was puzzled by what she saw at the edge of the street and Bonnie's driveway.

"Well, what do you think of that?" Bonnie asked.

Elaine was shocked. There was the silver convertible parked next to the beach access walkway right by Bonnie's house.

Elaine was now feeling apprehensive about the situation. "It's Teddy's car. That's who was walking on the beach!"

"Yes. It is kind of creepy, right? Even you must admit it."

Bonnie frowned. "I'm not sure, but it is not typical this time of year. I would think a tourist would want to take a beach walk on the island. Why is he so interested in Sabal Palms? And our beach is . . . well . . . small, semi-private, and without tourist attractions."

"Maybe he has an interest we don't know about," Elaine replied. "Not interested in the same tourist-type things but interested in something else."

Bonnie retorted, "Something sinister?"

"Let's not jump to any conclusions. Just the same, lock your doors. Do you still have your alarm system working?" Elaine asked.

"Yes, you?"

"Yes."

"Do me a favor?" Bonnie asked.

"Yes?"

"Text me when you get home and tell me everything is okay."

"Will do. And you text me back. I'll watch you go inside. Now, turn on your porch light tonight and leave it on all night."

"You do the same," Bonnie said.

Chapter Three

Elaine watched Bonnie go inside, close her cottage door, and turn on the porch light. She waited another few minutes making sure that Bonnie didn't rush back out in a panic. All seemed quiet at Bonnie's place. Elaine drove out of the driveway and down the lane to her own driveway.

Once inside her own cottage, Elaine texted Bonnie. "All safe."

"Okay, call me if you need anything. Set your alarm."

"Will do."

Elaine's inner turmoil revealed her true feelings about this man. She seldom felt this level of anxiety; and when she did, she suspected impending danger. This was the feeling she had when there was a tropical storm or hurricane warning issued before a storm hit. Yet there was no known impending danger. It must be something else. Maybe Bonnie's comments about Teddy being a questionable character were the root of her uneasiness. She wasn't one to be influenced by the power of suggestion . . . usually. But this seemed unusual.

Elaine set her alarm once she was inside the front door. "Come on, Bella. Let me try to write one more time today."

Elaine sat before the typewriter and looked at the clean white page. She felt the need to write a devotional tonight rather than work on her slowly evolving novel. She typed the title and the top: "Trust."

She rolled the paper up a line. She almost jumped out of the chair when the sound of Bella's vicious barking began. "What is it, girl? Bella?"

Bella's barking continued and morphed into a growl. Then another round of barking and growling. Elaine slowly pulled the curtain back and peered outside. There he was again. Teddy. He was walking on the shore right in front of her beach cottage. He walked past her cottage and continued walking north. He didn't appear to be doing anything but walking and gazing around over the sand and water.

"I think it is okay, Bella. But thank you for keeping watch. Thank you for warning me."

Elaine was shaken and couldn't focus back on her writing. She texted Bonnie to let her know Teddy was once again walking around outside.

Bonnie's response was quick. "Jeepers creepers. What is he doing out there?"

Elaine sent the shoulder-shrugging emoji back, indicating she had no idea what Teddy was up to at this time of the night on the deserted beach.

"Should we call the police?" Bonnie asked.

Elaine texted back, "He isn't doing anything wrong. Just walking. It's a public beach."

Bonnie replied in a text, "Could be planning to break in or worse."

"I'll watch and tell you when he heads back in your direction. Keep your phone on."

"Will do," Bonnie texted.

How can I write about trust when I don't feel any? When right now I'm not sure I trust this situation? Right now, all I feel is fear. At the moment, I feel I have no control over what might happen next.

That's when she realized it. She knew what trust meant. She whispered to herself, "But wait. Trust means knowing even in unknown situations, God is still with me. I can count on God to fulfill the plans He has for me. I can count on God to have the final word."

Reasoning in her mind, she knew the only thing she could trust 100 percent of the time was God. That was where her hope, trust, and faith were. She stopped her typing for a moment and remembered a verse in Proverbs: *The fear of man lays a snare, but whoever trusts in the Lord is safe* (Prov. 29:25).

She said a prayer for protection and asked that He keep her safe. She prayed for God to watch over Bonnie and all her friends. She felt a calmness wash over her in that moment.

At the end of her prayer, she looked out the window and saw Teddy had turned and walked in the other direction. She texted Bonnie, "He is heading your way. Watch for him to go to his car."

"Thank you. I'll text and let you know when he does."

Elaine, thankful for the calmness she felt after praying, sat back at her typewriter and began typing the devotional once again. She typed one complete sentence, then another. She completed the third sentence, and then Bonnie texted.

"He just walked by and is going to his car."

"Good," Elaine responded.

"Okay, he just got in his car and is driving down the road."

"Thank you. And thank God. We are both safe. Now, get some rest, and I will see you for our morning walk tomorrow," Elaine texted.

Bonnie replied, "See you then."

Elaine continued working on her devotional until she felt sleepy. She left the paper in the typewriter. The devotional was only half finished, but she wanted to think about it and continue it tomorrow. She wanted to feel more relaxed and that her safety was completely restored. She knew she needed a good night's sleep and would think more clearly tomorrow.

Bella yawned.

"You're right, Bella, it's time for bed."

With that, Bella got up from her spot beside the desk and crept into her fuzzy bed placed beside Elaine's.

At 4:31 AM, Elaine was awakened by a banging noise outside. Bella began her barking once again. Her heart raced. *Please, Lord, let this be nothing to fear.* She went to the window where she had a wide view of the beach and looked. *Nothing there. Nobody on the beach.* She heard the wind howling and then the banging noise again.

Bella growled and turned her head.

"Okay, girl, I'll go look."

Elaine grabbed her robe and took a flashlight from her night table. Her shaking fingers punched in the code and turned off the alarm system. She opened the front door; and the wind, howling harshly and blowing sand along the beach, yanked it out of her hands and toward the outside wall. The water's edge was almost completely obscure in the moonlight. She stepped out onto the deck, walked around the side of the cottage, and shielded her eyes from the blowing sand. With both relief and irritation, she discovered the origin of the noise. The side storage door wasn't latched properly. She tugged the door back into place and fastened the latch securely.

She turned to go back into her cottage. Then she saw it. Facing the shore once again, she saw a shadow in the distance heading north.

She could barely make out the shape because of the blowing sand. *Is it . . . It is. Why is Teddy back out here looking in the blowing sand in the middle of the night?*

She ran back inside the cottage, hoping she hadn't been detected by Teddy. She locked her door and shakily put the alarm system back on. Her heart was pounding as loudly as the storage door had banged. She went back into her bedroom, patted Bella, and climbed under her covers.

This is crazy. I can't even relax enough to fall back to sleep. Why is a strange man walking around in the middle of the night?

She said another prayer; and reluctantly, she got out of bed and switched on the coffee pot. Bella followed her into the kitchen, cried a soft cry, and turned her head.

"I know, girl. It's early. Still dark outside. I'm going to work a little while before we go outside."

Coffee in hand, Elaine returned to her typewriter and typed out a few more sentences. She read and reread the devotional. Then, like so many times before, she crumbled up the paper and threw it in the trash can beside her desk. She didn't think it was good enough for anyone to read. She felt uneasy again about this strange man walking on the beach in the dark.

"Okay, girl, the sun won't be up for a while yet. I'm going to read Scripture and finish this cup of coffee. We will go for our walk in a little while."

Sitting in her favorite comfy reading chair, warm mug of coffee in hand, she read several verses. Then she stopped. She listened. Something had changed. The gale force wind had died down to a murmur of a breeze.

When the first light of day was faintly evident through the window, Elaine dressed and went out on the deck. She unlatched the storage door and took her furniture back out onto her deck. She poured her second cup of coffee and took it outside. Bella joined her after making a quick stop in her grassy patch. A small sliver of light began to rise over the water; and within minutes, Elaine felt as if the morning breeze had wrapped her in the pink, yellow, and orange hues of the sunrise sky. The temperature was slightly cooler than yesterday, and the humidity didn't seem to be as thick. She looked south toward Bonnie's cottage and saw Bonnie trudging up the sand dressed for their morning walk.

"Morning," Bonnie called out.

"Good morning."

"Guess the other girls will be on their way out in a few."

"Yes. Want some coffee?"

"Sure. Had one cup but I think it is a two-cup morning."

Elaine went inside, then soon returned with a cup and handed it to Bonnie.

Bonnie took a sip. "Yes, I was right. Second cup should do the trick. The air feels a tad cooler today."

Elaine sipped her coffee and nodded. "I think so, too."

Bonnie put her cup on the table. "What was all that about last night? Why would that Teddy guy be walking back and forth?"

"No clue. But tell you something else. I heard this awful banging around 4:30 when the wind blew in and had to get up to see what was making that noise."

"Was it him?"

"No, it was the door on the side of the cottage. I didn't latch it correctly after we stored the furniture. Anyway, I latched the door; and then when I turned to go back inside, I saw him again. He was walking north again."

The sound of Mary's car driving over the crushed shell driveway interrupted their conversation. She walked up the wooden steps to Elaine's deck while Bonnie continued to pepper Elaine with questions.

Bonnie asked, "In the gale force winds? In the middle of the night?"

"Yes. I almost couldn't see him because the sand was blowing so hard. But it was a man walking back up the same way. It looked like him."

Puzzled, Mary asked, "Who? What are you talking about? Somebody walking in the wind last night? What's going on?"

"We were talking about Teddy," Bonnie said.

"What about him?"

Elaine said, "We saw him again last night on the beach. Walking to the north and the south again."

"Tell her the rest," Bonnie insisted.

"Around 4:30 last night, I got up to close the door of the storage room; and he was out there again."

"What in the world? That makes no sense whatsoever."

Undetected by the others, Adriana appeared on the deck. "What doesn't make sense?"

Bonnie and Elaine told Adriana and Mary about the visits during the night by Teddy.

Adriana gasped. "That sounds bizarre. Oh, my stars! Why would he be out here so late?"

Elaine sighed. "That's what we are wondering."

"Enough talking," Bonnie said. "Let's get some walking in. Gotta keep my blood sugar low."

Elaine agreed and glanced at her friends. Like each time the four women went walking together on the beach, her friends' individual attire brought a smile to her face. Their clothing was distinctive and said much about their individual personalities. Mary was dressed in an animal t-shirt and very casual shorts; Bonnie was dressed in a functional and somewhat athletic-looking set of matching shorts and a shirt; and Adriana was dressed in a striking, fashionable bright blue yoga top trimmed in white, black running shoes with blue trim, a black headband decorated with blue beads, and simple blue plastic bracelets that didn't jingle but made a rattling noise with each step she took.

Mary held up her hand. "Wait. Let's walk to the north. Maybe we can figure out why this Teddy fellow keeps walking up that way."

The others agreed and turned in the opposite direction. Bella scampered along in the sand beside Elaine regardless of the direction she walked. Her short legs meant she had to walk a fast pace to keep up with Elaine's stride.

The women walked and talked for thirty minutes. Most of the chatter was centered on two topics: the mysterious Teddy and the upcoming community garage sale.

Elaine checked the sun's position and realized they had been walking for a while. "Ladies," Elaine said, "should we turn around?"

Bonnie nodded. "Good idea."

"Nothing unusual up this way anywho." Mary shrugged.

Out of nowhere, Adriana screeched, "Oh!"

"What?" Bonnie asked.

"Just thinking about the garage sale in two days! Oh! There will be some bargains!"

"You scared the dickens out of me!" Mary scolded. "I thought you stepped on a jellyfish or something."

"No. But I have been thinking about the sale route. It might take most of the day to get through all the stops on the garage sale map. So many things to see! You know there will be some bargains! How can we make sure we don't miss anything? I'm wondering, should we prioritize?"

Mary shook her head. "How in the world do you prioritize people selling junk out of their garage?"

Elaine pondered the question. "We could prioritize by which ones are raising money for charity."

"Oh!" Mary exclaimed. "That's it! Let's go to the ones raising money for the wildlife organizations and the church first to be sure we don't miss those."

"Hmmm, anyone else notice she put the animals before the church?" Bonnie teased.

"You know what I mean!" Mary said. "Both are important."

"Good grief!" Adriana's high-pitched voice pierced through the morning breeze.

"Adriana, I was just teasing Mary about animals before church," Bonnie said. "Don't get worked up."

"No, that's not it. It's my toe! Look! What is this thing that nearly broke my toe?"

Bella ran to the protruding small, wooden stump and sniffed. The other three women circled around Adriana's foot.

"Goodness, that must have hurt," Elaine said. "Are you okay? Isn't that interesting? It isn't driftwood like from a tree or something."

Ignoring concern for Adriana's foot, Bonnie stooped lower and moved away some of the sand to expose the wooden protrusion. "That's crazy. It looks like a big wooden peg and a piece of a board."

"Don't suppose this is what Teddy was trying to find?" Mary asked.

"My foot is fine, thanks for asking." Adriana laughed.

"Baloney! Why would anyone be looking for a worn piece of wood?" Bonnie chortled.

Elaine wondered if Mary was right. "Now hold on, Bonnie. Maybe he was looking for this piece of wood, but why? What is it?"

"Piece of a wrecked ship?" Bonnie asked. "Or an old piece of furniture like a trunk or something?"

"Maybe so. He could be one of those treasure hunters that spends millions of dollars to find sunken treasure and ends up with a piece of rotten wood and a t-shirt that says, 'I'm a treasure hunter' or 'I'm Long John Silver' or some ridiculous pirate thing," Mary said. "In the meantime, the natural habitat of sea life and the shore is disturbed by their equipment and excavation of the underwater world. I mean there are 272 species of saltwater fish out there."

"Fiddlesticks! The wildlife again!" Bonnie laughed.

"Well, whatever this thing is, it should end up in the museum in Port Isabel, don't you think?" Elaine asked.

"I'll call the museum today," Mary said. "I know the curator. I can tell him where the wooden piece is and see if he wants to come over and take a look. We shouldn't disturb it."

Elaine looked at Adriana's foot. "You sure you're okay to walk back?"

Adriana, known to exaggerate everything, smiled, and replied, "Oh, yes. I just stumped my toe. But I am fine." Nevertheless, she limped for a few steps, moaned, and then returned to her brisk walking pace with the others.

Bonnie said, "Well, ladies, I'm ready to eat something. I'm getting hungry."

Two days later, Elaine collected Bonnie and Mary and went to Adriana's house to pick her up. The group decided they would carpool along the community garage sale route.

Elaine arrived in front of Adriana's house and honked her horn. No movement detected. Elaine, Bonnie, and Mary sat inside the car, waiting.

"Well, good grief," Mary said. "As excited as Adriana is about shopping, you'd think she would be standing on the curb."

Bonnie huffed, "Late as usual. She truly will be the only person late to her own funeral."

"I'm sure she is just locking up the house and will be right down," Elaine said.

Five minutes later, Adriana, dressed in a fetching new Hawaiian top and coordinated pants and sandals, joined Mary, Bonnie, and Elaine to begin the journey. "You ladies ready for this stop and shop?"

"Been ready the whole time we were sitting out here in the street." Mary laughed.

Adriana looked at Mary. "I'm sorry. Had to change earrings to go with this new blouse. You know, a girl can't go shopping in just any old earrings."

Bonnie rolled her eyes and looked at Adriana. "That's why I hardly ever wear them. Only have four pair of earrings, anyway. Less to worry about when I'm in a hurry—you know, a hurry to be *on time* somewhere. Ever done that?"

Adriana, changing the topic, said, "Haven't seen you girls in two days. Any news? Anyone seen that handsome new guy? You know . . . Teddy?"

"You mean the midnight stalker?" Bonnie snarked.

Mary sighed. "Adriana, you are certainly interested in that fellow."

Adriana's face turned crimson. "No, no. I'm not interested—just curious."

Elaine hadn't seen or heard from Teddy since the night he had walked on the beach at all hours. She was relieved she hadn't spotted him walking on the beach again.

"Say, I meant to tell you," Mary said, "the curator called me back. He said they took the pieces of wood from the beach and are sending them to be analyzed."

"Pieces?" Elaine asked.

"Yes, he said they found a few pieces near the one we saw just a couple of miles south on the beach. He is going to have them tested to find out more information."

Bonnie laughed. "I'll save them the trouble. I can analyze the wood for them. They are just rotten pieces of wood."

"The curator thinks it might be antique or pieces of an old ship. Guess we will wait and see."

Elaine wondered about the process. "When will they know something?"

Mary replied, "He said it could be weeks or months. Depends on how busy the lab of the Texas Historical Commission is I think."

"Horsefeathers, Mary! How do they determine anything about a piece of rotten wood sticking out in the sand?"

"He told me they will send it off and analyze it using a wiggle-match dating analysis—"

Bonnie blurted out laughing. "Wiggle-match? What in the world?"

"For your information, Bonnie, it is a method of dating a tree-to see how old the wood is."

"Oh. Who knew?"

"Interesting." Elaine turned toward the other women. "Where to, ladies?"

"Thought we were going to the sales addresses of the ones raising money for the animal shelter and wildlife refuge first," Mary reminded her.

"Ladies!" Adriana's bracelets jingled with every word. "I know we will visit those places, but I heard the other day that the Martinezes said they would be selling some of their furniture."

Bonnie turned to face Adriana in the back seat. "You mean the Martinezes who own the antique store on the highway?"

"Yes. The very ones. I'm hoping they have put some of the collectable pieces in the sale. Would be nice to see them up close. Maybe we should go there first so we see the best pieces. And it is the nearest stop on the map. Just down this block." She pointed. "Look, the cars are already parked down there."

"Sounds okay to me," Mary agreed. "Then we head to the charities stops."

"Okay with me, too," Bonnie said.

"Martinezes' it is. Trent asked me to text when we go to the animal shelter stop. He said he would meet us there, then maybe go to coffee shop?"

"Let's go!" Adriana exclaimed.

The street in front of the Martinezes' large Southern colonial-style home was blocked with vehicles, including trucks with their owners in progress of loading furniture.

Adriana sighed. "Hope there are some collectibles left for us to see."

The women walked down the sidewalk past two homes and a line of cars and trucks and joined the crowd at the Martinezes' home.

Elaine examined the remaining pieces of furniture. Adriana was right. These pieces were old—extremely old and no doubt very expensive. Nothing at all would go with furnishings inside her beach cottage and she was not shopping for furniture. Nevertheless, she looked each piece over, admiring the intricate details. Each piece had a card with information regarding the age and history. She was drawn to an unusual piece. It was clearly the oldest piece in the Martinezes' sale. The card described the piece as one made in the 1620s and said, "Only serious offers, not garage sale priced. Chest of Drawers Made by William Searle."

Adriana needs to see this, she thought. She left the piece, which was one of the few inside the garage, and scanned the outside yard lined with other pieces of furniture to find Adriana. That was when she saw him. Teddy was outside, talking to Mr. Martinez, who then pointed to the very piece Elaine had just examined.

What is he doing here?

Chapter Four

When she saw Teddy, Elaine hoped the look of shock on her face wasn't obvious to everyone at the yard sale. She looked around for Mary, Bonnie, and Adriana. They were walking toward her.

Bonnie grabbed Elaine's forearm. "You see him, too?" Bonnie asked.

Elaine nodded.

Teddy walked beside Mr. Martinez to the antique wooden chest of drawers. The unusual heavy-looking piece was unusual because it had doors covered with decorative carved swirls, plant stems, and leaves that hid the drawers. Mr. Martinez opened the ornate doors, pulled out each drawer, and continued the discussion.

Elaine stood to the side of the garage with the other women. She noticed an area, at the top of the typical sized drawers, was a compartment with individual slots and other smaller drawers. The top compartment looked like an old secretary type desk where one would keep important papers, keys, and the like. Teddy was particularly interested in that section of the chest.

Another customer approached Mr. Martinez and said, "Excuse me, can you tell me more about this dining table over here?" Mr. Martinez left Teddy and accompanied the woman to the antique piece on the other side of the garage.

Teddy continued examining the chest of drawers. He pulled out each individual drawer. Each time he pulled out a drawer, he attempted to lift the bottom liner of the drawer. Elaine wondered if he was testing the quality of the antique wood or if he was trying to determine if the drawers had false bottoms where something might be hidden underneath. Then Teddy examined each individual smaller compartment above the other drawers. He appeared to be searching for something rather than admiring the intricate carved work of the furniture.

Mary watched Teddy's every move. She moved closer to Elaine and tried to be discrete as she whispered, "What is he doing now? He's an interesting character, for sure."

Adriana gasped, placed her hand on her chest and said, "If he is interested in buying *that* chest, he must have a lot of money. And I mean a lot."

Bonnie couldn't let that remark go unanswered. "Okay, spill it. Tell me. What does a piece of old furniture like that go for? I mean, usually?"

Adriana mumbled, "Hmm, ah, probably $12,000 or more. No real way to know without doing some research."

Mary grunted. "I don't care if he does have money. He just seems . . . "

"Interesting?" Adriana said. "A discerning buyer with excellent taste?"

"Nope. I'm thinking more like sneaky," Bonnie said.

"Well, no matter what you think, I think he is charming and handsome." Adriana grinned. "And probably wealthy."

Elaine watched Teddy inspect every inch of the chest of drawers. Maybe he was perfectly okay, just quirky. She didn't want to judge him. She didn't know him. She watched him as he continued a thorough investigation of the chest. His examination of this unique piece of furniture was not what Elaine would expect of a potential buyer. He seemed to be searching for something specific, not merely inspecting the furniture for purchase. Elaine wondered if Teddy believed there was something valuable, or even sentimental, inside one of the compartments or drawers. He rifled through the entire chest again. With disappointment, he turned and walked out of the garage and down the street to his flashy silver convertible.

Adriana, looking like a lost puppy, wandered from the garage stuffed with antiques, followed Teddy with her eyes as he walked down the street, then turned to look at other more affordable pieces of furniture. Adriana touched a piece of furniture, but she continued looking beyond the furniture piece. Elaine believed Adriana was watching Teddy walk the full distance to his car.

Bonnie groaned and mumbled to Elaine, "He is such a weirdo."

Mary nodded. "Agreed. But don't say anything to Adriana."

"Why? It's not like she knows him personally or has a relationship with him. He's just plain strange."

Elaine didn't want to contribute to the negative perceptions already held by Bonnie and Mary. "Now, ladies, he might be okay. We don't know him at all. We shouldn't judge him."

Bonnie blurted, "Maybe he'll just go away. He has been in town now for . . . what? Four or five days?"

Mary huffed. "Yes, he has been here most of the week, I think. Anyway, I've seen enough of this old stuff we can't afford; and frankly, I don't even like it. Not my taste."

Bonnie agreed. "Let's move on to the first stop for the animal rescue center fundraiser."

"Ready," Elaine said. "Adriana, ready to move on?"

Adriana's arms brushed against her Hawaiian print shirt, jingling her bracelets. "Of course, I'm ready. Let's go."

Elaine unlocked the car for the others and sent a text to Trent. She let him know they were on the way to the next shopping destination and asked him to meet the group there.

After a short drive, they arrived at the next stop on the community shopping map. Elaine parked the car, noticing the lighter crowd. "Doesn't look like too many shoppers yet."

Bonnie remarked, "All the early curious shoppers are probably still back there looking at stuff that is older than dirt."

Adriana enthusiastically rebuffed the remark and waved her hands as she announced, "I never dreamed the Martinezes had such a unique collection of antique furniture! The items in the collection the Martinezes were selling were exquisite! Absolutely remarkable."

Mary replied, "Remarkably unaffordable."

"They were priced pretty high," Adriana agreed. "But considering those specific pieces are investments for people who purchase them, the prices are likely no higher than prices other antique dealers have on their furniture. It is a very high caliber of furniture, after all."

Elaine saw Trent and waved as he walked up the street to join the women. "Good morning."

"Hello, did you make it to the Martinezes' already?" Trent asked.

Adriana's arms waved about with her noisy bracelets jangling and burst out, "Yes! It was fantastic! Amazing, in fact. They had pieces there from William Searle."

"Seriously?" Trent asked. "Those hand-carved pieces are old. Very old. I'm surprised they were selling them in a garage sale."

Adriana put her arm in Trent's to walk up the sidewalk to the yard sale. "I knew you were a man of impeccable taste."

Trent smiled. "Tell me, Adriana, did they have the prices displayed on those pieces?"

"Sadly, no. Just that they would take serious offers. Not sure if anyone bought the William Searle or other rare pieces."

Bonnie interjected her own take of the situation. "No, no one bought those because most people have more realistic down-to-earth taste. They bought functional things, you know, like a kitchen table made in Mexico or a set of beach chairs and umbrellas."

"Makes sense in a coastal community this size," Trent said.

Elaine and her group of friends looked over tables of knickknacks, household items, clothes, baby toys, a highchair, tools, a hair dryer, old dishes, and pots and pans. Trent looked over a few of the tools and pieces of yard equipment.

Bonnie noticed the items Trent examined. "Guess you can't use much of that stuff in your townhouse?"

"No. But it brings back memories. Now that I have my own house here in Sabal Palms, I have been thinking about selling my townhouse and some of my other properties in Florida, Atlanta, and North Carolina. I do still like to use the townhouse for entertainment; but ever since the plane crash last year, I've been rethinking my life. I am just weighing out all my options to determine the best path forward."

"Seriously?" Bonnie asked.

Elaine, hanging onto every word, said, "I have read about people who believe they are given another chance at life to live their lives differently. I knew you had strengthened your own faith since the crash."

"Certainly have. And part of my increase in faith is closely examining how God wants us to live our lives every day. For me, I feel like I might need to slow down the pace. I began slowing down when I purchased the townhouse on the island and later when I bought my home here in Sabal Palms. And since then, it seems like I am here in Sabal Palms every day. The type of investment work I do and my work with the Christian foundation, I can work from anywhere. I don't have to be in Florida—or any of the places where I still own a couple of condos and houses. I have closed most of my large offices. I don't need as many staff for the type of work I am doing now. I'm more involved in charity work and helping others to make investments in companies with strong Christian values. Might as well sell the remaining properties I don't use as often. That said, the island townhouse is very nice to have for visitors of these organizations. I will likely hold on to that one for business and let the others go."

Mary and Adriana completed the round of sale items all along the yard and in the garage. They joined Elaine, Bonnie, and Trent, who were near the tools and yard items.

Mary held up a delicate glass dish with raised flowers around the edge. "Check this out. Isn't it beautiful? It is to hold deviled eggs."

Bonnie laughed. "Don't you have three of those already?"

"No, smarty, I had two. *Now* I have three." Mary smirked at her friend. "Besides, it is a lovely dish, the money from the sale goes to the animal rescue center, a great cause."

Bonnie laughed again. "Of course, the animals."

Trent interjected, "Ladies, I didn't have breakfast this morning. Anyone interested in joining me at the coffee shop?"

"Well, we can't let you go hungry! I'm in," Bonnie said.

"I could use a coffee!" Adriana exclaimed.

Entering Sabal Palms coffee shop, Elaine surveyed the empty wooden tables all around. None of the regular patrons sat at their usual tables, except for one table where Kristy and her four children were sitting enjoying their breakfast treats. The older children who did not have school and were dressed for basketball practice were busy entertaining the younger newly adopted boy. Kristy attempted to juggle her attention between the youngest boy, her three older children, and her computer.

Bonnie glanced around the coffee shop. "Guess most of the regulars are still shopping."

Alexa greeted the group as they entered. "Good morning, all. What can I get started for you?"

Trent, Elaine, and each of the other women gave Alexa their orders. Alexa executed her excellent barista skills and worked on all five orders at once.

Alexa, with her backed turned to Elaine and the others, called out, "Been to the community garage sale this morning?"

"Yes, we have," Trent replied.

She continued working the espresso machine. "See anything good?"

Adriana said, "Some amazing things! Are you going to get a chance to go?"

"Not today. Here you go." She handed each one their drinks.

Elaine glanced around the coffee shop and wondered about Kristy and her determination to finish her graduate studies. She approached Kristy's table. "Good morning, Kristy."

"Good morning, Elaine." Kristy smiled.

"I don't want to disturb your study time; but I've been wanting to ask you, what are you studying?

"That's okay, you're not disturbing me. I'm in a graduate counseling program."

"Oh, that's terrific."

"Thanks. I'm almost finished with my master's and will take the boards after that."

"Going to open a practice here?"

"Maybe part-time." She nodded toward her busy and talkative children.

"Yes, you have your hands full. Are you going into any specialty field?"

"I've been fostering children for quite some time. I want to help kids and families who are or have been in the foster system. I would like to support families, so they can keep their own children if they are able."

"Certainly needed in this world. There are many children and families who need support and help."

"Yes, there are."

Adriana and the others walked to their usual table.

"Well, nice talking to you," Elaine said.

"You, too." Kristy smiled and turned to the youngest boy. "Eat your fruit."

Elaine joined the others, who were sipping their orders while sitting at the regular table by the window looking out on the street.

"Well!" Adriana gasped and looked at Trent. "Did you hear the news?"

"What news?"

Bonnie sighed. "Oh, good grief. I think she is talking about that Teddy fellow."

"No, why? Wasn't he just visiting? I thought he left town."

All of the women looked at one another waiting to see who would speak first. Mary couldn't take the suspense. "Okay, Bonnie, tell him."

"Okay. Here's the latest. We saw him at the first garage sale this morning."

"Really? I haven't seen him in the last couple of days. Was he buying something?"

Bonnie shook her head. "No, but he seemed to be very interested in something at the sale."

Adriana, impatient to provide the details, blurted out, "It was the piece made by William Searle."

"William Searle, huh? I know that furniture. Had one of Searle's chairs at one of my other vacation homes. I never even allowed anyone to sit in it! That seems funny now. Nowadays, I wouldn't have something like that if I couldn't use it."

Elaine continued, "Yes. I feel the same way. But Martinez had just a few collectible pieces there, and Teddy was interested in a desk with drawers by William Searle. It wasn't really the desk he was interested in; it was more like he was interested in something he thought was inside one of the drawers."

"Is that what he said?" Trent asked.

"No."

"What made you think that?"

Elaine elaborated, "It seemed he was looking for something because he opened each of the side drawers and tried to see if there was anything underneath."

"Like a false bottom in the drawers?" Trent asked.

"Yes, and then at the very top was a section that looked like the top part of a secretary's desk, with individual compartments for mail or keys and such. He looked into each one several times. He felt around the edges of the drawers and checked out the bottom of the drawers."

Trent nodded. "It does sound like he might have been looking for something."

Bonnie fidgeted with the napkin beneath her coffee cup as if she were anxious to say something. "Elaine, don't forget about Teddy walking on the beach."

Trent turned back to Elaine. "Walking on the beach?"

"Yes. The other night after you all left, Bonnie and I finished the last of cleaning up the kitchen; and that is when we saw him walking on the beach."

"That's not unusual—a tourist walking on the beach."

Elaine paused for a moment and selected her words carefully. "I don't want to think badly of someone I don't know, but he was walking back and forth in the dark for quite a while."

Trent thought for a moment and added, "Maybe he was just lost in thought?"

"I thought that, too, at first, Trent. But later, he came back and walked on the beach at 4:30 a.m. the night the strong wind came through. I could see him walking north on the beach, even though he was being pelted by blowing sand in gale force wind."

"I suppose there is no way to understand what he is doing unless we get a chance to ask him," Trent said.

Mary nodded. "You're right. Let's hope he is not doing anything sinister in our community. But we won't know unless we see him again and ask him."

"I agree," Elaine said.

Trent looked at the group sitting around the table. "I, for one, think we should give him the benefit of a doubt."

Bonnie rolled her eyes. "Seriously?"

Elaine touched Bonnie's arm. "Let's think about this, Bonnie. Trent is right."

Bonnie couldn't take it. Her eyebrows furrowed right in the middle. "Well, then, if you think there is a logical explanation, tell me what it is."

"Okay. How about what I do before I buy a house in a new community. When I invest in a property, I want to know everything about it. I look at the surveys, the community plans, and the history. After all, there was plenty in the local papers about the time Evergreen wanted to develop the golf course and turn the beach by your quaint community into a tourist trap. Perhaps he knew that and wanted to see for himself and didn't want anyone to know what he is doing. Or if he wants to put a business in here, he may not want to go up against you ladies." He smiled broadly. "You certainly held your ground against Evergreen, and that was in the papers, too."

"Or," Bonnie refuted, "how about this? He was casing our houses for a break-in."

Mary and Adriana laughed.

Adriana belted out another chuckle and said, "Bonnie, did you see the car he drives and the way he dresses? He looks pretty well-off if you ask me. He would certainly not need to break into beach cottages of a couple of old ladies."

The others nodded, but Bonnie was persistent. "Oh, he could have stolen that fancy car."

Trent laughed out loud at Bonnie's comment. "Doubt it."

Elaine had had enough of this discussion. "I, for one, agree with Trent. Now, if possible, can we get on the road? We have more shopping to do."

When Adriana finished her muffin, she stood up and gathered up her paper plate, napkin, and empty coffee cup. "I'm ready! You all ready for another shopping stop?"

The others followed Adriana.

Elaine stopped, turned, and waved at Kristy before leaving. All the kids waved back, but Kristy had her eyes locked on her laptop.

The next shopping stop and the other stops on the community garage sale map had a variety of "gently used" items for purchase. Elaine purchased a stack of beach towels that were in very good shape, had bright colors, and showed very little wear. The extra towels were perfect for the beach when her family came to visit. Bonnie purchased two sturdy beach chairs, and Adriana purchased a "never used" makeup mirror that was still in the box.

Driving back to Adriana's house, Elaine asked, "Everyone going to church tomorrow?"

Adriana responded first. "I am going to mass this evening and will accompany you all to Church on the Shore tomorrow. Maybe walk on the beach afterward?"

"Sounds good," Bonnie said. "The weather should be great."

"I'm in," Mary agreed.

Elaine smiled. "Perfect."

Elaine dropped Adriana and Mary at their homes, and she and Bonnie continued to their cottages on the beach.

Elaine's phone buzzed and she handed it to Bonnie. "Can you tell me who is texting?"

Bonnie grabbed the phone. "Looks like it's Billy. Yep. It's him."

"Oh, can you read it to me?"

"Just says to call him."

"Thanks. We should update him on our fall equinox and other fall festivities. He will want to know the plans for our gatherings. He might be able to schedule to be here for all the events with enough notice. Would be a treat to have him sing for one of our parties."

"It would. And that's not all. We need to tell him about Teddy. He knows many wealthy people in Nashville and from the entertainment industry. He travels in those well-to-do circles now. Maybe he knows Teddy."

"Might be a long shot but it's a possibility. Trent knows a great number of people, and it would make sense that Billy does, too. He has contacts from Sabal Palms to Nashville and even out in Los Angeles. They might be able to help us figure out who this Teddy character is."

Bonnie added, "Billy usually comes to church when he is in town. It would be good to let Trent know if Billy plans to join us at church.

I mean, Trent did volunteer to be in charge of the entertainment. He can work out the details with Billy."

"I'll text Trent and let him know we are walking on the beach after church if he wants to join us. In fact, I'll throw a quick lunch menu together for after church."

"What can I do? I'm sure I have things for a salad."

"I have burgers and the fixin's already. I can grill some burgers."

Bonnie paused for a moment, then said, "How about if I bring over some of those healthy hamburger buns, no wheat or sugar, and a salad?"

"Great. I'll bake some beans and ask Mary if she can bring over an easy dessert."

"And Adriana?"

"She may already have chips and things we can add. I'll text her with our plans for lunch."

And just like that, an impromptu beach-style cookout was planned.

Chapter Five

Elaine was relieved to be back in her cottage after being away most of the day. Bella was more excited than Elaine when the door opened. The little furry dog jumped all around, wagged her little nub of a tail, and ran in circles around Elaine.

"Come on, girl, let's go for a short walk."

The air signaled change was coming—not just a change of the warm salty atmospheric air along the beach but also a change of the current state of affairs. It felt ominous—as if there was the threat of danger from someone or something. This was not the first time Elaine had felt a sense of change in her world. She was good at detecting when change was about to transpire. She remembered this feeling before Hurricane Jada hit, the major storm that had changed so many lives. She had felt similar feelings when the community of Sabal Palms was threatened by a large community development company, Evergreen Recreation and Conservation Industries, that had wanted to change the quaint settlement into a tourist resort. And she had felt the same threat when a new age religion group, disguised as a new preacher and his wife, had attempted to interject false beliefs to Sabal Palms and takeover the Church on the Shore. What was coming next?

Bella chased the ghost crabs emerging from their hideouts under the sand. Elaine watched as Bella ran north on the beach. She looked northward at the stretch of beach ahead and wondered what this mysterious Teddy had been interested in a few nights ago on this part of Sabal Palms beach. What was the attraction? Was the appearance of Teddy connected to her feelings of uneasiness about a change? It was beyond her. She would pray about it to ease her uneasiness. She didn't like feeling anxious.

"Come on, Bella. Let's turn around. I need to touch base with Billy."

Bella wagged her tail and scampered to catch up with Elaine.

Elaine noticed the quietness of the peaceful beach that stretched out in front of her house and down to Bonnie's cottage. The quiet was the opposite of how the beach felt at the height of the tourist season. Schools in Texas had opened in the last weeks, and families with young children had returned home until the next long weekend or Christmas break.

Elaine closed her beach cottage door and sent a text to Billy. "Are you coming to church tomorrow?"

He replied quickly, "Yes."

"We'll be having burgers at my place and walking the beach afterward. Interested?"

"Sounds like a perfect Sunday. See you at church."

Bonnie was right about catching Billy up on the news. Billy hadn't been to Sabal Palms in nearly a month, and Elaine had plenty of news to discuss with him. She knew he was ready to work on a new song. She wanted to write a few verses tonight and see where her heart and God's Spirit would take her. Maybe she'd write about change. That was on her heart at this very moment.

"Bella, come on. Let me get your dinner . . . and mine. Have a lot of work to do tonight."

Elaine fed Bella, ate a light dinner, then prepared a few items for the cookout tomorrow. She prepped the burgers for grilling and made a batch of deviled eggs. She laughed at the thought of calling Mary and asking her if she could borrow her new deviled egg plate she had bought at the garage sale. After a good chuckle, she decided she wouldn't disturb Mary with a phone call and reached for her own plate in the cabinet.

With Bella snuggled into a dog bed next to Elaine's desk, she turned on the light over her workspace, switched on her old electric typewriter, inserted a clean sheet of paper in position, and rolled it up to the correct top margin. Her mind was fixed on the topic of change. It wasn't good change that rips out our hearts and brings frequent tears of sorrow or frustration; it's bad change. The threat of bad change increased anxiety. And she knew where to find the best consolation for anxiety. She opened her Bible and went to her favorite passage that helped her in many times of anxiety and worry: *Do not be anxious about anything, but in everything by prayer and supplication with thanksgiving let your requests be made known to God. And the peace of God, which surpasses all understanding, will guard your hearts and minds in Christ Jesus* (Phil. 4:6-7).

Elaine continued her line of thinking, turning to Scripture in times of worry and praising God and being thankful for everything. She typed out a few more sentences, but something was missing. She knew the missing piece: she felt a threat in her own world but didn't know what from.

She turned off the lamp and went to bed. Like Billy said, tomorrow would be a perfect Sunday—church, a cookout, and a long walk on the beach. She was thankful for opportunities like worshiping where she wanted, being able to openly declare her Christianity, spending time with good friends, and fellowshipping with other believers. Indeed, she had many blessings.

As soon as Elaine let Bella out for her morning duty, she saw the billowing smoke. She smelled it the entire walk to Bonnie's cottage and feared it would get worse the further south she walked. She arrived at the cottage and was surprised Bonnie was not yet on the deck waiting for her. She walked up the wooden steps and knocked on her door.

Bonnie opened the door. "Criminy! I couldn't wait outside with the smell of that smoke. I was afraid I'd smell like a smoked turkey in church if I waited on my deck!"

Elaine nodded. "It is getting worse. Is it that time of year?"

Bonnie took out her phone. "Seems early. Hold on. I'll ask Mary. She will know."

"Hey, Mary. Yes, good morning. Elaine and I have a question. Is it already time to for the sugarcane fires in Mexico? Oh, okay. Thanks. Yes, we can smell it and see the smoke out on the beach. Yes, see you in church."

"What did she say?"

"Mary's sources told her it is a controlled burn over on the outside along the wildlife refuge. She said it won't last too long. Oh, and for future reference, she said the sugarcane burn starts in October."

Elaine knew the sugar cane burning for the harvest of sugar was an annual occurrence, but she had suspected it was too early for the annual fires. "That makes more sense. Hope they have it put out before we walk after church."

"Me, too. We'll probably see it from the church parking lot; and after church, we can see if it is still burning."

"Yes. You ready?"

"Yep." Bonnie locked up her cottage and joined Elaine on the deck. "Did you talk to Billy?"

"I did. He's going to meet us at church and spend the afternoon with us."

"Good deal."

"Adriana is bringing the chips and some other things for the burgers. I think she said she had some pickled okra and some garlic dill pickles, too."

Bonnie laughed. "Great. Tastes good and we'll all have dragon breath when we are finished."

Elaine chuckled. "That has never bothered us before. And of course, Mary said she'd bring a sugar-free cake."

"I knew she would come through for our impromptu cookout!"

"Sometimes, last-minute parties are the best, don't you think?"

"No question about that!" Bonnie agreed.

Elaine was grateful that the weather was beautiful and cooler than yesterday. Except for the lingering smell of the control burn near the wildlife refuge, the shore was pristine. They'd decided yesterday to walk to church instead of drive. Elaine wondered if it was the best idea.

The two trudged along the shoreline. Following standard practice at the little Church on the Shore meant the congregation wore casual clothes for the service. And for Elaine and Bonnie, that meant they could walk in the sand in sandals or even flipflops to church if the weather was pleasant. And here at Sabal Palms, except for a few weeks of cooler weather in January and February, the occasional hurricane, or a tropical storm, the weather was almost always perfect.

Bonnie must have been thinking the same thing as Elaine about the lingering smoke. "Maybe we should ask Mary or Billy for a ride back after church to escape this smoke."

"I'm sure either one would be happy to give us a lift."

Elaine and Bonnie were the first of the group to arrive at the Church on the Shore. Pastor Sam greeted them and welcomed them to enter the small, bright sanctuary. They took their usual positions near the front of the church.

A few minutes later, Mary joined them in her dressy Hawaiian muumuu, adorned with her silver whale tail necklace. "Good morning, girls. Did you walk in the smoke smell?"

Elaine nodded. "We did. It wasn't too bad. Not sure we will walk back, though."

"You can ride with me."

Bonnie blurted out, "Perfect! Thanks."

"You're welcome," Mary said. "I do worry about the environmental concerns."

Bonnie said, "Worried about the animals?"

"Animals? No, they mostly run or crawl out of the burning fields. I'm worried about the breathing problems for children and older people. There is an increased risk for individuals prone to respiratory ailments. Especially for older people."

Bonnie chuckled. "It's a good thing we aren't old."

Mary teased, "Well, I'm not, but have you looked in the mirror lately?"

Bonnie and Mary now both chuckled.

Elaine believed they were about to get a look from Pastor Sam for all their rowdiness. "Ladies, shhh," she admonished.

Billy sat down beside Elaine. "Good morning. Beautiful day, except for the smell of smoke."

Elaine replied, "We were just discussing that."

Trent appeared and sat by Mary. "Good morning, everyone. Where is Adriana?"

Bonnie rolled her eyes. "She will be here, at some point-on her own schedule."

Two minutes later, the strong scent of gardenia perfume traveled into the Church on the Shore at the same time Elaine heard the jangling of jewelry. "She's here."

Adriana's dressy sandals clicked on the white tile floor as she made her way up the aisle. She sat next to Trent and announced, "My stars! That smoke. How is a girl to breathe?" She fanned her face, clanging the bracelets once again.

Billy waved hello at Adriana and replied, "Good morning. It shouldn't last too long."

Adrian looked puzzled. "What do you mean? It usually lasts a couple of days."

Billy explained, "This morning, when I drove across the causeway, I heard some talk about what was happening here. It is a controlled burn—or so it was reported on the radio."

Mary nodded. "It is. Won't last too long, though."

Billy continued, "Well, if the smoke lasts much longer, it will be blowing in the other direction. And since the wind changed and is now blowing from the north, this lingering smoke should blow it away from Sabal Palms and toward Mexico."

The music began, and the usual people in the congregation who sang with gusto each week belted out the songs as loudly as ever. Elaine knew which people in the crowd had golden voices as they offered praise to God and those who . . . well, probably should turn their volume way down so others could hear the tune. But she knew God didn't care. God was happy when people offered songs of praise each Sunday, no matter how they sound.

As the music played for the third and final opening hymn, Pastor Sam walked up to the pulpit. After saying a short prayer asking God for his message of worship to be understood and applied by his congregants, he began his remarks.

"Good morning. As you can tell from the smell of smoke outside, it is almost that time of year. Although it is not quite sugarcane-burning time, it will soon be upon us. Today, we have the word of the fire department that this smoke is from a controlled burn, and it should end"—he glanced at his watch—"in just about an hour. Nevertheless, as we look forward and think about the sugarcane burning this fall, we know that fall will soon arrive. To help us to understand the purpose of burning the sugarcane fields, here is a reminder. Burning the sugarcane in the fall is to clean out the dead leaves and rubbish, making it easier to glean the sugar during the next season. And soon after the harvest of the sugar, the field can be planted again. Once planted, the field will grow and can be harvested once again when the time comes.

"In this way, we are all like sugarcane. We have bits and pieces of our past that should be thrown out. We should get rid of all the little bad pieces, the rubbish of our past, or the remains of past events. But do we? Do we ask forgiveness, clean out our hearts and souls, plant new faith seeds, nurture and grow faith, move on toward our own great harvest to come?

"Or, instead, do we hold on to those angry feelings? Grudges? Do we become so covered with rubbish that we can no longer grow our faith? Do we hide behind shame, rather than enjoy God's grace? Do we no longer have the "sugar" or the spiritual fruit of our hearts? Or can we forgive those parts of ourselves that somehow led to disappointment? Can we forgive those who wronged us; or do we hold on to those pieces, choking any possibility of forgiveness of our own sins and cutting off our future spiritual growth? And what is sometimes the most difficult of all, can we forgive ourselves for those past transgressions or when we fell short?"

Elaine listened to every word. Maybe Pastor Sam's words would help her to think about the devotional she had started writing last night. Maybe the change was for the purpose of cleaning out the old. Maybe she needed to clean out something in her feelings and begin something new, strengthen her own faith. She would think about it more when she worked on that devotional.

Pastor Sam continued with his sermon for another twenty-five minutes; and toward the end, he changed his tone. "Good people of Church on the Shore, this time of year brings up another event that happened in the not-too-distant past. The anniversary of the past event is upon us and is fast approaching. As you recall, our little church was threatened not long ago by false prophecy. But we fought it off. Thanks to the good people of Sabal Palms, those who have lived here all their lives and those new to the community"—he nodded toward Trent and Billy—"we did not let New Age religion get a grip on our community. We stood fast. You all helped in the battle.

As you also may recall, prior to the intrusion of the threat into our lives, I had planned to leave the Church on the Shore."

The church fell completely silent. Elaine dreaded what might come next. This subject had not come up since Pastor Sam had stood before the congregation and announced he would stay at the Church on the Shore indefinitely. But that was in the past.

"But when we had this threat, I agreed to stay on until things calmed down. I would like you all to pray and ponder about our church and my own calling. I am once again considering a change."

Adriana gasped. Bonnie put her hands on her cheeks, and Mary's eyes widened. Elaine's heart sped up, and each beat pounded from her chest to her head.

Pastor Sam continued. "I have had a call from another church, and I am praying about this. Please, keep me in your hearts and prayers. I am planning on accepting that call to move to the North, closer to my family. I will pray daily for the Church on the Shore. The time has come for the church to begin plans for a search committee to bring in a new pastor. And this year, we will take our time and make certain the right person will be selected. The decision will not be made in haste."

Was Pastor Sam's announcement about his departure the unknown change Elaine anticipated? Her mind was spinning. She felt her anxiety increase. But maybe her high level of anxiety was associated with what had happened before when the New Age pastor almost made his way into the church. She felt she needed to help the church this time in the selection process. She wanted a front-row seat to the process and would help however her church needed her. She wanted to assist and make certain a good candidate would be selected. She felt solid in her resolve. She would ask the executive committee how she could help.

Pastor Sam gave the benediction, and the congregation that had been silent erupted in conversations. No doubt, the entire sanctuary remembered the details of selection and the near-fatal miss of the New Age pastor. Elaine was certain every conversation that spontaneously erupted as soon as the benediction was said was about Pastor Sam's departure. Once the loud babbling quieted a bit, the congregation slowly spilled into the aisles and trickled out the front door. Each member of the congregation shook Pastor Sam's hand and said kind words as they departed the church.

Elaine followed Mary, Bonnie, Adriana, Trent, and Billy as they stopped to talk to Pastor Sam. When it was her turn to say a few words to Pastor Sam, she was surprised that he initiated the conversational topic she wanted to hear more about.

"Good morning, Elaine. I have asked the executive committee to invite you to their sessions. It would be a real blessing for the church if you would serve as a member on the selection committee this time around."

"Yes, Pastor Sam. I would be honored if the executive committee approves of me serving with them."

He gently shook her hand. "They will."

Elaine had hardly stepped off the bottom step of the Church on the Shore when Mary and Bonnie swarmed around her.

Bonnie began the interrogation. "Spill it. What did Pastor Sam want?"

Mary nudged in closer to Bonnie to hear Elaine's reply, then impatiently demanded, "Tell us!"

"He asked if I would be willing to serve on the search committee—"

"Oh!" Adriana, who wasn't even in view yet from the church porch, scurried down and threw her arms up in the air with all the Sunday bling jingling. She stepped in front of Mary and interrupted, "You absolutely must do it!"

"Yes!" Mary peeked her head back around Adriana and added, "You must! You can keep us informed on the search!"

Trent and Billy stood back smiling and watching the circus that transpired around Elaine. Elaine felt the vibrant blush fully engross her cheeks. "We can talk more about this later," she said and hastily walked toward Mary's car.

Trent yelled out, "See you at your place in a minute."

Billy waved and went to his truck.

The six gathered at Elaine's beach cottage within minutes. She would work hard to distract the entire group toward food and a nice long walk and away from the search committee conversation.

Elaine, Mary, Adriana, and Bonnie looked like a group of ants darting around the kitchen and back out to the deck and back into the kitchen. This back-and-forth continued for about ten minutes, and then the six good friends settled around the outdoor table with cool glasses of tea and lemonade before they ate and went for their walk on the shore.

"Billy, you were right. The wind shifted to the north and blew the smoke out of here," Mary said.

Billy nodded. "Yes, it doesn't take much to blow it the other way. I suspect the burn was about over with before we left church. But I noticed the breeze has cooled things off."

"It is great weather," Trent remarked. "We could walk five miles and not break a sweat."

"Five miles! I'd be sweating like a p—" Noticing Billy and Trent's glares, Bonnie opted to stop before the whole word "pig" was uttered. "Uh, a farm animal."

Mary chuckled. "I don't think Trent was serious about the five miles."

"Oh?" Bonnie said. "Sorry. But on the other hand, if we walked north, maybe we could see what Teddy was so interested in seeing."

"Teddy? Who is Teddy?" Billy asked.

Elaine began the report on Teddy by saying, "Billy, you've been gone a couple of weeks, and, well, there was a stranger who has been in town a few days. And he was acting—"

"Suspiciously?" Bonnie blurted.

Adriana waved her hands in the air while saying, "Oh my goodness! There was nothing suspicious about him. He was-"

"I was about to say he acted in a in a curious manner," Elaine remarked.

"I thought he was perfectly fine"—Adriana smiled—"just fine."

Trent laughed. "Adriana, are you sure that was all you thought? You sound a little bit . . . smitten."

Adriana blushed. "Why no, I'm certainly not smitten."

"Wait!" Billy insisted. "Will someone tell me what happened? I can't keep up with this conversation."

Bonnie was all too happy to divulge everything that had transpired. "What happened was this: when the stranger came into the coffee shop, Adriana's eyeballs couldn't stop staring at him. I thought her eyes were gonna pop right out."

Adriana waved her hand, dismissing the comments. "Now, Bonnie."

"Oh?" Billy asked.

"Billy," Elaine interjected, "what *was* strange was we saw him out here on the beach at all hours walking north, and we wondered why. He came back a few times and did the same thing."

Billy's eyebrows crinkled. "That does sound—as you said—curious. I agree with your idea. He has been here several times, huh? Then I agree; walking north, we could check if there is anything new there."

"Besides the pieces of wood we discovered last week?" Bonnie asked.

"Nearly broke my toe on that wood!" Adriana exclaimed.

"Now you really have me curious," Billy commented. "What did you find?"

"A wooden peg and a board together," Bonnie elaborated, "but it looked very old. Mary called the museum, and they came out and dug it up. Now, Texas Historical Commission is investigating the age and origin of the wood."

"That's quite a find," Billy noted. "Maybe there is more out there somewhere. That might be what this person is looking for—you never know. Sunken ship?"

Trent turned the burgers again. "I think these are almost ready."

The burgers were casting off their own delectable aroma. Billy and Trent both took charge of the grilling, and the burgers were placed on a platter on the outdoor table. The group soon filled their plates full of burgers, chips, deviled eggs, and baked beans.

"Billy and Trent, thanks for being the cooks today," Elaine said.

Billy placed a burger on his plate. "No problem. You ladies got everything else together."

"And, Elaine, you ladies are the bests hosts in Sabal Palms! All of you!" Trent added.

Elaine, holding her plate full of food, surveyed the table. "Anyone need anything else?"

Mary patted the space beside her. "No, come and sit here and eat."

Elaine and the others gathered around the table were completely quiet. But after the second or third bite, Bonnie initiated the conversation.

"So, Adriana, for the pool party, what do you want us to bring? I mean, it is this week."

"I'm so excited to be kicking off the fall festivities; and hopefully, we will have a good turnout. But don't worry about bringing anything—it is so soon, I think I will just have it catered. Mary, would you mind stopping off with me at the café in the morning to put in the order? You always remember a detail or two that I forget when ordering in a rush."

"I'd be happy to."

Trent took another burger and set it on his plate. "I could use a little help. I volunteered for the invitations and the entertainment. I can get some quick invites printed up this evening. How many should I make? And can you all help me with the delivery?"

Bonnie wiped her mouth and responded, "I would be happy to help. We aren't preparing any food for this week. It would give me something to do."

"We can meet tomorrow at the coffee shop—that is, if you think you can get invites printed by then, Trent," Elaine said.

Billy added pickles on his burger and passed the pickles around. "Guess I can't make the meeting tomorrow. I have a phone conference with Nashville."

"You will be missed," Elaine said.

"Thanks, Elaine. I am sure your meeting will be more fun than my phone call. It is about marketing."

"That does not sound fun at all," Trent remarked. "Back to the invitations, let me have a ballpark number; and I'll print a few extras in case."

Bonnie placed a deviled egg on her plate. "How about if we meet tomorrow around ten at the coffee shop? That gives us time for our walk, Elaine. And we can divide up the invites then."

Adriana replied, "Perfect. Now, as for the number—I am thinking thirty? What do you think?"

Mary said, "That sounds good. I know your house and pool area can accommodate that many."

"I'm happy to play a few songs for the party, but I also have a new recording—a collection of my songs. I can bring that, too."

Adriana put her hands up to her cheeks. "Oh! That would be amazing, Billy. I can set up the sound system ahead of time by the pool."

"I think we are all set," Elaine said.

Billy glanced around Elaine's deck and the view of the water. "Always good to be back on your porch, Elaine, and checking out this view. I miss this when I travel."

"No place like it," Elaine agreed.

Mary brought out her cake. Everyone ate a slice and, as always, told Mary it was the best cake she had ever made.

"I need to walk the full five miles after all that food," Trent said.

"Seriously?" Bonnie asked.

"Well, maybe three." Trent laughed. "You know, a mile and a half each way."

Elaine stood and began gathering the food from the table. "It will just take me a minute to clear the table, and we can get started on our walk."

Mary helped Elaine, and the others joined in and cleared the table of the remaining food. Bonnie carried the used paper plates to the trash can inside. The group soon returned to the deck.

Adriana waved her arms toward the beach and announced, "Let's get walking!"

Chapter Six

The group set out heading north on the beach with Bella walking at Elaine's heels. Bonnie and Trent seemed more determined than the others to discover something new about this area of the beach and link it back to Teddy somehow.

Particles of fine, strange grit found its way into Elaine's eyes. She blinked, attempting to find relief from the stinging. "Is this stuff in the air from the controlled burn? It wasn't this bad when we left to go to church."

Billy rubbed his eyes. "Not sure if it is from the controlled burn. But the wind might have shifted a little, bringing more of this grit back our way. The air should clear off soon."

Bonnie sped her pace and walked a few feet ahead of the group. "Well, let's get a wiggle on. This breeze should clear up the air on the northern part of the beach. I want to see if we discover anything unusual that might be what this grifter was looking for."

Once again, Adriana raised her hand in protest. "Innocent until proven guilty."

"But seriously, Adriana. Think about it. This guy is snooping around at 4:30 a.m., and then he searches the drawers of an old wooden collectable piece of furniture—some old chest of drawers."

"Bonnie, he was just interested in a piece of furniture! It was a collectable piece—an antique, after all," Adriana said.

"Just hope Martinez wasn't hornswoggled!" Bonnie insisted.

Trent walked at a determined pace and caught up to Elaine. "We can look for footprints out on this end where a few people come this time of year. If we see some fresh prints where people do not go, chances are it could be him."

"For the life of me," Mary added, "I cannot think of a reason anyone would be out here in the middle of the night during the off season, unless they were up to no good. There is nothing out this way except some sand dunes further north."

"Even if we find something else up this way," Elaine reasoned, "how do we know that it is what Teddy was looking for? Maybe he enjoyed the moon over the water."

"Or he likes to fish and was looking for a potential night fishing spot," Trent added.

"See, Bonnie? There could be plenty of reasons we haven't considered. I, for one, believe we should find out before we judge him," Elaine added.

"There she is," Bonnie said.

"Yep, Miss 'I Always Look on the Bright Side of Things,'" Mary agreed.

Billy gestured toward the aquamarine water. "There have been a lot of ships and vessels that have gone down in these waters. He could be wanting to find some sunken treasures or something—or, oh, maybe he is looking for evidence or artifacts of World War II Nazi submarines."

Mary turned to Billy. "What on earth? Nazi submarines! I never!"

Elaine added, "Well, Mary, there were submarines that sunk out there during the war."

"True story," Trent said. "Lots of history in these waters. Remember, I said I did a lot of research before I purchased my townhouse on the island? And later, I did more research before I bought my house in Sabal Palms."

"Nazi submarines that close to Texas?" Mary asked.

"Yes," Billy replied. "And of course, don't forget the most famous Spanish ships of 1554 that were sunk or run aground out here."

"Yeah, I've heard of those ships," Bonnie sputtered. "It has to be something shadier than looking out where a sunken Nazi submarine went down."

Adriana rebuffed, "That settles it! I'm going to find out."

"And how do you propose to do that? You could be placing yourself in danger," Bonnie insisted.

"Easy. If we see him again at the coffee shop or elsewhere, I will ask him. I'll strike up a conversation and find out his intentions for being here in Sabal Palms."

Mary joined in, "About what?"

"Oh, I don't know. Maybe uh . . . "

"I know! You can tell him there are over three hundred bird species that are seen here, if you include the migratory species."

"Oh, Mary, most people don't give a hoot about your bird species!"

Billy and Trent both laughed at Bonnie's remarks.

Elaine couldn't take anymore, and she knew Billy and Trent both appeared to be enjoying this sparring. "Okay, Adriana. Let's suppose he really is just looking around as a tourist or potential investor. What would we do to make him feel welcome?"

Adriana clapped her hands, which sent her bracelets flying up and down violently her arms. "I've got it! I will bring up the fall equinox!"

Bonnie shook her head. "And how will that help you discover his motives for being here and lurking around the beach?"

"Well, it won't tell me much about his motives, but it will give me a chance to invite him to the pool party the night of the equinox!"

"Oh, good grief! A perfect stranger coming over to our party!"

"Bonnie, correction, I am hosting it!" Adriana insisted. "I can at least find out if he is going to stay until then. Besides, if he isn't staying that long, I can find out when he is leaving and put all this nonsense to rest."

Billy nodded in agreement. "Adriana, you do have a good idea there. But I am surprised you ladies are so worked up over this guy."

Elaine replied, "You know, Billy, I wasn't concerned until we saw him around our houses along the beach in the middle of the night."

"I understand that would be troubling, and you are right to be concerned. Maybe he isn't staying long. But like Adriana said, if he is leaving soon because he is a tourist, she will find out by inviting him to her party."

With the bright sunshine, the temperature heated up in the afternoon. The sand was not too hot to walk barefoot, and Elaine quickly shed her flip flops and walked along the water's edge darting in and out of the water. She loved to feel the foam rolling over her toes, and Bella liked to try and catch the piping plovers, which were able to fly away before the pooch reached them.

The chatter about the suspicious visitor died down on the route back to Elaine's beach cottage. Instead, Mary was concerned about spotting shore birds; Adriana spoke of the days when she and her dear Antony used to go to the beach; and Bonnie and Billy were looking for lightning welks.

Bonnie picked up a shell and showed Billy. "You know what is so strange to me about these shells?"

"That they are called left-handed?"

Bonnie laughed. "Yes! Except I heard once that there are some right-handed ones, too."

Elaine knew as soon as Mary heard this topic, she would be joining in. If nature was involved, particularly animal or sea life, Mary would be in the middle of any conversation.

"Technically, most right-handed ones are not lightning whelks but knobbed whelks or other kinds of whelks. And did you know," Mary noted, "some lightning whelks can be fifteen inches long? I think the record is sixteen inches."

"Is that right?" Billy asked.

"Yes. And these fellas—these lightning whelks—are carnivorous," Mary continued.

Bonnie jumped back in the conversation. "Wait, they eat meat? What in the world do they eat?"

"Oysters, things like that."

Examining the shell, Bonnie asked, "How in the world can this thing eat an oyster?"

"For starters, they usually pry it open using this edge. But if that doesn't work, they can use their own shell and grind a hole in the oyster."

"Then what?" Bonnie asked.

"They have a tongue, and they use it. They get the goodies out!"

Bonnie's eyes widened as she listened to every word. "Get outta here!"

Elaine knew Mary loved being their nature encyclopedia and prided herself on being able to share tidbits of information about sea life and nature.

"Not only that but the females are also larger than the males, and these whelks can live for years."

Adriana shrugged her shoulders. "That is news to me."

"Speaking of news," Bonnie said, "I haven't heard any of you talk about Pastor Sam's news."

Mary shrugged her shoulders. "What are we supposed to think? I mean, I am not surprised. We knew he considered taking a call to another church in the past—before the New Age church tried to take over. And since the church is now on firmer ground, I am not surprised he is reconsidering a move to be near his family."

"Well, that is not exactly what I am talking about, Mary," Bonnie blurted.

"Oh? What then?"

"The fact that our own dear Elaine will be on the committee to select a new pastor."

Billy laughed. "No one is surprised about that."

Trent agreed, "I'm not surprised. An excellent choice."

Bonnie continued, "And you will tell us everything, Elaine. I mean everything."

"Oh, Bonnie, you know there will be some business I will have to keep confidential."

"Oh? Like what?"

"I would suppose the initial list of individuals who might be interested in the position—or those we might want to invite. I am sure we will be asked to keep all the information confidential until a later time."

"You won't share with your best friends?" Bonnie insisted and gave Elaine a puppy dog look.

"I will make a deal with you, Bonnie."

"Okay. Spill it. What?"

"I will tell you everything I am allowed to tell. And yes, I will tell you and the rest of the group before anyone else. But only after I have the okay from the executive committee."

Bonnie sighed. "Oh, okay. I knew you wouldn't budge, even a tiny bit."

The group gradually made their way back to Elaine's cottage and said their goodbyes.

The next morning, Elaine dressed quickly to meet Bonnie for a short walk on the beach. She was anxious to go on their walk early and get the day started. She glanced down at Bella bouncing along beside her. Bella's tiny paws patted along in the sand and left a trail of doggy prints behind them.

Bonnie walked more slowly looking for shells along the shore.

"Are you going to start collecting shells, Bonnie? A new hobby?"

"No. But after the discussion yesterday, I am determined to find a right-handed lightning whelk. I will find one and show Mary that there are some around here on the coast."

"I read they are pretty rare," Elaine noted.

Bonnie shook her head. "I know. I didn't know until we had our marine biology lesson yesterday."

Elaine laughed. "Mary loves talking about sea life."

"Or anything else that breathes!"

Elaine stopped in her tracks. "Look up there, ahead of us."

Bonnie glared. "There is Teddy again."

"Wish I knew what he is so interested in."

Bonnie nodded. "Me, too. But I guess Detective Adriana is on it. If he shows up today—whether at the coffee shop or anywhere in town—she will hunt him like a heat-seeking missile and invite him to her pool party."

"I, for one, think it is a good idea."

"Really, Elaine?"

"Yes. End this investigation once and for all. At least we can find out if he will be here through the week. And if he does come to the party, we can get to know him."

Bonnie studied this stranger, Teddy. "What is he doing out there?"

"I think he has binoculars around his neck. Yes, see, he is looking out to sea."

"Maybe waiting for his ship to come in?" Bonnie laughed.

"Good one, Bonnie. We'd better head back."

"Yes. I want to be back at our own cottages before he comes this way. Don't want to have to talk to him about anything going on this week in Sabal Palms. We will let Adriana handle his invite."

Elaine said her goodbyes to Bella and left her cottage to go into town. She stopped on the way at Bonnie's beach cottage to pick her up. She parked at Bonnie's drive and waited.

Where is she? Elaine glanced at her watch. *Not like it for her to be late.*

Elaine debated for a moment about getting out of her car to check on Bonnie. She put her hand on the door handle; but before she opened the door, she saw Bonnie's screen door open.

Bonnie, looking disheveled, made her way down the wooden steps spanning from her deck to the walkway. She quickly opened the car door.

"There you are. I was worried."

Out of breath, Bonnie said, "Sorry."

"You okay?"

"Well, yes. I got out of the shower and had just put my clothes on when I glanced out the window toward the shore. And there he was."

"Who? Teddy?"

"Yes. I watched him for a while to see what he was doing."

"And?"

"He stood out there, on the beach right in front of my house, and looked through the binoculars again. But something was different."

"Oh?"

"Yes. I couldn't stop watching him. He looked through the binoculars out to sea, and there was a boat in the distance. The boat looked like it was sending a signal of some kind."

"A signal?"

"Yes. It was like a mirror reflecting or a light blinking or something. I don't know if the boat was signaling to him or if he just noticed it and stopped to watch."

"Guess we won't know unless we get to talk to him at some point. Maybe the light just caught his attention. Anyway, if he stays around town, we will find out later this week."

"Yes. At the pool party, if not before."

"Let's get to the coffee shop. Trent is expecting us to help with the invitations."

On the way into town, Elaine had a thought. "Hey, Bonnie, if we do see this Teddy guy again in town, maybe we shouldn't confront him about being on the beach just yet."

"Oh? Why?"

"I don't know. Maybe we should wait until we learn more about his reason for being in town. Then we can try to put things together and figure it out. The walks on the beach, the middle of the night walk on the beach. It must all be connected. And if it is something sinister, we might want to let the authorities handle it."

"Hold on a minute. Is this the always-positive Elaine? The look-on-the-bright-side-always Elaine? The same one wanting to give Teddy the benefit of the doubt?"

"And I am also the one who wants to be safe. All I am saying is if Teddy is on the up and up, we will find out soon. If he is up to something, we should collect our evidence, talk about what we find, and then go to the police."

"Well, that is a switch. But I have to admit, I think your approach is right. We should take it slow and gather more information. Collect more evidence."

"I'm proud of you, Bonnie. Taking a wait-and-see attitude requires some patience."

Elaine drove straight to the coffee shop and found a parking spot in the front by the door. "We lucked out."

"Perfect spot!"

"Makes a difference when the tourist season is over—lots of empty spots on the street."

Trent pulled his car in behind Elaine's and hopped out. "Good morning, ladies. Let me grab the invitations."

Trent collected a stack of invitations from the passenger seat, closed the door, and caught up with Elaine and Bonnie.

Elaine glanced over the papers in Trent's hand. "Those look lovely. Green palm leaves around the edge of the front. Nice—tastefully done."

"Pretty easy using a program I had on my home computer."

Bonnie looked at the invitations and touched the edge lined in palm leaves. "Those are very classy, Trent."

"Well, ladies, let's go inside and see if Mary and Adriana are here."

Bonnie laughed. "I'm sure Mary is early, and I am also certain Adriana will be late."

The familiar jingle of the bell on the door of the coffee shop was met by a cheerful welcome from Alexa, the barista. "Good morning. Come on in. You want the usual?"

"Yes, thank you," Elaine replied.

Mary waved to the group at the counter from the back table by the window.

Bonnie laughed. "See, Trent. Like clockwork. Usually, the first of the group to arrive."

Elaine took her cup to the table and sat beside Mary. "Hi, Mary. Looks like beautiful weather for delivering invitations around town today."

"Yes, it is. Can you believe the fall equinox is this week? Seems like yesterday was the Fourth of July!"

Elaine laughed. "Yes, and watching all the fireworks over the water!"

Mary continued, "You have a great view from your deck—and it was a great party. Had trouble getting up the next day, though. Not used to staying out all hours of the night."

Elaine laughed.

Bonnie took her seat. "What's so funny?"

"We were talking about the Fourth of July, and Mary said we stayed up all hours."

Bonnie chortled. "Horsefeathers! It was only 10 p.m. when we left Elaine's house!"

"Like I said, all hours." Mary chuckled.

"Might seem like it was late for you old people," Bonnie chided.

Trent brought the stack of invitations and his coffee and sat down at the table with the chattering group. "Lots of cheerful laughing over here. What are you ladies up to?"

"Nothing," Mary said.

"This old person here"—Bonnie gestured to Mary—"just said 10 p.m. was late!"

Trent laughed. "I understand what you mean, Mary. I'd rather go to bed early, too, and get going early the next morning. Here, Mary, have a look at these."

"Those are lovely, Trent. Very pretty colors. Now, let's make the list and divide up who is taking invites and to which locations."

Bonnie held her hand up to the group. "Hold on. Miss Sunshine isn't here yet."

"Well, we can get the list made out and then divide it between us when Adriana arrives," Elaine suggested, reaching inside her purse. She found a tablet and placed it on the table. "Here, I brought a small tablet of paper."

"Oh"—Mary fumbled in her purse—"I have a pen."

The bell announced Adriana's arrival before her perfume permeated the coffee shop.

"Adriana and her perfume are here." Bonnie rolled her eyes.

"That is on time for her." Mary laughed.

Adriana ordered her flavored specialty coffee of the day. "I'll wait over there, Alexa." She gestured toward the table.

Adriana arrived at the table shortly after her perfume. Her bling-laden arm pulled a chair out from the table. Taking her seat, she greeted the group. "Ladies, Trent, how is everyone this morning? Ready to roll?"

"Been ready," Bonnie said.

"We were about to list the names of individuals to invite for the party and divide and conquer the invitation delivery," Elaine said.

Adriana's eyes opened wide as she reached across the table and took an invitation from the stack. "These are amazing, Trent! You simply outdid yourself! My stars!"

"Thanks, Adriana. It was easy to design on the computer."

"I love these palms on the font of the invite. It is stunning!"

"Thank you, Adriana."

Alexa called out Adriana's name and held up her coffee drink.

"Hold on. Let me get my drink. Now, don't start talking without me."

Bonnie shook her head. "I think we should list the names of the people right here on Main Street first—you know the shop owners we usually invite."

Returning with her coffee, Adriana motioned toward the group to get started. "Okay, ready. I can take anyone in my neighborhood."

"Got it," Elaine said. "Now, Bonnie suggested the shop owners first. Let's list those."

Swallowing a sip of her coffee, Adriana suggested, "Mary and I will deliver the invitation to the café—we are going there to place the catering order after we leave here."

Mary nodded. "Yes. And the boutique, Ship Shape, is right next door. You know the owner well, Adriana."

"Indeed, I do." She glanced down at her shirt and smoothed it out. "Got this Hawaiian shirt there."

Elaine jotted the names of the shops on the paper. "And Bonnie and I can go by the bookstore on our way back to the beach."

"I can take the invitation over to the real estate office. I know those people well," Trent suggested.

Mary put her finger to her forehead, "Oh! I had a thought. Adriana, after we go by the café and get the catering order in, I'll run out to Ramon and Maria's house—"

"Wait! I have an idea," Bonnie exclaimed. "Do you think Maria can make tamales? And bring the salsas?"

"I will ask her if she has time to help us out."

The bell of the coffee shop door rang out. All eyes looked forward.

Chapter Seven

The coffee shop door closed. Adriana turned toward the door and gasped. "There he is—Mr. Tall, Dark, and Handsome."

Bonnie rolled her eyes and tapped Adriana's arm. "Remember Antony?" she whispered.

Adriana crossed her chest. "Forgive me. Oh, poor Antony."

Teddy went to the counter, gave his order to Alexa, and walked over to the table where the group sat. All eyes fixed on him. Teddy smiled and nodded. "Good morning. Good to see you all again."

"Good morning," Adriana replied, batting her long eyelashes. "How are you?"

"Doing well."

Adriana continued, "We have seen you a lot the last couple of days, Teddy. You must be enjoying Sabal Palms."

"Oh . . . yes . . . oh, that's right. I saw you at the garage sale the other day—the place where the furniture was displayed."

"Yes," Adriana replied.

Alexa called out, "Order for Teddy."

Teddy nodded to Alexa.

Trent gestured to an empty chair. "Care to join us?"

"Thanks. But I can't stay. I just stopped in to get my coffee to go."

Adriana's wide eyes looked up at Teddy. "Say, I am curious, Teddy. Did you buy that William Searle piece Martinez had?"

"Oh, no, I didn't. But you know Searle's work?"

Adriana nodded. "Yes, I do. I like fine furniture—you know, antique collections like those."

Bonnie looked at Mary, then Elaine, and rolled her eyes once again. "The rest of us bought beach chairs."

Ignoring Bonnie's remark, Adriana continued. "Say, we were discussing the fall equinox."

"Oh? Is it the fall equinox? I had no idea. Must have missed that."

"Well, it's not yet. The equinox is on the twenty-second."

"Oh. I didn't miss it. That's in just a few days."

"Yes, and"—she reached across the table took an invitation from the stack—"we are having a party to celebrate the equinox that night. If you are in town, maybe you want to come by?" Adriana's eyes twinkled.

Examining the invitation, Teddy replied, "I will consider this."

"So, you will be in town?"

"Not sure right now. But if I am, I will try to stop by."

Adriana nodded. "Hope to see you then."

"Thank you for the invitation. I'd better run. Have a few things I need to do." Teddy nodded and returned to the counter to retrieve his coffee.

Bonnie broke the silence. "Well, that was strange."

Elaine nodded. "Bonnie, I think I agree with you."

Trent finished his coffee. "Anyone else finished? I'll take your cup."

Elaine handed Trent her cup. "Thank you."

Glancing out the window, Elaine watched Teddy and wondered what this man was really doing in Sabal Palms. He didn't seem like the typical tourist. He seemed to be scheming or investigating something.

Trent returned to the table and divided the invitations between the group. "Does everyone have enough invitations to cover your names on the list?"

Adriana thumbed through her invitations. "Let's see, one, two, three . . . "

"I think Bonnie and I both have enough, and I have an extra one."

"Okay. Shall we get started? And let me know if you need me to do anything else before the party, Adriana."

"Thank you, Trent. I'll call if I need anything."

The group stood, pushed in their chairs, gathered their invitations, and took the remaining cups to the counter.

Elaine and Bonnie worked their way up and down Main Street delivering the fall equinox party invitations to the various shop owners. When they approached the café, Elaine saw Mary and Adriana inside.

Elaine looked through the window for a moment. "I think they are working on the party order in the café."

"Hey, Elaine, let's go see how it's going. Curious to find out what Adriana is ordering."

Elaine opened the café door. They entered and saw Adriana at the counter speaking with the owner. Mary motioned for Elaine and Bonnie to come to the counter.

"You two can help us with something," Mary said.

Adriana turned. "Oh, hey there. Now look at this catering menu. They have added these new items. What do you think about having heavy hors d'oeuvres, rather than any sit-down type of meal?"

Elaine replied, "Excellent idea. With that many coming over—and some guests will want to swim—the informal approach is better. And I like these new choices."

Bonnie nodded and laughed, motioning toward Elaine. "What she said."

Adriana waved her blinging hand across the menu. "It's settled then. Sid, I think we should go with charcuterie board, and these appetizer trays, and a variety of breads and crackers." Turning back to Elaine, she asked, "What do you think?"

"Looks amazing."

"I like it," Bonnie added.

"Great. Mary, think of anything else?"

"No. Oh, Sid, you know it's for thirty people?"

"Yes. Got it."

Elaine had another idea. "Ladies, should we stop by Miriam's bakery and order some cookies or other types of little sweets? She bakes sugar-free ones, also."

Mary nodded. "Yes, and I need to take her invitation to her."

Adriana turned to Elaine, Mary, and Bonnie. "Thank you, ladies. Let's go down to the bakery . . ." Adriana stared out the front window with wide eyes. "Well, well."

The other three women spun their heads toward the window.

Bonnie blurted out, "Now who is that guy talking to Teddy?"

Mary replied, "Never seen him before."

Elaine looked out the window. Across the street, Teddy stood talking to a fellow in a sweatshirt with longish hair and glasses.

"Bet he is hot in that sweatshirt," Bonnie uttered.

The other man pointed down Main Street and then to the left. Teddy replied, pointed out something on Main Street, then looked at his watch. The other man nodded and looked at his watch.

Mary's eyebrows squeezed together. "What are they up to?"

"Bank robbery," Bonnie sputtered.

Adriana gasped. "Bonnie!"

"Okay, not a bank robbery. A white-collar crime at the real estate office?"

Gasping again, Adriana said, "Seriously?"

"Okay, okay. Wait, I know! Auto theft? To drive cars across to Mexico and sell them for parts?"

Mary hollered, "Bonnie! That's a stretch, even for you!"

"Ladies, it is none of our business. If we are meant to find out, we will," Elaine reminded them.

The women were quiet.

Mary broke the silence. "You're right, Elaine," Mary noted. "We may never know what he is doing here or if he is planning anything at all. For all we know, that guy just asked him for directions."

Adriana signed the catering order and put the receipt in her designer Hawaiian purse. "That's right, Mary. We just don't know but whatever those two were doing out there might be perfectly reasonable. Ready, ladies? Mary and I have invitations to deliver, and then we will run out to Ramon and Maria's house to give them their invite and see about the tamales."

Elaine closed her car door and turned to Bonnie. "Ready? Need to run by the store?"

"No, I think I have what I need for the rest of the week. Say, still think Teddy is okay?"

"I must admit I am curious about his midnight walks on the beach. If he comes to Adriana's party this week, we can find out more about him-get to know him. And, if he doesn't show up because he left town, we won't have anything to worry about."

Bonnie huffed. "Seems like he dodged the party invite—like he didn't want to say yes, but he didn't want to say no, either."

"Sounded like he didn't know how long he will be in town. Guess we will find out at Adriana's party."

"Guess so."

After Elaine returned from taking Bella on her late afternoon walk, she decided to work on her devotionals again. She could not shake the same feeling of anxiety. She turned to her Bible and decided to take the rest of the day off and study. She knew her peace of mind was inside the Scriptures.

The rest of the week went without any surprises. No sightings of Teddy walking on the beach or in town anywhere. Elaine believed the town of Sabal Palms had escaped a close call with some shady character up to no good—or, at least, someone who had no true investment in the community.

A few days later, Elaine dressed for the party in capris and a three-quarter sleeve length Hawaiian blouse. She put on a simple pair of earrings and a casual pair of sandals. Any other pool visits to Adriana's house, she and the other women would plunge into the pool. But as assisting hostesses, the women would be all hands-on deck to help Adriana entertain and cleanup.

Elaine and Bonnie agreed to arrive at the party an hour early and help Adriana with any last-minute details. She knew Mary would likely arrive even earlier.

Pulling up the driveway at Bonnie's cottage, she found Bonnie already on the deck ready to go. She scampered down her steps, opened the car door, and plopped down.

"Hi, Elaine. You ready to kick off the fall?"

"Yes! It will be wonderful to visit with everyone! Haven't seen Cara, Juan, Carlos, and Miriam in a while."

Elaine turned out of Bonnie's drive and ambled down the road toward town. There was no traffic, and they arrived at Adriana's house earlier than anticipated.

"Here we are. I'll park over here out of the way for others to get into the driveway."

Bonnie closed her door. "It feels funny to arrive and not be juggling platters of food of some kind or bags stuffed with drinks, chips, and whatever."

Adriana swung open the front door. "Ladies! Ladies! Come in! Haven't seen you two in a couple of days. Mary is just inside. You can help put all the food around on the buffet and the counters. I set up another small table for all the paper plates, utensils, and such. And a separate smaller table for the desserts."

Scanning the house, Elaine noticed the extra decorations on the table. "Nice fall center pieces. Love your matching party plates, napkins, and cups."

"Thank you, Elaine. Let's decide about where to put this food. The caterer just came by. Of course, Sid's son offered to place it all out for me; but . . . well, you know, we girls always have the party touch!"

Bonnie laughed. "Well, I know I do!"

Everyone chuckled.

Adriana added, "Think I will wait to start the music once we get the food staged. And . . . I wanted your complete attention because . . . wait for it . . . "

"Spill it! What?"

"Well . . . " Adriana seemed to be enjoying torturing Bonnie.

"Stop all the hooey! Spill it already!"

"Okay, okay. But we shouldn't say anything about it to Teddy."

Bonnie shook her head, "Teddy again, is it?"

"Let her finish," Mary said.

Bonnie frowned. "Who knows if he will even show up?"

"Word on the street is he and that other fellow were overheard talking about making a movie here."

Mary put the tray of appetizers down and stared at Adriana. "Word on the street? Are you kidding me? Rumors? How do you know it is true?"

Elaine agreed. "Yes, Mary is right. Remember playing that game in school where everyone was to repeat a secret and by the time the 'secret' went all the way around the room, the whole message was different?"

"Oh yes, I remember that game. But I'm telling you, they were overheard talking about making a movie!"

"Adriana!" Bonnie squawked. "Maybe they were talking about going to see a movie! Or they were discussing a movie they both liked!"

Adriana continued. "All I am saying is if Teddy shows up today, listen for any details."

Elaine thought this discussion had run its course. She opened another carton of food and set the plastic cover on the counter. "How about this fruit and cheese, Adriana? Where would you like it?"

"Let's put two of those trays over here. Oh, and the dessert items can go over there. Bonnie, can you get those boxes from the bakery and set the cookies out on this tray?"

The doorbell rang.

"Hmm, that is early," Mary said.

"Probably Maria and Ramon with the tamales. Elaine, do you mind letting them in?"

"No problem."

Elaine walked through the kitchen to the large foyer and opened the door. "Maria! Ramon! So good to see you."

Maria, laden with foil-wrapped packages full of tamales, entered through the door. "Hello, Elaine. It is good to see you, too."

"Oh my, those tamales smell amazing! Ramon, can I help you with those containers?"

"Thanks. Brought all the salsas."

"Wonderful. Come on in and go through to the kitchen."

Elaine followed Ramon and Maria to the kitchen, where they joined the rest of the group.

Adriana waved her arms in the air and exclaimed, "Oh my! I am so glad you are here—and these tamales! I am sure they are just as delicious as always! I have a warming tray over here to keep them nice and steamy. Oh, and the salsas we can set right beside this tray.

Elaine, would you mind taking this smaller fruit and cheese tray out to the table by the pool?"

"No problem."

Elaine placed the tray on the poolside table and looked around the setting. A beautiful, large pool was not the best feature. Nor the decorated patio tables or even the small cabana for guests. No, the best part of the view was the one provided by God. The gentle breeze rustling through the palm fronds, the lacy pink clouds and striped sky of the sunset, and the smell of the gardenia and honeysuckle added to the beautiful setting. Although she could hear the guests arriving, Elaine paused for a moment and said a quiet prayer of gratitude.

Bonnie's abrupt clamoring to get out of Adriana's patio door interrupted Elaine's peacefulness. "Elaine!"

"Bonnie, what is it? What is the matter?"

"He's here."

"Who?"

"Teddy. You'd better get in here and diffuse Adriana before she embarrasses herself!"

"I'm sure it is not as bad as all that."

"Her voice went up to a higher pitch; her face turned red as a beet; and she is frantically fanning her face with her bracelets dinging loud enough to wake the sleeping people in China."

"Let's go invite him to come see the pool."

Before Bonnie and Elaine made their way to the patio door, Adriana and Teddy exited the house and stood on the patio. Elaine attempted to keep the shock from showing on her face as she watched Adriana, arm in arm with Teddy, walking out to the pool.

Bonnie whispered, "Oh, dear."

Elaine discreetly grabbed Bonnie's arm and gently pushed her toward Adriana. "Hello, Teddy. Bonnie and I were just observing the sunset and discussing God's artwork."

Teddy politely disentangled himself from Adriana and walked toward Elaine. "Ladies. How are you this evening?"

"We are doing well," Elaine said.

Bonnie looked sternly at Adriana. "Adriana, I think we should go greet the other guests."

Adriana, visibly not happy with Bonnie, was reluctant to go back inside the house.

"And I think we need to check on the food." Bonnie nudged. "Let's go."

Adriana gave Teddy another look and flashed a smile before she went inside.

Teddy walked around the side of the pool and examined the perimeter. "Nice-size pool. And great cabana."

"Yes. Adriana has done a good job with the landscaping and all the finishing touches."

"She has impeccable taste. This house must be worth a fortune in today's market and in this location." He looked over the property and back to the house. "Yes, this house would cost a pretty penny in today's market, wouldn't you think?"

Elaine felt the hairs on her neck standing up. Teddy's remark was a strange one. In the first few minutes of his visit to the home, he was sizing up Adriana's worth. Why would he care about the value of Adriana's home? "I am sure I wouldn't really know the worth."

"And where exactly is your house, Elaine?"

Part of Elaine's thought process was to tell Teddy it was none of his business. Then she realized she wasn't sure she wanted Teddy to know where she lived. After all, he had been at the edge of her property and didn't even know it.

Thankfully, before Elaine could answer, Carlos, Juan, and Cara appeared.

Cara quickly approached. "Elaine!" She hugged Elaine. "I haven't seen you in a while."

Bonnie returned to Elaine's side and greeted Cara.

"Good to see you, Bonnie. How is your son?"

Although Bonnie was typically not a hugger, she briefly hugged Cara and Juan. "He is doing very well, thank you."

"Miss Elaine," Juan said, "so good to see you—and Miss Bonnie."

Carlos added, "Miss Elaine. You doing . . . eh, good, yes?"

"Oh yes, thank you. It is so good to see you all."

Elaine looked at Teddy, who seemed mildly curious about what was happening. But apparently, he was not curious enough to ask about these people-or to want to meet them. But Elaine knew it would distract him from his question about where she lived. "Teddy, this is Cara, Juan, and Carlos. Teddy is visiting Sabal Palms."

Carlos and Juan shook Teddy's hand, and Cara nodded. "Es nice to meet you, eh, Teddy."

"Likewise."

"If you all will excuse me, I need to see if Adriana needs help," Elaine returned to the house.

Once inside, Elaine made a beeline to Adriana. "You need any help?"

"No, I think everything is fine in here. But we can encourage everyone to go poolside. I see several are dressed to swim."

"Okay."

Adriana stepped toward the living room. "We are so glad you all came today. There is plenty of food, so please help yourselves. And as we are greeting the fall equinox tonight, please enjoy the pool for a last-summer-first-fall swim! You will find plenty of towels in the cabana and lots of chairs poolside."

As if the cattle had been called to feed, the herd of people in the living room found their way outside to the pool.

Elaine took Adriana's arm and held her back. "Adriana, I wondered if you learned anything about Teddy?"

"Like?"

"What is he doing here in Sabal Palms?"

"I didn't get to that, but I will."

"Be careful."

"Why?"

"I am not sure of his motives, but he was curious about the value of your property. We have been down this road before-when Evergreen wanted to buy the houses here, remember?"

"Oh, I am sure it is nothing like that." Adriana waved her hand, seeming to dismiss the comment.

"What makes you certain?"

"Just think he might be, you know, trying to make friends here."

"Adriana, just be cautious. Not everyone who wants to be friends with us are people we want to have as friends."

Adriana's jaw dropped wide open.

Elaine patted her arm. "I don't mean to say anything to upset you. I just worry about you—about all of us."

"Don't worry." She waved her hand, downplaying the seriousness of Elaine's concern.

But Elaine didn't think Adriana was convinced at all. Her words had not changed Adriana's thinking about Teddy.

Elaine and Adriana joined the others outside and were greeted by splashing, laughing, and multiple conversations around the pool.

Teddy walked around the pool and nodded at the guests. He stopped to speak with Cara.

Feeling somewhat like a mother figure to Cara, Elaine moved to Cara's side. "How have you been doing, Cara?"

"I have been well, Elaine."

"Good to hear."

"Cara just told me about how she met you. She said it was around the time of Hurricane Jada."

"Yes. Most of these people here either met each other during Jada or became closer because of the hurricane. We learned to depend on each other."

Cara nodded. "Elaine helped so many people during that time. And now, because of Elaine, my faith is stronger; and I have a church home at the Church on the Shore. I know that I can depend on Jesus."

At this point of the conversation, Teddy's attention appeared to wander. He shifted from one foot to the other and looked around the crowd. He seemed disinterested in wanting to continue the conversation. "Excuse me for a moment."

Teddy made a beeline to Adriana. He engaged her in conversation, tilting his head away from the crowd. He appeared to be wanting to pull her away from the other guests by the pool. He talked in a very low voice and once even looked as if he whispered in Adriana's ear. Adriana nodded, and they went inside the house.

Elaine felt her heart pounding. What was this guy up to?

"Cara, I think I'll go check on the tamales Maria brought. Want to join me? We can see if everything is ready."

"Tamales sound good. I am hungry."

Elaine opened the patio door and entered the kitchen. She watched aghast as she realized her fears for Adriana were well-founded.

Chapter Eight

Elaine hoped her face did not convey the feeling in the pit of her stomach when she saw Adriana and Teddy standing at the kitchen counter. Adriana batted her eyes at Teddy and smiled as she wrote something on a scrap of paper. He touched her arm, flashed his glistening smile, and thanked her. She walked him to the door, turned, and twinkled her eyes again; and he left.

Adriana turned to the kitchen, where Elaine was waiting. "Oh! Elaine! I am so excited!"

"Adriana, were you giving him your phone number?" Elaine hadn't meant to pounce on Adriana, but she couldn't stop herself.

Before Adriana could respond, Bonnie opened the back door and blundered into the kitchen, promptly followed by Mary. "What is going on?" Bonnie asked.

With hands moving more rapidly in the air than her lips, Adriana exclaimed, "I am just so excited! I can't believe it! Who would ever have dreamed this would happen to me?"

Bonnie's face scowled. "Did I hear Elaine say you gave him your phone number? Adriana, whatever for? Why did he want it?"

"Girls! Girls! He *is* making a movie right here in Sabal Palms!"

"Horsefeathers! I don't believe it! I don't!" Bonnie replied. "He doesn't look like the movie-making type."

Adriana shook her head. "And whatever does a movie-making type look like? Flashy car? Great smile? Money? Well, he's got all that!"

Mary tilted her head and looked in Adriana's eyes. "Now, Adriana, sweetie, why in the world do you believe him? You don't even *know* him!"

"Well, he explained to me, and then he asked me to be in the movie," Adriana protested.

"What a bunch of rubbish! Oldest trick in the book!" Bonnie said.

Elaine calmed down. She wanted to be a voice of reason; someone had to do it. "Okay, Adriana, suppose this is true. What kind of movie?"

"A documentary!"

"Hogwash! Documentary! About what?" Bonnie blurted.

"About the history of our gulf here in Sabal Palms and the Laguna Madre region."

Elaine wanted to flesh out the story to see if there was any validity to it. She needed more details. She needed credible facts without letting Adriana know she was probably using poor judgment. "And what type of history? The storm history? The history of the settlement of the island?"

"No, no, more exciting than that. He wants to make a documentary about the ships that have gone down in the gulf."

Mary frowned and mumbled under her breath, "I was hoping the documentary would be about birds or wildlife of the coastal region."

Bonnie shook her head, "Oh, malarky, Adriana! Let me just say, I'll believe it when I see it! He probably wants to find a pirate ship and hunt for gold! You are too gullible! After all, for years, you believed a fish killed Antony!"

Elaine turned to Bonnie in disbelief. "Bonnie! That was not very kind at all."

Mary added, "Uncalled for Bonnie! Below the belt."

Adriana reached for a tissue and dabbed her eyes. She crossed her chest. "God rest his soul."

Mary looked at Adriana with a sympathetic gaze. "Now, Adriana, dear. Let's think about this for a moment. I don't want to upset you. But I . . . well"—she gestured, encircling Elaine and Bonnie—"all of us—we don't want you to be hurt. Now, if he was making a documentary about sunken ships, exactly what part did he say you would have in this . . . movie?"

"He wants to interview me. I would be one of the people from Sabal Palms he would talk to in the film. And he said, depending on my voice on the recording, I might be asked to narrate the entire documentary!"

"Fiddlesticks! I suppose he wants to come to your house for this so-called 'interview.'" Bonnie said, using air quotes.

"Yes, he said he would call me in a couple of days to set it up."

Bonnie took Adriana's arm. "You know, Adriana, when things are too good to be true, it is because they *are not true*."

"Oh, Bonnie! All of you! Let me at least see if I can find out more about it before you all judge."

Elaine felt awful for Adriana. She walked to Adriana's side and touched her arm. "Oh, Adriana, I am sorry we sound like we don't believe him, but—"

"We don't!" Bonnie screeched.

"Now, Bonnie," Elaine admonished, "let's think about this a little more for Adriana's sake. We should offer to help Adriana. Let's help her figure out any warning signs she needs to listen for that mean it is a scam."

Adriana's face dropped. "Scam?"

Elaine added, "Or on the other hand, listen for statements to indicate this is a viable movie project." Elaine wanted to continue to reason with Adriana, but the opening of the back door interrupted her.

Juan held the door open as guests, some wrapped in beach towels and others sporting swimsuit cover-ups, burst through into the kitchen. The numerous partygoers now made their way around the tables and counters loaded with party platters. Each took a small decorative paper plate and filled it with the vast variety of appetizers.

The doorbell rang; and Adriana hurried to answer it, temporarily escaping Elaine's reasoning, Bonnie's frowns, and Mary's doubts.

Adriana swung the door wide open. "Trent, Billy! Glad you are here."

Trent entered. "Sorry we are late."

Billy placed his guitar against the wall. "It's my fault. I had another last-minute phone conference."

Adriana touched Billy's arm. "Oh my, Billy. I hope everything is okay."

"Yes. All good. It was a good conference call. My agent booked another concert for next spring."

Adriana's expression changed from disappointment to delight once again. "My stars! That *is* great news! Come on in." She took wide sweeping motions toward the kitchen, which sent bracelets skittering up and down her arms. "Join the others in the kitchen and help yourselves to some food. We'll be going back out to the pool after food and refreshments. Billy, do you want to set up out by the pool to sing?"

"Yes. That would work. Thanks again, Adriana. I'll grab a bite to eat after I sing. Tonight, I am trying out a new song just for your party."

Adriana's face seemed to light up hearing this news. She waved her arms again toward the kitchen with the jangling bracelets echoing in the foyer. "How exciting, Billy! Come out to the backyard."

Elaine, Bonnie, and Mary greeted Trent and Billy when they entered the kitchen. Mary and Bonnie followed the other guests, filling their individual plates with the succulent assortment of foods.

Adriana turned to the group, put her hands together, and faced the guests gathered in the kitchen. "People, people"—she moved about the kitchen clanging her jewels—"don't forget these amazingly scrumptious desserts on this table near the end of the counter. I am sure you will love these delectable sweet treats from Mariam's Bakery."

Trent, nodding and greeting the other guests by the table, took a small paper plate and eyed the party trays. "Wow, Elaine, this looks outstanding. I believe Adriana outdid herself on providing party food this time."

"She always comes through for our parties," Elaine agreed.

"She certainly does. She uses the café downtown for her catering?"

"Yes. She has used others in the past, but I think the café has had the best appetizer trays."

"I will remember that next time I have business guests from out of town."

Elaine followed Trent to get in the food line behind other guests. She selected a variety of appetizers and placed each one on her plate and whispered, "Trent, when you have a few minutes, I'd like to speak with you about something."

"Of course. Let's fill our plates and step outside."

"I'll be right behind you."

The evening air was the perfect temperature for a pool party. Elaine followed Trent to a small poolside table that was nestled in front of several palms and a large plumeria tree. A flameless candle, encircled with a small plumeria lei, flickered, providing a warm glow.

Trent placed his plate on the table and hurried to pull the chair out for Elaine. "Thank you, Trent."

"You are welcome. Where to start on this plate? Too many choices." He grabbed a skewer of shrimp and pineapple. "This one is calling me."

"I wanted to let you know Adriana has been approached by Teddy—"

"The new guy?"

"Yes."

"For a date?"

"Worse, I'm afraid."

"Oh?"

"He was here earlier but left the party before you arrived. He dropped by to tell Adriana about a documentary he would like to make about the sunken ships in the gulf."

"Is he a filmmaker or a producer? A writer, perhaps?"

"She didn't say exactly, but she is under the impression he is a filmmaker. I don't believe he told her many details. He asked her for her phone number and said he would call her."

"Hmm . . . what is your feeling about him?"

"I am trying not to judge—we don't have all the facts. I want to be fair. But I also want to protect Adriana if he is not legitimate."

"Well, I have to say, I haven't heard about any kind of filmmaking happening here—not that I would know about all media plans. But as far as my own business sources go, I haven't heard anything. Has he done anything that makes you unsure?"

"This may sound like I am forming a hasty opinion about him without anything to warrant negative thoughts; but earlier this evening, I was out here alone when he came out by the pool. He first seemed to be measuring the pool and commented about it being a good-sized pool. Then asked me questions about Adriana's house."

"What did he want to know?"

"He was curious about the value of the house."

"That seems like a strange question to be asking, especially since he doesn't know you or Adriana. If he was in the real estate business or other type of investment business, he would likely have a ballpark estimate of the value and wouldn't be fishing for information."

"I thought so, too. And there was something in the tone of his voice that just didn't sit right with me."

"Well, Elaine, you are an excellent judge of character. You go out of your way to give people the benefit of the doubt. And goodness knows you are a person of integrity yourself. What bothered you?"

"Trent, the other thing that made me feel uneasy was he followed up the question about Adriana's house by asking me where my house is—like, exactly where I live. I didn't want to tell him he had already been by there a couple of times and once was at 4:30 a.m. I didn't want him to know I had spotted him when he was on the beach on the north shore, either."

"I understand why you and Bonnie would prefer that he not know where you live until you know him better. What did you say? How did you answer him?"

"I didn't. Thankfully, we were interrupted. But here is the thing. When Cara, Juan, and the others arrived, he was not at all interested in mixing with the crowd. I introduced him to Cara, and she told him just a bit about how we met and that she now goes to the Church on the Shore. It was as if he either didn't know what to say or the topic of Christianity was one he wasn't interested in discussing. He left abruptly and returned to talk to Adriana."

"I know the topic of religion, and especially Christianity, can make some non-believers very nervous. I encounter that often when I meet new people. But as a Christian, talking about my faith is one thing God expects me to do."

"That is an expectation for all of us, and you are right—people who do not share our faith may not welcome the conversation. Teddy seemed uncomfortable when Cara brought it up."

"Whatever his motives are, everything we know he has done so far in Sabal Palms doesn't quite add up. But if he really is going to make a documentary about Sabal Palms and if he is a true filmmaker, somebody should be able to back up his story. There should be information about him that is available to the public and investors. Tell you what, I will check around quietly to see if anyone in the field of corporate business has had any history or knowledge about Teddy Carter. I will begin checking tonight when I get home; and if I don't find anything tonight, I'll keep checking tomorrow morning when other businesses around the country are open.

"Until then, we should probably keep this between you and me. If he is legit, we will find out and not need to worry. No one else will know we have been checking up on him. On the other hand, if no one has ever heard of him or there is no history of him online, we can establish that quickly. You want to check online? Check your writing and media sources and friends. We will compare notes and see what we find out and what our next steps might be. How about you and I touch base tomorrow at the coffee shop? Say around ten?"

"Thanks, Trent. I didn't want to ask Bonnie or Mary about this guy because they already have their doubts. I believe they would see things through their already-negative lenses where Teddy is concerned. And after what happened in the past when those New Age characters came to Sabal Palms, Bonnie and Mary are more skeptical than ever about new people with unsavory motives."

Trent laughed. "It is understandable. I am sure Bonnie is about to have a fit over this. I can just imagine what she would say."

"She suspects Teddy already! Now, on to more important things." Elaine pointed to her plate.

"Yes! This incredible food!"

The other guests at the fall equinox party found their way back to the poolside tables with glowing flameless candles. Soon, the entire group of partygoers were scattered around the perimeter with their loaded plates, eating and chatting in the warm evening air.

Billy Wrangler exited ahead of the others spilling out of the door out to the pool. He walked to the opposite side and set his guitar case down. Adriana had arranged a small clearing and set up her adequate sound system she used for entertaining at pool parties.

Billy opened his guitar case, took out his guitar, and placed the leather strap around his neck. "Good evening, everyone. I think I have had a chance to speak with most of you when I came into the party this evening. But in case I didn't, hello to all my good friends here in Sabal Palms. I'll catch you after a few songs for a good visit. Now, I'm gonna play a couple of songs you are familiar with—the ones you have heard on the radio or on TV. And then, to close out, I'll be introducing a new song. The last song is one I wrote for the good people of the great town of Sabal Palms."

The group of partygoers clapped.

"If you are familiar with my music, you know I sing to bring glory to our Lord and Savior, Jesus Christ, Who saved me from the perilous journey I was on . . . and . . . well, He saved me from myself." Billy plucked a few notes and checked on the tuning of his guitar. "So, here we go."

Elaine listened to the first few songs Billy sang and recognized the lyrics she had written for Billy to put to music. In the beginning of Billy's singing career, very few people had known that Elaine was the songwriter behind Billy's hit recordings. She had sworn Adriana, Mary, and Bonnie to secrecy. But gradually, others in town got wind of her writing because Billy didn't keep it secret when he was in Sabal Palms.

The people around the pool clapped and sang along with every song. Some of the people around the poolside swayed along with the songs. One couple broke out in a dance on a corner of the patio.

Elaine had not heard the new song and was anxious for Billy to play it because typically, if Elaine didn't write all the lyrics to a song, Billy wrote the lyrics for his songs *with* Elaine. But this time, he told her he was writing a song by himself because he wanted to write a song in her honor.

After Billy sang a few of his well-known hit songs, he cleared his throat and addressed the partygoers. "Some of you know that Elaine collaborates with me on my lyrics for my recordings. And in fact, the very first song that was a big hit was one that she wrote before I knew her"—he tipped his cowboy hat to Elaine—"and I added the music. This song is for the people of this town and especially for my good friend, Elaine. The new song is a surprise to her. And I just want to say, this is the first run; so, Elaine, feel free to offer changes."

Elaine laughed. "I am sure it is wonderful, Billy."

"I wrote this new song about Sabal Palms because, well, when I am here, this feels like home. But it is not just the town because you see, when I am here, I have special feelings for the good people here on the southern coast of Texas. This place is special to me because, as you may know, Elaine here is the one who brought me to Jesus when I was on the road of no return. So, Elaine, the last song is dedicated to you."

Elaine listened intently to the lyrics and felt her heart grow warm and her face turn red. The entire song was heartfelt, and Elaine's eyes were filling with tears when she heard the words. The chorus was her favorite part of the song; it was a verse from Romans. "'For everyone who calls on the name of the Lord will be saved'" (Rom. 10:13).

When Billy finished singing, the crowd erupted in applause, turned to Elaine, stood up from their chairs, and continued clapping. Elaine preferred to fly under the radar, to be unknown, undetected, in the shadows. In this type of situation, her heart pounded; and her face turned crimson. "Thank you, thank you, Billy, for such a beautiful song."

Billy put away his guitar, nodded, and spoke to other guests, then joined Elaine at her table. "Elaine, I hope the song was okay. I'll bring the lyrics over tomorrow afternoon if that time works for you. I'd like you to check them over and see if there are any words that need to be changed. Always room for improvement."

"Oh, Billy, you know I am willing to help, and tomorrow afternoon is perfect. But I am not sure the song needs any work. I am happy to look it over for you, though."

Trent chimed in, "I liked it, Billy. It captures many of my own thoughts, especially the verse about Elaine's words touching your own heart and helping you to change your life."

"Thank you, Trent. Glad it meant something to you. Elaine is going to help me polish it up a bit. Elaine, about tomorrow, will three o'clock work?"

"Yes. I will be home."

"Great. Now"—Billy rubbed his palms together— "I'm going inside and pile a load of food on my plate. I worked up an appetite, and it all looks delicious."

***

Elaine, Bonnie, Mary, Trent, and Billy were the last remaining guests. Elaine and Billy carried the extra chairs around the pool and put them away.

Trent brought a heavy basket of wet beach towels into the utility room and set it down. "Adriana, want me to start a load of these towels?"

Adriana's dressy flip-flops clapped along the floor from the kitchen to the laundry room "Oh no, Trent. I hate for you to go to all that trouble."

"No trouble at all, Adriana."

"Well, thank you. If I can get one load finished tonight, that would give me a head start for tomorrow."

Trent began to load the machine. "Say, Adriana, I heard Teddy stopped by before I got here tonight. Sorry I missed him."

"Me, too. You should be able to catch him in town, though. He is hanging around Sabal Palms for a while."

"Oh?"

"Yes. He wants to make a documentary about the old sunken ships."

"Oh yes, Elaine mentioned he might be doing a film. Sounds like an interesting topic. Do you know much about sunken ships or anything else about him?"

Adriana laughed. I don't know a thing about sunken ships really. He wanted to interview me as a resident of the community. I don't know much about him. But I should be talking with Teddy again soon. If I find out the juicy details about the film"—she laughed— "you know I'll tell you everything."

The conversation was halted by Bonnie clunking dishes into the sink. In a loud voice, she announced, "There, now, the mess is confined to only a couple places instead of the whole house and backyard."

Elaine and Mary followed Bonnie from the patio through the doorway of the kitchen. Each carried large plastic bags of trash.

Adriana's dressy flip-flops clomped out from the laundry room, and she waved her hands about. "Girls, girls, that is plenty of help. Don't worry about the rest. I have the cleaning service coming in the morning."

Elaine put her trash bag in the hall leading out in the garage and returned. "Are you sure, Adriana? We don't mind at all."

Bonnie, out of breath, said, "Well, if you have help tomorrow, we can call it a night. What do you say, Elaine? Ready to go back out to the beach?"

"Adriana, if you are certain?"

Adriana shooed her company out of the kitchen. "Of course, Elaine. Go home. It is all under control."

***

The full moon cast a light onto Elaine's wooden steps up to her deck. She glanced out over the glassy waves reflecting the light and the gently waving palms. "No place like home," she whispered. She put her key in the lock and turned the handle.

Bella greeted Elaine at the door as soon as Elaine entered the beach cottage. "Hello, girl."

Bella ran in circles and jumped up on Elaine's leg, wagging her little tail. Elaine turned off her security system.

"I know, girl, you need to go outside. Let's go."

Bella scampered down the wooden steps and promptly ran to her little patch of grass in the back. Elaine watched Bella and scanned the yard. She remained uneasy about the middle of the night visits Teddy made to the beach. She didn't want to worry, but she did.

Heavenly Father, watch over us, she prayed.

Bella walked up the steps and back beside Elaine on the deck, her tiny paws pitter-pattering across the wooden slats. Elaine ambled from one side of the deck to the other. *No sign of anyone on the beach tonight.* "Come on inside, Bella."

Now, to get some work finished.

Sitting at her desk, Elaine knew she should work on her devotional about trust. But she was more worried about Adriana and the trust Adriana placed in Teddy without even knowing him. She wanted to be sure Adriana's trust was not placed in someone with evil motives. "I'll do a little online investigation, Teddy. Let's see who you really are."

She turned on the computer, waited a minute for the browser to open, and entered the name "Teddy Carter."

"Wow, there are a lot of people with that name."

Bella, sitting beside Elaine in her fuzzy bed, turned her head and looked at Elaine. She laid back down and wagged her tail.

"It's okay, Bella. Just talking to myself."

Elaine turned her attention to the screen. "I'll just click on each one of the listings for Teddy Carter until I find the one who is visiting Sabal Palms. I'm sure most of them will have pictures. Now, let's see. Nope, not that one. No, no . . . " After going through multiple pages on the browser, she stopped. "Let me try something different. What happens with a search for Teddy Carter and movies?"

A few names popped up on the search. "Now, let's see, is this you?" She clicked on the name. "You don't look like that—not you." She clicked the next one. "You are deceased." Again and again, she opened the links. After exhausting every name associated with movies—whether movie, TV, or Broadway actors—she came up empty.

"I know! Teddy Carter and documentary. Let's try those terms." Once again, nothing came up matching the Teddy currently visiting Sabal Palms. Any of the names she clicked had pictures of people who looked nothing like Teddy. Some were thirty years older. A couple were already deceased.

She had a more sinister thought. "Maybe I can find something under Teddy Carter criminal charges." Once again, she entered the search terms. Several entries popped up. She clicked on each one. "Hmmm . . . assault? Nope, you don't look like that." She clicked another one. "Real estate scammer." She clicked on the entry. "Nope. I would have thought that would have been a match, since you are so interested in Adriana's property. Hmm . . . how about this one?" She clicked on every link listed. The others were not matches for this particular Teddy Carter hanging out in Sabal Palms.

"Okay, Bella, this one is going to be really creepy. But just in case . . . " Bella looked at Elaine then laid back on her bed. "Here we go. FBI most-wanted." She clicked and gasped. "My goodness! These pictures give me the creeps! Cybercrimes, fugitives, capital crimes—these are awful!" She looked briefly. She could see the evil in some of the eyes of these people. "Oh! I can't look at any more of these pictures." She said a quick prayer for protection and turned off the computer, thankful she had not seen Teddy in any of the horrible pictures.

"No luck. I hope Trent has more luck talking to his contacts. Maybe he will have good news for me tomorrow."

She took a deep breath. "I will read a few Scriptures and get my mind off of these pictures."

She opened her Bible, studied for another thirty minutes, and said another prayer.

Elaine turned off her desk lamp. "Okay, Bella, time for bed."

Chapter Nine

Elaine, with Bella by her side, knocked on Bonnie's door at her beach cottage the next morning for their regular walk. Elaine hoped to take a shorter walk this morning. She was anxious to get to Main Street and meet Trent at the coffee shop.

Bonnie locked her door. "Good morning, Elaine. Ready to get going?"

"Yes! I need to walk off that food from last night."

Bonnie agreed. "I know! I ate way too much! I was a real porker! Gotta walk and keep this blood sugar down. But my sugar wasn't too bad this morning."

"Good deal. I feel the need to walk off the desserts—even if they were sugar-free! Can you imagine if Adriana had served a multi-course meal?" Elaine asked.

"I ate too much of those appetizers and the sugar-free cookies. I ate everything I am allowed to eat that wouldn't mess up my sugar. I ate two of some things. Okay, three. I really need to get moving this morning. What a spread she had!"

Elaine and Bonnie moved from the dry sand to the wet sand, where the high tide had brushed over and left a splay of seashells. They were able to walk faster on the firm sand.

Elaine glanced down at the sand. "Don't see any whelks here."

Bonnie nudged Elaine and pointed. "Look over there."

"Is that Teddy again?"

"Can't tell from here," Bonnie replied. "He is pretty far up the beach-that is quite a distance away."

"And he is walking away from us-further north," Elaine noted.

"He seems to be."

Elaine couldn't wait to hear what, if anything, Trent found out from his contacts. She didn't feel right keeping anything from Bonnie; but at this point, until they knew more, she thought it best not to encourage gossip. Elaine had only looked up Teddy's name online and found nothing. No need to talk about that.

Elaine and Bonnie neared Bonnie's cottage. "Got any plans today, Bonnie?"

"Mary is coming by in about an hour to pick me up."

"Oh? Where are you two off to?"

"She wants to take me to the wildlife display about the monarch butterflies. She thinks it will help me figure out more about how to decorate for the party. I know Adriana already has a stash of some decorations for the fall theme, but I need to add some of the butterfly festival ideas."

"That will be helpful since you are hosting the festival on your deck in just a couple of weeks. That visitor center always has great displays; I'll bet you will get some great ideas."

"Yes, and you know Mary—all about the butterflies, or birds, or alligators, or wildlife in general."

"She does love nature!"

"Love it? Hogwash! She is obsessed with it!"

"It keeps her busy. And that is a good thing. Remember how she was after her husband died?"

"How can I forget? I thought she would never be the same. She didn't leave her house for six months. But she started back to church, and that helped-you played a big part in that, Elaine."

"And you helped her, too, Bonnie. Then, once she went to church with us, she began visiting the wildlife refuge; and everything changed. She had a purpose again."

"We always stick together," Bonnie said.

Bella darted from one plover to another, but the speedy shorebirds flew off before she could catch one. She returned to Elaine's side, panting from all the running around. Elaine and Bonnie continued to walk for a while in silence.

Bonnie stopped and looked at Elaine. "You know, Elaine, thinking about what you said. You are right. Her husband and her home served as her only purpose until he passed away. It was a hard adjustment for her. But preserving our coastal wildlife is her purpose now. And speaking of purpose, we'd better get back. I have to get ready before Mary comes over."

Elaine walked with Bonnie back to her cottage. Bonnie bounced up the wooden steps and turned at the top. "Any plans this afternoon, Elaine?"

"Billy is coming over around three. Nothing after that."

"Want to come over for a dinner on the deck? Nothing fancy—especially after all that party food last night. I have a few things that are easy to throw together."

"Sounds good. I'll see what I have on hand that I can add. Say around five?"

"See you then."

"Come on, Bella, let's get back."

Elaine entered the cozy coffee shop on Main Street overwhelmed by the aroma of the strong brew. "Good morning, Alexa."

"Hi, Elaine. Usual? Coffee of the day?"

"Yes, thank you, Alexa." Elaine took the cup of bold, roasted coffee and a dollop of heavy cream and took a sip. "This is tasty. What is this one?"

"Dark roast Blackbeard's Delight."

Elaine smiled. *Everywhere I turn, there is talk of pirates.* She walked to the table at the back of the coffee shop, pulled out her chair, and took a seat. Hearing the jingle on the door, her eyes found Trent entering the coffee shop.

The coffee shop was quiet. It was unusual for this time of morning. Trent collected his order and made his way to the table.

"Good morning, Elaine."

"Morning. Awfully quiet in here this morning."

Trent nodded. "I was thinking the same thing. Some of the regulars parking on the street. They will be in soon." He took a sip.

"Did you find out anything from your contacts?"

"Not much. You?"

"I searched all kinds of terms on the internet last night—I didn't find a thing. I couldn't find anything using his name. I tried terms associated with movies and moviemaking, documentaries, criminal charges—you name it. I even searched the FBI's most wanted list. It was creepy. You know what is funny, though?"

"What's that?"

"I never knew how common the name Teddy Carter was. That name turned up several links. None of the people sounded or looked like Teddy. And there was an actor, football player, and all kinds of famous people. A couple of people with that name were already deceased. Some of the links were for people who had committed crimes. There was a real estate swindler, someone with a history of assault, a variety of crimes and people. But none of the entries matched this particular Teddy Carter."

"Interesting. It has been my experience that some criminals who seek another identity pick a very common name. Makes it harder to find the person you are looking for among many people with the same name. I did a search once for another common name that had fifty-six thousand links."

"Really? I had no idea."

"Yes. Then you must sort them out to find the right one. It delays law enforcement a while. Certainly does delay those of us who are just curious. But now, with computers, it is faster for the police and other agencies to go through all the names."

"Never thought about that."

"As far as my own contacts, I asked everyone around my business— the real estate business I used to be so involved with and my nonprofit businesses I work with now. No one had heard of him or his idea about making a documentary here in Sabal Palms. But walking down Main Street this morning, I had an idea."

"I'm all ears."

"When I was in the corporate real estate and development business, back with companies like Evergreen, large companies had issues with people stealing corporate secrets, embezzling, all kinds of white-collar crimes."

"Hmm . . . I never realized you had to deal with those issues."

"We didn't have it happen often, but I know some people in high places in businesses who had to use detectives or private investigators to find out about criminals in all kinds of white-collar crimes—fraud, identity theft, embezzlement . . . you name it. I can reach out to some of my friends and ask them about these investigations. Not sure the people they used would be in this region, but I can ask."

"Will that be a problem?"

"No. And, if they can't provide me with a local contact, I can hire a private investigator for us. I also have used a PI from time to time. I haven't talked to him in a year. But he comes down here to work with some of the corporations in the tourist industry. I can give him a call, too."

"I hate for you to go to all that trouble and expense."

"Not a problem. We aren't going to be investigating an actual crime—at least, not at this point. We are only going to ask a PI to find out Teddy's true identity. And besides, it is better to be safe than sorry. My fear is that Adriana might get in over her head. She could be in jeopardy."

"How so?"

"I would expect if this Teddy fellow is not on the up and up, his next move will be to ask people for money, especially Adriana and any people in the community with means. It won't sound like he is asking for money, but that will be what he is doing."

"Well, what would that sound like? Look like?"

"He will sell Adriana on this acting bit or being in the documentary. He will play up how important it will be to have her and tell her it is because she is local, well-known in the community, or whatever. Once she is convinced that he is sincere and wants her for the movie, he will come to her with some information about these sunken ships. He wants to sound like he is knowledgeable."

"For what purpose? After all, he will be researching the sunken ships by interviewing and surveying Sabal Palms. I would think he wants to appear like he knows everything on the topic, like an expert who wants to make a documentary."

"Oh, he will sound smart. To have credibility, he will want to sound like he has been studying this area for years and is very close to finding out the information. But he is just missing one piece of his well-researched puzzle. To find that missing piece of information, he will need something from Adriana. He will need to go out to sea and visit these ships to find the answers for part of his documentary. And that is when he will take his next step—if he is up to no good."

"What will the next step be?"

"To convince her to invest financially in the movie. He will tell her this investment will allow him to complete his research by conducting dives. These dives cost a great deal of money. He will tell her he needs to charter a boat or even more than one boat. He will need to get equipment, hire other divers; he could make up all kinds of things he needs to make this movie. And he will tell her she will be thanked in the movie credits at the end. He might tell her she will have her picture at the end with some comments. Basically, if he is a scam artist, he will tell her whatever she needs to hear to be convinced."

"Uh oh. I see how Adriana might fall for this—if he is one of these con men. She is already excited about the project. And Teddy behaves like . . . well, like he is trying to charm his way into her life. But he had no interest in any anyone else at the party."

Trent took another sip of his coffee. "My guess is he won't be interested in any of the partygoers unless he sensed they had money."

"Okay. I see your point. In our particular group, she was the only one he knew for sure had money. And you hadn't arrived to the party yet, or he might have approached you."

"Maybe not. A widowed, attractive, wealthy woman might have appeared to him to be low-hanging fruit, an easy target."

Elaine paused and thought about Trent's comments. "A PI sounds like a good idea-if we can't find out anything else on our own. But I wouldn't feel right not telling Adriana what we are thinking. I wouldn't feel right asking him to investigate without bringing Adriana in on our plans."

"Let's cross that bridge when we get there. First, I will ask around, If it is okay with you, I'll call a few friends who have dealt with this as soon as I get into the office this morning. I'll call you later if I can arrange for someone to help us out."

"Okay. If your contacts haven't heard of him or don't know anything about this filmmaking, then you will see about a PI?"

"Yes. I will check with all my contacts first and see if they can help out. Now, while I check with my contacts, maybe you can do a couple of things in town."

"What's that?"

"You have lived here for a long while and know all the shop owners, the so-called pillars of the community. This includes people and places you might not think about."

"Such as?"

"The locals who keep this place going, including the people who keep the tourist establishments going. And not just here in Sabal Palms but Port Isabel also."

"Like the gift shops?"

"Like the libraries, bookstores, museums—anyplace with information about the local area. A tourist would look in those places to see about sunken ships. So will a con man."

"Do you mean, like the Port Isabel Museum? Or the Pirate's Landing tourist area with the pirate ship rides? And the tourist information center?"

"Yes, the tourist attractions. And don't forget about the dolphin-watching cruises and any business that takes tourists out."

"I'll need to cross the causeway and go to the island. There are many establishments here in Sabal Palms and Post Isabel. But the tourist boat industry is on the island."

"If you need me to go with you, let me know."

"Thank you. Typically, I would ask one of the girls to go with me—or all of us. But under these circumstances, I'll ask around myself and get back to you."

"How about this? Just think it over, Elaine. I will ask my contacts. Because time is important, if they don't have any information on Teddy, I will ask the PI I know. He is a guy we used before for corporate investigations, and he does assignments here in the area. If he is around, we can at least talk to him. Depending on what he says, we can consider hiring him to help us out."

"Before we tell Adriana?"

"We won't ask him to take this on unless he thinks Teddy sounds fishy. And then, if you must tell her, we will let her know."

"Okay. Hopefully, your contacts know this guy. I wouldn't feel right not telling her."

"I will ask around; and if he is in the area, you and I can meet with the PI on the island. Less chance of us getting discovered over there until we know what we are up against. And, Elaine, we need to move fast. If he is planning on contacting Adriana for an interview, it will be soon. The longer he waits to approach her for money, the greater risk he takes of being discovered. Of course, this is only if he is not honest. Maybe we will learn good news, and we will find out this guy is legit."

The ringing of the bell on the door ended Elaine and Trent's conversation.

Adriana—and her perfume—walked into the coffee shop. She turned and waved at Elaine and Trent. After ordering a caramel macchiato with a double shot and extra whip, she waltzed to their table. Adorned in a leopard pattern shirt, capris, three difference necklaces, jeweled sandals, and jangling bracelets, she made it to their table with a brown bag swaying on her arm. "Well, good morning, dears!"

"Good morning." Elaine smiled. "That was quite a gathering last night. The music, the food, and the swimming—it was all fun."

"Thank you. It seemed like everyone enjoyed it."

Trent added, "And that food was tasty, Adriana. You said the café added those new appetizer items?"

"Yes."

"Tasting them at your party convinced me to use the café at my next business meeting with the people from out of town. Speaking of people out of town, I have some phone calls I need to make this morning. I need to run."

"Good to see you," Adriana said and patted Trent's arm.

Trent pushed his chair up to the table and carried his cup to the counter. "Elaine, Adriana, good to see you both."

Adriana set the large paper bag on the table and adjusted her bracelets.

Elaine asked, "What's in the bag?"

"Believe it or not, these are extras from the party last night." Adriana shuffled through the items. "Extra plastic utensils, napkins, paper plates, and a few table decorations. Mary called and asked if I had any leftover party supplies. She and Bonnie are planning the monarch butterfly party today. She said they would use the same fall patterns and buy additional butterfly decorations since it is a fall migration of the monarchs—or so she informed me. Told her I'd drop these by her house this morning. But first, I needed my usual coffee drink to get me going."

"Makes perfect sense. Do you know if the t-shirts Mary ordered for the festival have arrived yet?"

"She didn't say. Oh! I wanted to tell you; I enjoyed that new song Billy wrote for you last night. It was just precious. Very touching." She touched Elaine's arm.

"I thought it was heartfelt. It is the first time Billy had written the lyrics on his own. He asked if I would look over the words again today and make suggestions. I think what he wrote was beautiful. Although he is very talented, he feels unsure about writing all the lyrics by himself."

"Please tell Billy how much I loved the song."

"I will."

Alexa called out Adriana's name for her to pick up her to go order. "Well, I guess I'll get that drink and be on my way to Mary's. Want to tag along?"

"Thanks, but I need to get back. Have a couple of things to do before Billy arrives today.

"Okay, doll." Adriana patted Elaine's hand. "Do tell him hello."

"Will do."

Elaine drove back out to her beach house. She didn't feel very good about keeping things from Adriana and the others; but right now, she thought it was best. If Trent felt they should hire a PI, she would tell Adriana then.

The knock on her door came before Elaine was ready. She looked at the clock. *I thought he wasn't coming until three.* "Hang on, Billy."

Bella ran from the bedroom to the living room and barked an unusually fierce bark. "Hold on, Bella."

Elaine opened the door. "Billy—Oh, excuse me, you're not Billy."

"Hello. I am sorry to bother you. Wait, you're Elaine? Right? I met you at the party."

Elaine worried that Teddy could hear her heart pounding. "Yes, Teddy. Can I help you?"

"I was wondering about the beach out here. Well, to be specific, the gulf itself."

Elaine attempted to quell her fear and suspicion. "Yes? What would you like to know?"

"Have you ever picked up anything on the beach that looks like it could be . . . well, it might sound strange . . . but anything that looks like it is from the remains of a ship?"

"No, I haven't. I know many people see things along the beach and wonder about that. Mostly tourists."

"I suppose that is true."

"Are you looking for something?"

"No. Nothing in particular. Just wondering about the history of this place. And that cottage down there. Is it also occupied?"

"Yes."

"I am surprised."

"Why?"

"I suspected these were just vacation homes."

"Were you looking for a vacation home?"

"No, not really. I am staying in a hotel on the island. Pretty crowded place. Thought maybe this area had fewer people."

"The island is the number one tourist spot here."

"So, I have discovered. I might look around for another place to stay. Well, thank you."

Teddy turned and went down the steps to the walkway.

Elaine closed her door and looked out the window. She was relieved to see Teddy close his car door and drive away. *Strange visit.* She was glad he didn't stay long, and she was happy to see Billy pulling up in his truck.

Chapter Ten

Elaine went out on the deck to wait for Billy to walk up the steps. He glanced back at the car pulling down the road, and asked, "Visitor?" He followed Elaine and settled in a chair on the deck. He placed his guitar case next to his chair and faced the shore.

"In every sense of the word."

"How so?"

"You didn't get to meet him at the party last night. He left before you and Trent arrived. He said he is visiting, but no one seems to know exactly how long."

"Oh, and that is unusual because? Some tourists come here and never leave. Me, for one."

"You weren't really a tourist. You came here to—"

"Meet you and tell you about my new life and how you helped me turn my life around. I know. I was not the typical tourist. But once I saw this beautiful place, I knew it was going to be my new home. Maybe he felt the same way."

"He could be one of the people who immediately falls in love with the peacefulness of Sabal Palms. But on the other hand, he mentioned starting to work on a film project."

"I can understand that, for sure. I realized this place"—he gestured toward the beach—"was picturesque when I first came to your door that day. A pristine beach here. Perfect setting for a movie."

"It is. Just curious if you have heard anything about Teddy or seen him in town?"

"No. This is the first time I have seen him. You met him last night at the party, and then he came here today? I don't want to be nosey, but why was he here?"

"I have seen him in town and on the beach before he came to Adriana's party. He asked if we ever found anything out here on the beach that looked like it was from a sunken ship."

"Strange. Let me guess—his movie is about pirate ships. Looking for buried treasure, I imagine."

"Sunken ships in the gulf. So far, he hasn't mentioned treasure. But isn't that usually why people want to look for sunken ships? Anyway, if you hear anything, let me know."

"Sure will."

"Did you bring a copy of the lyrics?"

"I did. Right here inside my guitar case."

Billy opened the case and took out the tattered pages with handwritten lyrics. "Here you are."

Elaine examined the words on each page. "This is even more beautiful than I remembered, Billy. You speak of redemption, second chances, and grace. It is wonderful."

"How can I improve the lyrics?"

"I wouldn't touch a single word of this song. Not a single word. It is so heartfelt, sweet; and I sense the precise emotions you felt when you were being saved yourself. In each verse, you tenderly tell people of your struggle and your new life. Your emotions change throughout the song and reflect what new believers feel when they are going through the repentance, redemption, and grace thought process."

"Can I improve on the rhyming or the beat of the words?"

"Billy, trust me when I tell you this. This song, these words, written exactly as they are, will touch many people. I believe this song might be better received than any of your other songs."

"Seriously?"

"Yes. Can you play it for me once more? If I hear anything else in the rhythm that needs to be changed as you sing, I'll let you know."

"Okay. Here goes."

Billy played and sang the song from the beginning to the end. When he finished, Elaine once again had tears in her eyes.

"So beautiful just like it is, Billy. It needs no improvement. It's perfect."

Elaine and Bella met Bonnie for a quick easy dinner around five o'clock. Although she enjoyed the meal and the company, she and Bella were ready to call it a day. "Bonnie, can I help you clean up?"

"No. Paper plates are easy enough."

"Want the leftover casserole in a container for the fridge?"

"Sure. Here. Just put it in this one."

Elaine placed the small amount of casserole in the fridge. "How was your meeting with Mary today? And your trip to the wildlife center?"

"It was interesting. I saw a few interesting displays about the butterfly migration. And Mary and I decided we could make a small replica for the center piece of the buffet for the party."

"Great idea."

"Yes. She is a whiz at making little butterflies out of paper. Then, she uses colored markers to copy the monarch pattern. That girl can whip those paper butterflies out in minutes."

"She is crafty. Do you need any help with the menu?"

"Mary will call you about that. We are going to meet and go over our plans—the ones we outlined when we first met to plan the fall festivities. Should be a quick meeting at the coffee shop in a day or two."

"Okay. Guess Bella and I will walk back home. Oh, I wanted to let you know something. I am just thinking about this now, and it was pretty strange."

"Oh?"

"Teddy stopped by my house today."

"What? You're just thinking about this now? Were you expecting him?"

"Guess I got distracted once Billy came over and didn't think about Teddy the rest of the day. I certainly was not expecting him to come to my house. He knocked on my door a few minutes before I was expecting Billy."

"Whatever did that schemer want?"

"We don't know yet if he is a schemer—"

"Swindler? Stalker?"

"Bonnie! He didn't know it would be me answering the door, so he isn't a stalker. He didn't know I lived there. And we don't know if he is a swindler. Anyway, back to the point. He was surprised people lived in these cottages on the beach."

"Cottages? As in your cottage and my cottage?"

"Yes."

"Good grief. That . . . that . . . buttinsky!"

"He said he thought they were vacation properties."

"What? That is strange. He was thinking they would be vacant? Was he just snooping around?"

"He said he was staying on the island, and he wanted someplace less crowded. He likes our beach."

"Hmmm . . . something about him. Can't quite put my finger on it. Let me think . . . I know, scoundrel?"

"Oh, he had another question, too."

"And?"

"He wanted to know if I had ever found anything on the beach that looked like it was washed up like it was from the remains of a ship."

Bonnie shook her head. "He is up to no good. I feel it in these old bones. No good whatsoever."

"I just wanted to make you aware he is still in Sabal Palms, and he is looking around in our little area here on the beach. Just be careful. We should both be cautious."

"I agree."

Elaine turned to leave. "Okay, Bella and I will head back. Come on, Bella. Let's go home."

Bella scampered to the door.

Bonnie followed Elaine and Bella to the door. "See you in the morning, Elaine?"

"Yes. We will be ready for our walk."

The next morning, Bella tagged along behind Elaine and Bonnie along the wet sand, leaving tiny paw prints on the way. Elaine breathed in the salt air. She felt invigorated and ready to get her day underway. The daily exercise, the seaside views, and the company along the way contributed to lifting her energy each day.

"Always great sunrises out here. Something about the light reflecting on the water, those wispy clouds, and the colors of the sky. And this morning, I would call this cotton candy and deep blue stripes across the horizon—one of my favorite combinations of color for sunrises on the beach."

Bonnie stopped and looked around. "I agree. The colors are magnificent this morning. Great views of the sky and the water. And today, for a change, no one is out on the shore but us. I'm going to spend some time out here looking for that special righthanded lightning whelk."

"They are very rare."

"I have set my mind on finding one of those lightning whelks and showing it to Mary. She doesn't think I will find one."

Elaine laughed. "You have your mind set on it. If you do find one, I want to see Mary's expression when you show it to her."

"I'll let you know. Be prepared! I'm gonna shock her and find one."

"Okay, Bella and I are going to walk back. Have a few things to do today and want to find some time to write."

"Sounds good. I'll check you later." Bonnie turned and walked back out toward the water darting back and forth, avoiding the waves while checking for shells.

"Come on, Bella."

Bella scampered along the wet sand, crossed over the dry sand dunes sprinkled with sea oats, and ran up the wooden stairs.

Elaine unlocked the door and stepped inside just as her phone buzzed in her shorts pocket. She took out the phone and checked the caller ID. "Hello, Trent."

Trent sounded excited. "Elaine, I couldn't find any other information about Teddy, but good news. I have a PI lined up for us."

"Okay."

"He was in the area finishing an investigation for one of the hotel chains on the island. He can meet with us over there today at lunch."

"On the island? Today?"

"Yes."

"Where? What's the hotel?"

"He doesn't want to meet in the hotel where he just finished his job."

"That's understandable. Name the place, and I'll meet you over there."

Trent cleared his throat. "He wants to meet in an open-air café on the south end of the island. It's called the Half-shell Hideaway."

"I know the place. Great décor of parrots and palm trees everywhere. What time are we supposed to meet him?"

"Can you make it by 11:30? He wants to beat the crowd of winter Texans and tourists coming in for lunch."

Elaine glanced at her watch. "Sure. See you there."

Elaine spent the rest of the morning inquiring about any potential documentary film making projects in the shops of Port Isabel. She stopped first in the local museum and then the bookstore across from the lighthouse of Port Isabel. She asked in two other gift shops. No one had any idea of film projects or individuals doing research about the topic of sunken ships in the gulf for the purpose of making a documentary. Her good friend at the bookstore at first asked if Elaine was going to write a book about sunken ships. That question brought an uncontrollable laugh. Then she thought maybe someday she might write a Christian book about sunken ships. Maybe something about stormy seas and sunken ships? She would think about it.

Elaine thanked the bookstore owner, museum personnel, and the other shop owners. She started her trek to the island. Steering her car back onto the street, she hoped Trent had some good news for her.

No matter how many times Elaine drove across the causeway, she never tired of the panoramic view. The bridge, spanning over two miles across the bay, provided a postcard picture of the skyscraper condos, hotels, fishing boats leaving from their docks, and the bayside restaurants. A formation of pelicans glided above the water, and a single parasailing tourist floated by. Reaching the end of the causeway, Elaine slowed and turned right. The restaurant, located on the far south end, provided an excellent view of the Space-X launches and the more distant channel to the Port of Brownsville.

She parked the car and grabbed her purse, small writing tablet, and a pen. She moved along the crushed seashell parking lot and up the wooden steps to the deck wrapped around the building. A tall, wooden pelican statue, surrounded by shorter posts or pilings, wrapped in rope, stood near the front door.

A host opened the restaurant door. "Welcome. Come on in. Table for one?"

"No. I'm meeting others. I believe there will be three of us."

"Oh, a gentleman over there said he was waiting for two others. Is that who you are looking for?"

Across the restaurant, Elaine saw Trent sitting at a window table overlooking the bay.

"Yes, thank you."

Elaine glided across the room. Trent stood up and held the chair out for Elaine. "Thank you, Trent."

"I didn't have any luck with the other contacts I know. No one seemed to know anything about a film project in this area. Our PI just called and said he was on the way. I think you will like this guy. Very down to earth. He can tell us the procedures he will use to help us identify this Teddy person."

"Trent, do you think we are overreacting?"

"In my experience, no. A new person doesn't insert himself into a situation or place in the way this guy did. His mysterious appearances, strange questions, and unusual behaviors whether night or day. You know the one thing I didn't see or hear about him?"

"What's that?"

"He doesn't appear to be on a vacation. There has been no sign that he is enjoying himself. It is like he is on a mission of some sort. Anyway, it doesn't hurt to check him out. You know what they say, better safe than sorry. But I think Mr. Case will be able to find out for us." Trent's eyes scanned over to the entrance to the restaurant. "Here he is now."

An unassuming, medium-height man dressed in a Hawaiian shirt and khaki shorts walked to the table. "Hi, Trent. Good to see you." The man extended his hand.

Trent shook his hand and turned to Elaine. "Elaine, this is Mark Case, Private Investigator."

"Nice to meet you." Elaine shook his hand.

Trent motioned to the chair. "Have a seat, Mark."

Mark tapped on the menu. "Did you already order?"

"Oh, no, we just arrived," Trent said. "Do you have a recommendation?"

"I usually get the fried oyster basket with fries." He laughed. "I don't follow healthy eating while I'm on the island."

Elaine looked over the menu. "This shrimp Caesar sounds wonderful."

"It does," Trent said. He looked at the menu once more, and his eyes locked in on something. "Wait, I think I changed my mind. The shrimp po boy looks great."

The waitress returned to the table. "Ready to order?"

Trent said, "I believe we are. Elaine, after you."

After their orders were placed, Mark began. "Elaine, I have known Trent the past several years."

"Oh. Did you work with him in his real estate development company or in his corporate businesses?"

"Yes, as a matter of fact, I worked in both the real estate and the corporate businesses. And once Trent began working in the nonprofit sector, I helped him a few times to sort out some scam artists."

"I see."

Mark continued, "Yes, it has been pretty simple work to find out if these people were scammers or had sincere interests. I was glad to find out you were on the island."

Elaine felt better about the process. "That's good. That is the kind of work we had in mind."

"Oh? Another potential scammer for the nonprofit, Trent?"

"No, not this time, Mark. It is a bit more personal. Elaine, would you like to provide the details?"

"Of course."

Mark explained, "Okay, Elaine, I need to know a little bit about what is going on so far with the person you want me to investigate. What is the situation?"

"There is a new man in Sabal Palms that has been making his presence known to a good friend of ours. Our friend's name is Adriana Manale, and she is fairly well-to-do in our community and well-known."

"Got it. And this new person is interested in her, and you don't trust his motives?"

"Yes. And I am afraid he is going to ask her for money."

"So, not just a romantic kind of interest? Not concerned if he is already married?"

"No. Nothing like that. I mean, I hadn't thought about that at all. But here is the thing. He has been here for a few days showing up in the same places looking around. He said he is going to make a film—a documentary about sunken ships."

"And you think he might want to ask Adriana to invest in this movie? You don't think he is really making a movie, do you?"

Elaine replied, "I'm not sure. And now he says he wants Adriana to be in this movie. He wants to meet with her personally for an interview."

"This sounds like a typical scam routine. Someone convinces an unsuspecting person they can star in a movie if they will help finance the movie. He might mention a specific project for the investment-like to make a trailer of the documentary to show to other investors. Or he might tell her he needs the money for equipment or to hire a cameraman, rent a studio, and so on. Of course, the movie will never be made. But he will want investors just to grab some money and disappear. A true filmmaker won't ask for funding from individuals who have no history in this industry unless they are extremely wealthy."

Trent said, "That is what I thought. And Adriana—she will give him the benefit of the doubt. I'm afraid she will invest her own money and then be hurt—not to mention the financial loss."

"This may sound like a strange question, but I need to ask you, Elaine. Has your friend, Adriana, ever been in the news? Like national news where this stranger might have found her?"

Elaine thought for a moment. "Why, yes. She was in the news. It was close to two years ago. There was a story picked up by national news about how her husband was killed."

The waitress brought their individual plates and set each one on the table. "Anything else?"

"Nothing for me," Elaine said.

"It all looks good," Trent replied.

As they each began to eat, Mark motioned to Elaine, "Go on. What was the story in the news?"

"There were a couple of stories that made national news about Adriana. The stories were about Adriana's husband being killed by Frankie the Gun."

Mark's eyes widened. "Oh, yes. I heard about that. Hold on a minute, are you *that* Elaine? The Elaine who wrote something, and Frankie the Gun found it? Then he confessed?"

"Yes, that is me."

Mark paused a moment, leaned forward, and talked in a lower voice. "It all fits together now. Frankie the Gun is on TV telling his story. Now, any story about a mobster like Frankie the Gun will draw the crooked elements like a magnet. Your strange man sees the story on TV and decides to find out a way to cash in on the poor widow with money. He starts by studying anything that would build up a good story for an investment. He probably learned Adriana was from this coastal area and that started him thinking about pirate ships, sunken treasures, and so on. But the real treasure he seeks is Adriana's bank account."

"You mean this guy, this Teddy Carter—"

"That's his name?"

"Yes, this Teddy Carter could have sought Adriana out in the beginning because of that story?"

"I don't know for sure. In my years of experience, these con men take any angle and use it. It wouldn't surprise me one bit if the whole thing started with that news story. He might have seen her as a grieving widow who would be an easy mark. Gullible. And vulnerable to being exploited, taken advantage of, an easy swindle."

Trent added, "By the way, we have not been able to verify his name."

"So, Teddy Carter is the name he has told you?"

"Yes."

Trent added, "And we have checked around a little. I asked around with my contacts. Elaine checked online."

"Okay. I will do a few standard things PIs do and see what turns up."

Elaine was concerned that Mark might upset Adriana once she learned what would be going on in the next few days. "Exactly what are some of the things you would do? I don't want Adriana to be upset about the investigation."

"I will be discrete. No one will notice me. Much of what I will do is check, like you did Elaine, with online sources. I have some connections and can investigate using law enforcement databases."

"Like the police database?"

"Yes and a few other connections that I can't reveal. My sources just help me out . . . informally, so to speak. And I will be undercover. Adriana and your friends won't notice me. You and Trent probably won't recognize me either. But if you think you see me, just ignore me."

"I understand."

Elaine asked, "Anything else? Or can we help you in any way?"

"Can you tell me anything else about this fellow? Does he have a car?"

Trent nodded. "He is driving a car, but it may be a rental. It is a new silver convertible."

"Sounds about right. Didn't happen to get the plate?"

"No, I didn't," Elaine said. "When he showed up at my house, I just wanted him to get away from me."

"So, he knows where you live?"

"Yes. He discovered it accidentally."

"Not sure about that. He might have wanted you to think that. Another ploy to follow up about Adriana's friends."

"Elaine, I want you to be careful. If you need anything at all or suspect something is going on, contact me or the police. Meantime, I can run down that car. Now, one more thing. Are either of you on social media? Any way he can be investigating you, Elaine? Or your businesses, Trent?"

Elaine said, "I didn't think about that. I can check on the sites I have in case he has made any comments. I doubt he found me there because my posts are usually Bible verses and prayers."

"Do you know if Adriana is on any social media sites?"

Elaine shook her head. "No. Not anymore. After all the commotion with the Frankie the Gun story, she hasn't been online at all as far as I know."

"Okay. That is probably for the best, given her situation. Now, tell me some of the places you have seen this fellow, and you said he has shown up more than once at some places?"

"Yes."

"Okay, then, tell me the times he has been at each place. I will use this as a starting point to get eyes on him. Since you can't find him online, I want to see his face in case he is a con I've worked with in the past, unless either of you have a picture of him."

"I don't have a picture, but it makes sense for you to go find him in the places he visits," Elaine said.

Mark pushed his empty plate toward the middle of the table and took a small pad of paper from his pocket and a pencil. "Tell me the first time and place you saw him."

"Uh, okay. The first time was, I believe, at the coffee shop. He has been there a couple of times around ten in the morning."

"Anything else about these coffee shop visits?"

"One time, he talked with another man briefly out on the street. I had not seen that man before either."

"Okay, so he might have a behind-the-scenes partner. Where is the next place you have seen him?"

"He has been on the beach—the beach where I live."

Mark hastily took notes as Elaine talked. "I will need your address."

Elaine gave Mark directions and the address on her beach cottage and explained, "But he hasn't been in the exact same place on the beach. He has walked to different places."

"Tell me more about the beach visits."

"We have seen—"

"We? Who has been with you?"

"Oh, Bonnie, a good friend—she lives out on the beach also."

"So, Bonnie knows who this person is and has witnessed him on these same occasions?"

"Yes. She has seen him most of the times on the beach. But I also saw him a few times when she didn't. He came out one night at 4:30 a.m., and she didn't see him that time. And he came and knocked on my door yesterday. I don't think he knew it was my cottage—he looked surprised when I opened the door."

"You have seen him several times out on the beach, and the times are not predictable."

"Correct."

Mark continued writing his notes after Elaine had provided the answers. He looked up and asked, "And these are the only times you have seen him?"

"No. He came to the party."

"Invited?"

"Yes. One of his visits to the coffee shop, Adriana invited him. We had the invitations out on the table, and she handed him one."

"Okay. Thanks. How was he at the party?"

"That's when he first told Adriana about the movie and asked for her phone number. And he left shortly afterward. Trent had not even arrived to the party yet."

"I see."

Trent waited for Mark to finish writing before he asked his question. "Mark, what is your plan?"

"When I leave here, I will start with the online investigation and see what data is out there on this guy and attempt to verify his real name. Next, I'll be hanging around town and out on the piers and the marina."

Elaine asked, "Piers?"

"Elaine, if he is actually doing a documentary, he will be checking out local resources—boats to charter, talking to boaters, fishing guides—that sort of thing."

"Okay. That makes sense."

"And heads up, I will be going around town and out by your house. You might not recognize me; and if you do, just go along with the idea that you don't know me. I will be a tourist, fisherman—"

"I understand."

"Any other questions for me, Elaine? Trent, can you think of anything else?"

"No. Not right now."

Mark put his tablet in his pocket. "Oh, either of you know where this guy is staying? Island? Hotel?"

"When he knocked on my door, he said he was surprised people lived in the cottages because he was hoping to rent one and get off the island."

"Good. We know, at least for now, he is on the island. I will get back to you both in a couple of days. Well, it was nice meeting you, Elaine. And, Trent, good doing business with you again."

"Likewise, Mark."

Mark pushed his chair up to the table and left the restaurant.

"Well, Elaine, what did you think?"

"I think Mark will be a big help for us to determine if Teddy is credible. I am relieved to know we can get some answers."

"I agree. He is very good at what he does."

"Trent, you know I could never had put the pieces together like Mark did. It makes sense that someone would seek out Adriana because of the story on the news."

"Now, I have just a couple of questions for you, Elaine. When will you tell Bonnie and Mary what is going on? And what are you going to tell Adriana?"

"I think I need to pray about this one, Trent."

"I would imagine so. May I make a suggestion?"

"Of course."

"It is so hard to keep things from your best friends. I know how close you all are. It might be best to tell them sooner rather than later. Mark will begin his work today."

"Do you think I should tell her today?"

"Maybe best to go ahead and let her know. I wouldn't make a big to do about it but the next time you see her . . . "

"Trent, this just feels so . . . sneaky."

"I know. The sooner you tell your friends, the easier it will be for you. And remember, if Teddy is legit, you will be relieved knowing Adriana is safe. But if he isn't, we can warn her before she gets into trouble."

Elaine patted Trent's arm. "You're right, Trent. I know you are right."

"And, Elaine, if you or any of the others need anything, you know you can call or text me."

Elaine winked. "I have you on speed dial."

"Okay. Good. I am staying in Sabal Palms at the house until we get this resolved."

Elaine looked on the table around the dishes. "Did the waitress bring the check?"

"Don't worry. I got this."

"Thank you so much, Trent."

Chapter Eleven

Elaine's trip back over the panoramic causeway was not as peaceful as her trip to meet Trent and Mark earlier. She had mixed feelings. She knew in her heart that Trent was right. She knew she would need to tell Adriana about the investigation right away. Adriana had been duped before, believing that her husband had died in a fishing boat accident. She believed her husband had been killed when he attempted to reel in an enormous fish. But when Frankie the Gun confessed to the killing, she knew the truth. She knew her husband had been murdered by very bad actors. It was hard for her to accept that her husband experienced such a traumatic and violent death.

"Was Adriana better off knowing that Antony was murdered?" she murmured to herself. That was a question she couldn't answer. But one thing she knew, as far as Adriana's present life was concerned, she didn't want Adriana to be hurt again. The investigation was necessary.

By the time Elaine returned to her beach house, she had talked herself into believing telling Adriana about the PI was the best thing to do. Obtaining the services of a private investigator was for Adriana's protection. Elaine had no plans to see Adriana again for two more days. That would be the night of the monarch butterfly party. She thought it would be better to tell Adriana in a different setting, not during a party.

Elaine decided the best thing to do was to invite the girls over for an impromptu dinner. She wanted to tell Adriana about the PI before Teddy tried to take advantage of her. And she thought telling Mary and Bonnie might help decrease their anxiety. She felt more at ease herself knowing Mark was checking on Teddy and would get to the bottom of things.

Elaine opened her front door and found Bella anxiously hopping around and spinning in circles. "Hello, girl. Need to take a run out to the back?"

Elaine tossed her purse on the counter. Bella planted herself by the door.

"Okay. Let's go."

Bella hopped down the steps, and Elaine wasn't far behind her. She watched Bella make her rounds in the small patch of yard behind the beach house. Bella ran back to Elaine, wagging her tiny tail.

"Ready to go back inside? I need to call the others and ask them to come over for a cookout."

Elaine laughed knowing Bella wouldn't answer her, but she always asked the little dog questions as if she was a little furry person. Elaine turned back toward the beach house and noticed puffy storm clouds towering over the water some distance away. "Hmm . . . wind out of the south. You know what that means, Bella? Warmer temperatures. We might have another storm later tonight, Bella. Let's get inside."

Bella walked an inch away from Elaine's ankles, eagerly waiting for a sign that Elaine truly was going into the kitchen to get the dog food. Elaine felt the fuzzy miniature schnauzer's face bump against her. "You must be hungry. Come on."

She poured the food made especially for small dogs into the bowl, put the bowl on the floor, and watched Bella zero in on the food.

Elaine looked at the clock on the kitchen wall. "Good. A couple of hours until dinner. I'll text the girls."

Elaine grabbed her phone and typed out a group text.

"Hi, ladies. Having an impromptu potluck cookout today. My place. I have shrimp to grill. Want to bring sides and come over around five?"

From Mary: "I was just wishing I had something good for dinner! I can bring a big salad and dessert."

From Adriana: "Girl! Great idea! I have some great deli treats for appetizers."

From Bonnie: "Bringing some healthy squash casserole and sugar-free cookies. Thanks!"

Elaine turned to Bella, "That worked better than I expected. Now, to get the shrimp ready."

Bonnie, toggling a large casserole dish in one hand and a tray of cookies in the other, tapped on Elaine's door with her elbow. "Hey, Elaine," she called out.

Elaine ran to the door. "Sorry. Here, bring those inside. I could have picked you up."

"No bother. It wasn't hard walking over—just couldn't open the door."

Elaine took the tray of cookies from Bonnie as she stepped inside. "Delicious-looking cookies—and that casserole looks wonderful."

"Just needs to pop in the oven at 350 degrees for about thirty minutes to bring it all together."

"I'll preheat the oven. Just set it here," Elaine tapped the counter.

"Okay. Want me to get the cookie tray out of your way? I can put it over there on the table?"

"Sure."

"Guess Adriana is late. And Mary probably picked her up." The glare from the car traveled through the window and across the room. "Oh, looks like they are coming in the drive."

Car doors closing confirmed the arrival of Mary and Adriana.

"Can you get that door?"

"Sure thing."

Adriana entered the door, appetizers in hand. "Dear! So good of you to throw this last-minute soiree. My, but I needed a treat today!"

Elaine's mind beelined to her task at hand. She was not sure Adriana would like the reason for the impromptu dinner. She said a quick prayer all would go well.

With their plates filled with grilled shrimp and the extra sides of the potluck, the women decided to take their plates outside on the deck. Bonnie ran inside, grabbed the cookie plate, and set it on the outdoor table.

Everyone found their places at the table and pulled up their chairs.

Bonnie scooted her chair closer to the others. "Elaine, this view. Are we blessed or what?"

"Great weather, good friends, and delicious food. Indeed, we are!" agreed Mary.

Adriana placed her tea glass on the outdoor table. "Tell me, Mary, all the final plans made for the party this week?"

"I believe so. Finished up the center piece today, and the t-shirts will be ready tomorrow. I ordered for kids, too. We will sell a ton of them at the monarch festival this Saturday."

Elaine wasn't quite certain how to open the topic of Teddy for discussion. She said a quick prayer that God would provide an opening and that all would go well. He listened. Adriana opened the topic herself.

"Oh," Adriana said waving her hand toward the water, "it is no wonder Teddy wants to make a movie here. Just look at the view. It is incredible here."

Mary and Bonnie glanced at each other and rolled their eyes.

"Speaking of Teddy," Elaine began, "has anyone seen him around today?"

Adriana quickly answered, "No, doll. Did you?"

"No. Not today."

Adriana continued cutting her shrimp into smaller pieces, "I'm sure he is just making arrangements. He should be calling me any day for an interview."

Elaine locked eyes with Bonnie and Mary and then fixed on Adriana. "About that . . . "

Adriana's eyes popped wide open; and with a questioning expression, she asked, "What? Do you know something?"

"No, I don't. But, Adriana, I am concerned. I think we all are."

"About what?"

"Please listen to my words and know that I am speaking out of the utmost concern and love for you."

Adriana stared at Elaine. "Okay. What?"

"It's just that we—all of us—don't know anything about him. I don't want you to be hurt by a stranger who just shows up in Sabal Palms and hangs around without telling us much about himself."

"Like what?"

"We don't really even know where he came from."

"I imagine Los Angeles or somewhere out in California."

"But he didn't tell you?"

Bonnie and Mary's eyes bounced back and forth watching this dueling conversation.

"No, he didn't say. But I didn't ask either."

"I was wondering if he gave you a business card or something?" Elaine asked.

"No. What is this all about? Is there something you are not telling me?"

"I am going to tell you because I want you to understand my concern."

Bonnie and Mary both stopped chewing and watched to see what Elaine was going to say.

"The other night at your party, Teddy asked unusual questions. He seemed interested in your house and its value. And he has been visiting the beach in front of our cottages at all hours."

Adriana waved her hand as if to dismiss what Elaine said. "I'm sure he was just visualizing what he wanted to do in the documentary."

Mary blurted, "I'm bumfuzzled!"

Bonnie couldn't take it any longer and the words spewed out, "Oh, Adriana! Why would he come out to the beach at 4:30 a.m.?"

Adriana looked stunned.

"Mary, Bonnie, please. Let me have just a moment," Elaine said.

Bonnie nodded, and Mary stared with her eyes wide.

"Adriana, the next morning, you came into the coffee shop briefly, and I was having coffee with Trent. We are both very concerned for you. He suggested that we try to find out more about Teddy just for your protection."

Adriana remained silent.

Elaine continued, "He asked around, and I searched the internet."

"Did you find something bad?"

"No. In fact, we both came up empty."

"See? He is perfectly harmless."

"The point is, if Teddy was in filmmaking or known for making documentaries, we would have found out something about his work."

Mary pointed to Elaine. "You have a point." She turned to Adriana. "She makes a good point, Adriana. He should have social media or something out there on him."

"I can ask him when he calls me to set up the interview."

"I don't want to wait until then. And I hate to say this, Adriana but if he is up to no good, he will tell you something that sounds innocent but could be a lie. He might tell you whatever he thinks you need to hear."

Adriana looked down momentarily, then asked, "So you are saying I shouldn't be interviewed?"

"I am saying that I would like to find out more about him. Trent agrees with me."

Bonnie and Mary simultaneously said, "Me, too."

Elaine could tell Adriana felt defeated. "But don't give up on the idea. He could be perfectly legit. But the point is, we need to find out for sure."

Bonnie said, "Yeah, before he swindles you out of some money."

Adriana protested, "Wait a minute. He didn't ask me for any money."

"Not yet," Elaine replied, "but he might in the future."

"Can't I just tell him no?" Adriana insisted.

Elaine paused and gave Adriana a moment. "Adriana, he could be legit. Trent suggested we need to investigate this further, and I agreed with him."

Mary asked, "What kind of help?"

"Trent hired a PI."

"What?" Adriana gasped. "A PI snooping around in my business?"

"Oh my," Mary said.

Bonnie blurted out, "Good grief! Not your business, Adriana. Teddy's business."

Adriana's face turned ghostly white, and she fanned as fast as she could with a paper napkin, causing her bracelets to clink.

Elaine waited until Adriana ceased fanning and rested her arm back on the table. Elaine placed her hand on Adriana's arm and looked into her eyes. "Adriana, here is the thing. If Teddy is on the up and up, a PI will find out soon; and you can go ahead with the interview for the film. But if he has a history of bad actions with others or complaints against him and so on, we will know that, too. I am just asking that you trust us, all of us, to watch out for you and as soon as we know something, we will go from there."

Without saying a word, Adriana nodded. A tear emerged, and she wiped it away. "Thank you, Elaine. I know you mean well."

Elaine patted Adriana's hand and said, "Promise not to mention this to Teddy or anyone else?"

"Of course."

Turning her gaze to Mary and Bonnie, she repeated the request. "And you ladies, no mention of this to anyone else."

They nodded.

"But, Elaine"—Adriana wiped another tear and sighed—"what do I do if Teddy calls me?"

"Just see what he has to say. Act as you normally would act. And for all of us, if we see Teddy in town or out along the beach, don't say anything out of the ordinary."

Mary asked, "How long will this all take?"

"The PI said probably only a few days to confirm Teddy's identity. If he needs longer, he will let Trent know."

Bonnie finished her plate and reached for a cookie. "And until then, mum's the word."

"Yes."

Bonnie put the cookie to her mouth and hesitated for a moment. "Elaine, if we see him around or notice anything out of the ordinary, should we let the PI know?"

Elaine did not answer immediately. She wanted her words to be the right ones. Then she said, "In that case, I think we contact Trent. He has had experience with white collar crimes associated with his former businesses. He can tell us if what we see or hear should be reported to the PI."

Elaine continued, "I think we are all in agreement. Anything else?"

Adriana seemed bothered by her thoughts. "Elaine, if he wants to do the interview and we haven't heard anything yet, what should I do?"

Mary smiled and replied, "That's easy. You schedule the date further out."

Elaine could see that Adriana was not pleased with Mary's solution. "You could offer to do something else with him if we don't know anything yet."

"Oh? Like what? Dinner?"

"No, I was thinking something more along the lines of meeting him down at the Port Isabel Museum and taking the tour. He might enjoy seeing the ship exhibits down there."

Bonnie swallowed another bite of her cookie, then replied, "Good idea. We could all go."

Adriana laughed and dabbed tears from her face. "If you all show up there, it might seem a bit strange."

"Adriana, let's take it one day at a time," Elaine suggested.

Adriana gathered herself. "Okay."

Elaine needed to continue her discussion about the PI. She wasn't sure how the next part would go over. "This PI—I met him and he is a nice fellow."

"What?" Bonnie shrieked. "You met him already? When?"

"Trent knew the PI from other investigations. He was on the island. He invited me to meet with them today."

"And?" Mary asked.

"He is very nice and experienced in these kinds of things—you know, helping to find out people's identity and background."

Elaine noticed that Adriana remained upset. "Adriana, I am so sorry if all this upsets you. We will find out who he is and put this behind us. It could be nothing to worry about at all."

Adriana's trickle of tear evolved into full on boo-hooing.

Mary put her hand on Adriana's arm. "Now, now, dear. It is all going to be okay."

Adriana put her napkin up to her face and blew her nose in a loud, honking fashion, which sent Bonnie launching back into the house to retrieve a large box of tissues. She put the tissue box in front of Adriana. "It's okay, really, Adriana."

"It's . . . it's just that . . . " Her sobbing continued.

Bonnie, Mary, and Elaine exchanged glances back and forth.

Elaine placed her hand back on Adriana's arm. "Is it more than just Teddy?"

"Yes," she sobbed. "All of this reminds me of . . . "

"Antony?" Elaine asked.

She nodded. "All this talk about deception and lies and so forth. It reminds me of the mob and how they killed my sweet Antony and lied to me, to everyone. No one found out beforehand what was about to happen to Antony. It reminds me of the deceit, the evil people of the underworld." She wiped her face again.

Elaine got up, walked around the table, and hugged Adriana. "It will be okay. We are all here to help you this time. Don't worry about anything."

She wiped her eyes and hugged Elaine. "I know. I am thankful for that. And"—she sniffled—"in some way, I think dear Antony is watching, too."

Bonnie shifted back in her chair and asked, "Elaine, what is the next step? What happens now?"

"We just go about our usual business. The less concern we have about all of this, the better. When Trent hears from the PI, he will call."

Elaine did not want her impromptu dinner to end on a sour note. "Now that we have a plan, anyone want to take an after-dinner stroll on the beach? The sun will be setting soon."

Mary said, "I could use a walk after that delicious dinner. Adriana, wouldn't a walk be nice?"

Adriana wiped her eyes again and nodded.

"Let's go," Bonnie said.

The next morning after their usual morning walk, Mary texted the group. "Can we meet at the coffee shop at 10:00? Need help with invitations and last-minute items."

Elaine text a thumbs up emoji. "Come on, Bella. You need to eat before I go into town."

She poured the dog food in the bowl and headed to take a quick shower. *I will be glad when all this PI business is behind us.*

Once she dressed, she texted Bonnie. "Need a ride to the coffee shop?"

"Yes," she replied. "I'm ready."

Elaine put the alarm on her cottage and locked the door. She checked from one end of the beach to the other. No sign of Teddy. *Good.*

Bonnie was waiting on her porch when Elaine wheeled up the drive. Bonnie opened the door, took her seat, and fastened the seat belt. "Let's get this monarch butterfly party business done."

"Yes. I agree. We have had a lot going on, and I'm ready for a relaxed evening celebrating the migration of the butterflies."

"That was quite a bomb you dropped on us last night," Bonnie said.

"About the PI?"

"Yes. I never thought you would be the one to call in the troops for help on this guy."

"Bonnie, I am just very concerned about Adriana and don't want her to get hurt."

Bonnie's tone seemed to soften about Adriana and Teddy. "Elaine, you know Adriana; well, I love her like all the rest of the group. I know it took me a while. She was a little . . . uh, not sure how to say it . . . overwhelming when we first met her."

"I think she was just not sure how we felt about her when we first got together."

Bonnie agreed. "Yes, I think that is true, but . . . "

"But?"

"I have heard that sometimes people that are . . . overwhelming . . . what do they say? They take up all the oxygen in the room? Anyway, sometimes, it is just because they are insecure and want people to like them."

"Why, Bonnie, how very insightful of you."

"Yeah, I know I still have a lot to learn about people. But, hey, I'd better hurry up and learn it! I'm no spring chicken, you know."

Elaine and Bonnie both laughed.

The main street through town was quiet when Elaine turned. She parked the car on the street. "Mary's is already here. Let's see what she has for us to do this morning."

Mary waved at Elaine and Bonnie when they entered. They placed their orders for coffee.

"It is quiet in here this morning. I'll bring your orders to your table," Alexa said.

"I've got yours today, Bonnie. Thank you, Alexa."

Mary sat at the usual table with a stack of invitations sitting next to her coffee cup. "Good morning, you two. I think Adriana will be along soon. She wanted to shop after our meeting and insisted on coming in two cars."

"She must be a better mood this morning if she is going shopping," Bonnie stated.

The door opened, and the bracelets jingled right along with the bell hanging on the coffee shop door. "Alexa, be a dear and whip me up a frappe this morning."

"Changing it up today?" Alexa asked.

"Yeah, I figured why not live on the wild side." She laughed, waved her hand, and then got her money from her purse.

Mary waved at Adriana. "She does seem to be chipper this morning."

"Good. I was a bit worried after last night," Elaine confessed.

"Hello, dears," Adriana said, taking her chair.

The group nodded and greeted Adriana.

"Oh, Mary, let me take a look. Oh, my stars!" She held one up to the others. "These are lovely. Did you make these invitations yourself?"

"I asked the print shop to put it together for me. They used the same butterflies they created for the t-shirts."

"Grand idea!"

Mary passed out the invitations to the others to review.

Elaine opened the invitation. "And look, a tiny butterfly on the inside."

Bonnie looked it over. "And what can we do to help you out?"

"I think we can divide these up like we did before and get them to the shop owners and others we usually invite. Same people. What do you think?"

Elaine nodded, "Good idea. Do you need help with anything else? Last minute concerns about food or anything else?"

"I think I am all set," Mary said. "I've got Adriana's extra party supplies from her pool party. I can't think of anything else."

Bonnie stacked her invitations in a pile. "I'm ready to get busy. Elaine? You ready?"

"Sure am."

The four women exited the coffee shop, invitations in hand. Elaine followed the others out of the coffee shop. She noticed a somewhat-familiar-looking face entering the coffee shop at the same time she went out the door. She searched though her mind, then recognized the man in glasses, a beach hat, swim trunks, and a t-shirt. *That's Mark.*

After walking up and down the street handing out the monarch butterfly party invitations, Elaine was ready to get back home and spend time writing. "Bonnie, are you ready to go back to the beach?"

"Yes."

Chapter Twelve

The remaining days until the monarch butterfly party at Mary's house to celebrate the butterfly migration passed quickly. Elaine and Bonnie did not discuss Teddy or the PI and, of note, no one else did either. No one mentioned seeing Teddy in town or on the beach.

The monarch butterfly party was successful, and Elaine believed the guests enjoyed every minute. The most important thing that happened, in Elaine's opinion, was that Mary had a wonderful time entertaining and the guests said they would attend the monarch butterfly migration festival the very next day at the wildlife center. She was also thankful no one had seen or heard from Teddy and Adriana did not seem to be bothered about Teddy's sudden disappearance.

The next morning before the festival at the wildlife center, Elaine planned to take a quick walk with Bonnie. Elaine had been to the festival every year since Mary had been involved in the wildlife center. She knew the festival was important to Mary.

Elaine waved at Bonnie who waited on her porch for their morning walk to commence. "Hey, Bonnie."

Bonnie waved back. "Morning. Let's get some steps in."

Bonnie's doctor had suggested a watch with a step counter at the last office visit. Elaine wondered if Bonnie had become obsessed with the number. It seemed Bonnie looked at her step counter more often than she looked out over the water on their morning walks. Attempting to change the subject from step counting, Elaine asked, "You know what is strange?"

"What's that?"

"I haven't seen Teddy in town or on the beach lately."

"Come to think of it, I haven't either," Bonnie replied. "It's like he disappeared or something. Good riddance."

"Maybe he *was* just a tourist and decided to go back home."

Bonnie stopped walking and turned to Elaine. "If he was a tourist, I wonder why he told Adriana he wanted to make a documentary? Where was his home, anyway? Did he ever say where he came from?"

"His entire visit was curious. He didn't tell me anything about where he was from, and Adriana didn't mention hearing anything about that."

"Interesting. And just think, Elaine, Trent hired a PI to investigate Teddy a couple of days ago; and now he is gone. Coincidence? I think not."

"Bonnie, you mean you think he found out there was a PI investigating him, and that is why he disappeared?"

"Yes. I don't know how he found out; but if he was up to no good, he would skedaddle."

"At least, we don't have to worry anymore for Adriana. I honestly feared he would ask Adriana for money."

Bonnie continued, "And I'll bet there never was any movie project in the first place."

"Guess we will never know more about him now. Oh, hold on. Looks like Pastor Sam is buzzing. Hello . . . Yes, of course . . . Thank you . . . See you then."

Bonnie's curiosity got the best of her; and before Elaine knew it, Bonnie blurted, "Spill it. What did he want? Search committee news?"

Elaine knew the details were confidential, but she had to tell Bonnie something. "Yes, he wants to touch base after church this week. Said it would just take a few minutes." What Elaine didn't share was that Pastor Sam told her they had five applications to consider and the committee would be given information on each of the candidates this week after church.

"Sounds like the fun will begin. Since Teddy seems to have disappeared, maybe we can focus on the search committee news now." Bonnie turned and looked at her cottage. "I'd better get changed out of these walking shorts. Pick me up for the festival in about thirty minutes?"

"Yes. See you soon."

Elaine opened her door, and Bella followed her inside. "Okay, girl, I've got to run. Here, let me get you some fresh water."

Her phone buzzed. She took it from her pocket. It was Trent calling.

"Hello, Trent. How are you?"

"Good. You?"

"Doing well. You going to the festival?"

"Yes, but I wanted to talk to you before we meet up at the wildlife center. Just had a call from Mark."

"Oh?"

"He tracked down the name we gave him—Teddy Carter. He thinks it is an alias but still verifying that through a couple of databases. He determined there was a rental car, a silver convertible, rented from the Harlingen Airport under the name of Theodore Williams."

"Mark thinks Theodore is Teddy Carter?"

"Yes, he does. He is checking his sources. He wants to meet on the island this afternoon after the festival. Can you meet us over there?"

"Yes. I would like to hear what he has found out. Doesn't sound like he is certain about Teddy's identity; I won't tell the others yet. Bonnie and I haven't seen Teddy in a few days."

"Me either. Let's meet at the coffee shop on the island at 3:00. Will that work?"

"Café Karma?"

"Yes, it is close to Mark's hotel. I have some other business after the meeting with Mark; then we could ride over together. That okay?"

"Of course. I'll drive over right after I drop Bonnie back home from the wildlife center. See you at the festival in a bit."

"Okay."

The Monarch Butterfly Festival was a hit again this year. Mary flitted around from one visitor to another as she explained the annual migration and helped them to purchase the butterfly t-shirts. The fundraiser was a success, raising just under three thousand dollars in a matter of hours. The money would go to the wildlife refuge and help with the upkeep and the overhead.

Elaine, Bonnie, and Adriana walked through the center together and noted the new displays.

Adriana's bracelets rang out as she pointed to the new display about alligators in the area. "Oh my! This is interesting. Sounds like most of the alligators have been relocated back to their better habitats after Jada."

Bonnie agreed. "Took a while. And according to this, most of the new alligators they found were the smaller ones."

Adriana touched Bonnie's arm, "Girl, I don't care what size they are, I don't want them in my yard."

Bonnie and Elaine both laughed.

Elaine, Bonnie, and Adriana each bought another t-shirt to support the wildlife center and then said their goodbyes to Mary. Mary planned to stay until the last visitor left.

Elaine dropped Bonnie at her cottage, and they agreed to meet and walk to church the next day. Elaine left Bonnie's house and went on her way to the island.

Turning into the parking lot at Café Karma, Elaine parked in the last remaining spot. She got her purse and closed her car door. The salt air was thick, and the temperature had risen to a sweltering ninety-five degrees, warm for this time in the fall. She opened the coffee shop door, went inside, and found Trent and Mark sitting at a table in the back. She waved, stopped at the counter, and ordered a cup of coffee with heavy cream before she joined the two men.

"Glad you two could make it," Mark said. "I thought this was a conversation best to have face to face."

"Good to see you," Elaine replied.

"And you also, Elaine. Now, let's get to it." Mark pulled a folder out from a brief case and opened it. He tapped a large photograph of a man in a police lineup. "Have either of you seen this man?"

Elaine studied the picture. "Yes, I have seen him. That is the man I saw talking to Teddy on the street one day. Who is he?"

"He is bad news; that is who he is. He goes by several names. I think the name he used while he was here was Camillo Brown."

Elaine was puzzled. "Camillo Brown? And who is he?"

"He doesn't really exist. This is just one of his aliases. The name is the male version for the female name Camile, but he uses Camillo. Now, here is what I found out about Camillo's history. He is wanted for suspicion of murder in Louisiana and has a history of theft and assault in several states. He is also suspected of being involved with a counterfeit operation run by the mob. He travels the country and commits crimes wherever he goes."

Elaine gasped. "And he was right here in our little town of Sabal Palms?"

"Yes. He *was* here. But he has since left, according to my sources. But you did see him?"

"Yes."

"He is known for pulling people, vulnerable people, into his schemes to make money and has robbed banks in the past. He served time and got out for good behavior."

"My goodness. But he didn't turn himself around after all?"

"My sources don't think so. It appears he left your area of Sabal Palms, at least for now. And even though we found out Teddy's car was a rental and his name is Theodore Williams, he is in the wind. The rental car was returned. He probably returned to Louisiana."

"Louisiana?" Elaine asked.

"Disappeared?" Trent asked.

"Yes, but I wanted you to be aware of this other man, Camillo. I wanted you to see his picture and to notify the authorities if you see him again.

"Now, this is the picture we tracked down for Theodore. It is from the car rental place at the airport, and it is a copy of his driver's license. Is this him? I never saw him in town. I checked the coffee shop, the beach, the piers, and tourist boats. He returned the car the day I started looking for him."

Elaine took the paper with a small picture printed on it in black and white. "I think that is him. It's a small picture." She handed it to Trent.

"Yes, this is the man I spoke with briefly in the coffee shop that day."

Mark continued, "Okay. My theory is this fellow"—he tapped the picture—"Camillo, found Theodore while he was traveling in Louisiana. He had been released from the David Wade Correctional Center in the northern part of Louisiana. Once he was free, he traveled to the southern part of the state. We think during his wandering around in Louisiana, he met Theodore—or Teddy, as you know him. He probably talked up this scheme about buried treasure and your friend, Adriana. Camillo either heard about Adriana from his connections to the mob and Frankie the Gun, or he saw the news report about Adriana while he was in prison."

Elaine gasped again. "Camillo has quite a history. I mean he has past convictions, and he knows people in the mob. And wanted for suspicion of murder? Let's hope Teddy and Camillo are both gone for good."

"They are both gone," Mark confirmed. "But in my experience, these bad pennies tend to show up again and again. Maybe not in Sabal Palms, but likely somewhere around the Gulf Coast."

Elaine turned to Trent. "I guess we are safe for now."

Trent nodded. "It seems so. Mark, what should we do now?"

"My associates are on Camillo's trail. They will keep searching for him. As for this so-called Teddy Carter, or Theodore, he may not show up again. He doesn't have a criminal history and might have figured out that Camillo was bad news and bugged out. But no way to know for sure. He will be more difficult to track—not as well-known. But I will keep checking. My advice to you is to go about your usual lives; but if you should see Camillo in the area again, contact the authorities. If you see Teddy again, you can give me a call. Unless he commits a crime, the authorities won't bother with him."

"Good news, I guess?" Elaine said.

"I think so," Trent agreed.

"And, Elaine, you probably should go ahead and tell your friends what we know so far. They might spot Teddy or Camillo in town. Here, I brought you a smaller picture of Camillo. Show it to the others who might be contacted and warn them."

"Okay. I will let them know."

The day had been a long one. Elaine was glad it was over. She walked up her wooden steps to the deck and looked out over the water. Another beautiful sunset was about to happen. She went inside and got Bella.

"Come on, girl. Let's go for a walk." She quickly put on her walking shorts, grabbed her phone, put her alarm on the cottage, and walked down to the shore.

"Look at these clouds, Bella." The clouds had an orange cast and were like nothing she had seen before. "Very unusual, huh?"

She looked across the water. Ships were coming in toward the Port of Brownsville. "Must be expecting a storm. No worries, Bella. It is out to sea and will take a while to get here. Let's walk a little further to the north."

Elaine walked along the shore, in and out of the warm waves trickling over her toes. Nothing but beauty all around. She was inspired to write a devotional and thank God for her many blessings. "Let's head back. Need to write, and you, my sweet pup, need some dinner. Come to think of it, I could eat a bite myself."

Bella gobbled up her dinner while Elaine made a sandwich. She sat near the bay window and watched the lightning from the approaching storm. She had no way to know that in a future, a storm of a different sort would be approaching the people of Sabal Palms once again.

Elaine finished her sandwich and went to her desk. She put a clean piece of paper in the old-fashioned electric typewriter. "Now, let's see, Bella. So many thoughts racing through my mind. Gratitude for blessings. Thanking God that Adriana is safe for now from the scandalous character, Camillo."

"When I can't settle my mind, I turn to the Scripture. Works every time."

Bella walked to her bed beside the desk and plopped down.

"Exactly how I feel, Bella. Might be a long night."

Elaine skimmed through the verses. "Always loved this one—Psalm 107:1: 'Oh, give thanks to the LORD, for he is good, for his steadfast love endures forever!'"

Bella wagged her little nub of a tail.

"You like it, too? Okay. I will start with that one. And now, all the things I am thankful for today."

Elaine soon realized the list of things she was thankful for was extensive. "This might be longer than I first thought."

Bella's eyes blinked and then closed.

"Okay. I get it. I will finish this one later. Time for bed."

The next morning, Elaine met Bonnie to walk along the shore before they got ready for church. She decided to wait and tell Bonnie about what Mark had found out when all the group was together. She would ask them for an impromptu dinner tonight. Then, with no distractions, she would inform them of Teddy's alias and the details of Camillo. She would follow Mark's advice to warn the girls in case Teddy or Camillo was spotted in town again.

"Good morning, Bonnie."

"Hey, Elaine. I'm ready to get going! I can't wait to hear what you learn today at the search committee meeting. You will have to tell me."

"Bonnie, you know I will tell you what I am allowed to say."

Bella darted back and forth between the waves, chasing the shorebirds.

"Okay, okay. Speaking of hearing things, did you hear the storm last night?"

"You know what? I must have been tired. I saw it out to sea but never heard it after I went to bed."

"Don't think it came all the way to the shore. At least not here. And the lightning show! Wow! It was more significant than the thunder."

"You watched it?"

"I did. It was something else. It looked more like fireworks popping off. I saw several ships coming in at the last minute. Not sure they started back in time, though."

"Think some of them got caught in it?"

"No doubt. But it wasn't as bad as a tropical storm or hurricane. They probably got back in okay. I didn't see any flares or anything like that. Anyway, the storms late in the fall aren't as bad as the summer ones."

"That's true. Let's walk up just a little further before we get back to dress for church."

"Okay."

Bella skipped ahead and chased another sandpiper and a seagull. She stopped momentarily.

"What is she sniffing?" Bonnie asked.

"I'll go check it out."

Elaine increased her pace and joined Bella. "What's that, Bella? What do you have there?"

Elaine bent over and examined it. Bonnie joined her side. "Looks like another piece of that old wood. I think we should leave it there, girl. I'll let Mary know. She can ask the Texas Historical Commission if they want to come pick it up."

"Looks like an old piece of wood if you ask me."

"They can check it out. Don't want to disturb it. Hold on. I'll text her." Elaine texted Mary.

"Mary, another piece of old wood washed up just north of my cottage. About the same size as the other one."

Mary replied in a text. "Okay. I'll let the historical commission know. See you at church."

"Okay," she texted back.

"Bonnie, she said she will let them know. Now, we'd better get going."

Bonnie checked her watch. "Yes, and I got my morning steps done."

Elaine and Bonnie arrived at the Church on the Shore within an hour after their walk. They found Mary waiting at their usual pew.

"Hello, girls," Mary said.

"Good morning," Elaine replied.

"Oh, I already heard back from the Texas Historical Commission. They are on their way out to the shore."

Trent and Billy walked in together and sat behind the three women. "Ladies, good morning," Trent said.

Elaine, Bonnie, and Mary said, "Good morning." Then the three women's heads turned upon hearing the clicking of dressy, strappy sandals on the church tile floor. The floral perfume arrived about the same time. Adriana stopped at a pew, said her hellos, and then stopped at another one.

Bonnie rolled her eyes. "Here she comes."

Pastor Sam was already taking his position at the podium when he announced, "Let's begin by singing our first hymn today. Turn to page 367 and join us."

Adriana made it to her place. She patted each of the three women's knees, one at a time, and smiled. "Good morning," she mouthed without uttering a sound.

Following the first song, Pastor Sam stood and addressed the congregation. "Let's 'give thanks to [our] LORD for he is good.' What a glorious morning we have after a stormy night. Did you see the lightning show?"

Heads in the congregation nodded.

"I couldn't help but look up at those clouds being lit up by God and think about how beautiful Heaven must look from where He is. Right? Just astounding. Now, for an announcement about the search committee actions so far. I have informed the committee that we have received five applicants, people who are seeking to come interview with our committee and present a sermon to us."

Bonnie nudged Elaine and gave her a scornful look. "You didn't tell me, you sneaky girl."

Pastor Sam observed Bonnie and Elaine in the first row. "Let me remind you all, our committee work is confidential. That said, they will review the applications this week and determine if the candidates meet the standards set forth. We want to be especially careful in our selection this time around."

Elaine remembered the New Age applicant who wanted to take over the congregation in the previous search. She believed God had intervened, and the congregation was spared from the New Age philosophy that was not consistent with Christianity.

"Therefore, it will be up to the committee to make the determination of who will be invited to speak. I would urge you all to let the committee do their work. The early deliberations will be confidential. Now, on to today's message. Here is the reading of the Scripture for the day. Let us open our Bibles to Matthew 7:15. *'Beware of false prophets, who come to you in sheep's clothing but inwardly are ravenous wolves.'*" And this is what our committee will be concerned with. We should all beware of those who might want to reach us without pure intentions. Our job as Christians is to reach out to others. We might forget, in our world today, there are sheep in wolf's clothing still wanting to commit evil deeds. Beware and trust in God."

Pastor Sam's words echoed in Elaine's mind. So true. *We should each be aware of the evil in our world.*

Elaine looked at Adriana and couldn't help but think about Teddy and Camillo. She prayed they were gone from Sabal Palms for good. She focused on the remainder of Pastor Sam's sermon.

Chapter Thirteen

As soon as Pastor Sam concluded the last words of Scripture, the music began for the last song of the day. The congregation stood and sang along to one of Elaine's favorite hymns, "Praise to the Lord, the Almighty." Once again, Elaine sang with every breath in her. She felt the Holy Spirit was alive in the Church on the Shore.

Elaine walked to the back of the sanctuary. "Ladies, you all want to come over for a quick dinner. We can talk about my party the night before the shrimp cookoff."

"What do you say, girls?" Bonnie asked.

"Yes, doll, I think it is a grand idea. What can I bring?" Adriana asked.

"You can each bring whatever you like. I am going to cook some steaks on the grill," Elaine said.

"Steaks?" Mary asked.

"Yes, I picked up on sale the other day at the meat market. Billy, Trent, want to come over?"

"Wish I could," Trent said. "I have to work tonight. I have some new potential donors for the nonprofits."

"Sorry, Elaine. It sounds wonderful, but I need to head out for a few days," Billy said. "I'm off to Nashville first thing in the morning and need to work on a few things this evening. But the shrimp cookoff is in a few weeks, right?"

"Yes. First Saturday in November."

Bonnie nudged Elaine. "It will be here before you know it."

Billy replied, "I'll be back before then."

"Okay, Bonnie, Mary, Adriana, see you around 4:30 or 5:00?"

They agreed.

The church search committee meeting was like nothing Elaine had been involved with in her life. When she was a professor at the university before she had retired, the search committees were based on applicants' credentials and publications. The church committee reviewed the applications with the goal of searching for anything indicating the basic Christian beliefs and making certain the beliefs and experiences were consistent with the mission and goals of the Church on the Shore. In the end, the committee decided four of the five applicants would be extended an invitation to come and provide a sermon. But before the invitations were extended, the committee agreed to conduct telephone interviews and screen for any red flags.

The committee decided at the meeting next week, they would finalize the interview questions and begin the telephone interviews. At the conclusion of today's meeting, each member was reminded to keep the names of the applicants confidential until after the telephone interviews. After the telephone conference calls, the names of the interviewees would be announced to the congregation.

Elaine opened her cottage door and greeted Bella. In her mind, she could not stop thinking what she would tell Bonnie about the meeting. She knew Bonnie would be full of questions and that she would not be able to answer most of them.

"Come on, Bella; let's go outside for a bit. Then I will need to get the steaks ready for the grill. You can chase the birds for a while before our company gets here."

Bella hopped around in circles causing her two little floppy ears to bounce with each hop. She followed Elaine out the door. After a short walk in front of the cottage, Elaine and Bella went inside to prepare for the cookout.

Bonnie traipsed up Elaine's cottage steps precisely at four-thirty. She banged on the door with her elbow.

Elaine opened the door and found Bonnie, hands full of two casserole dishes and dangling a bag of sugar-free after-dinner mints.

"Come in. Sorry, I should have been watching for you." Glancing out the door as she closed it, Elaine said, "Oh, Mary and Adriana are just arriving right behind you."

"That's a first! They're on time! Well, that means Adriana was ready when Mary picked her up." Bonnie laughed.

Bonnie marched inside and placed her casserole dishes on the counter. "Well, do tell. How was the meeting?"

Elaine thought quickly, and a satisfactory response immerged. "Just procedural, really. We decided any acceptable applicants will have telephone interviews first. Pastor Sam wants to be sure we don't have any problems with questionable applicants this time around."

"Makes sense to me. Don't want to be hoodwinked twice."

Adriana and Mary joined the group in Elaine's kitchen. Mary brought the sugar-free chocolate cupcakes for dessert and a side of fresh veggies with dipping sauce, and Adriana brought a large salad and an appetizer tray.

"This all looks delicious! All I have to offer is a few steaks," Elaine noted.

"Listen to her, girls," Adriana said, waving her hands in the air. "Just a few steaks! Look at those beautiful steaks!"

"Ladies," Elaine continued, "there are pitchers of tea and lemonade over on the table. Grab a glass and come out to the deck while I grill these steaks. We can watch the shorebirds. Pelicans should be coming by."

The ladies gathered outside along the deck, and Elaine got the grill going. She knew now was the right time to let the group know what the PI had found out about Teddy and the Camillo character.

Adriana sipped her lemonade; Mary and Bonnie drank their iced tea and watched Elaine.

"I wanted to tell you that I talked with the PI."

"What?" Mary asked.

"You did?" Bonnie asked.

"Tell us, Elaine. Don't keep us waiting," Adriana chided.

"Okay. Here is what he knows at this point. Teddy is actually Theodore Williams from Louisiana. And he turned in the rental car and left the area."

"Imposter!" Mary blurted.

Bonnie laughed. "Ha! I knew it! I knew that fancy car wasn't his!"

Adriana looked down at her glass of tea; then her eyes focused on Elaine. "Is there anything else about Teddy?"

Mary added, "Yes, anything else we need to know about Teddy?"

"And," Adriana asked with a desperate look in her eyes, "what about the movie?"

"The PI doesn't know anything about the movie at this point. None of his sources had heard or seen anything about a possible movie project. But do you remember the day we saw Teddy down the street from the coffee shop talking with another man?"

Bonnie nodded. "I do. I thought he was giving that guy directions or something."

Elaine went on. "The man Teddy was with on the street used the name of Camillo Brown while he was here. He's bad news. Mark found out this Camillo is a con man, a bank robber, and is wanted on suspicion of murder."

Adriana gasped.

Mary's eyes bugged out as she yelled, "What? A killer?"

Bonnie rolled her eyes and said, "It just figures! I knew that Teddy was no good. I knew he was a scoundrel."

"Now wait, Bonnie. See, here is the thing. Mark is not certain Teddy is the one who is the troublemaker. Of the two men, Camillo and Teddy, Mark said Camillo likely pulled Teddy into this scheme. Camillo was released recently from the David Wade County Prison in Louisiana and probably met Teddy soon after his release."

"What?" Mary gasped. "A prisoner? A recent prison release? Here in Sabal Palms?"

"Good grief!" Bonnie exclaimed.

Elaine continued, "He thinks—just his theory, at this point—that Teddy might have figured out Camillo was up to no good. Of course, he couldn't confirm this because Teddy disappeared before Mark could question him."

Elaine's friends sat with their eyes wide opened, and Bonnie's mouth was gaping in a perfect circle.

"Hold on, let me grab the picture Mark gave me of Camillo."

"Picture?" Adriana asked.

Elaine went inside and lifted the picture from inside her purse. She took it outside. "Here, this is Camillo."

Bonnie examined the picture. "Yes, that is the same guy we saw on the street." Bonnie passed the picture to Mary and Adriana.

Elaine resumed the explanation. "Mark found out that Camillo had ties to the mob—"

Adriana moaned and shook her head. "No! No! Not again."

"I'm sorry, Adriana. Mark thinks Camillo might have either known about what happened to Antony or saw the story on the news when he was still in prison."

Adriana put her head in her hands and began to cry. "Will it ever end?"

Mary jumped up from her chair and put her arm around Adriana. "There, there. It's okay. We will watch out for you."

Bonnie launched into the kitchen and got a napkin and took it to Adriana.

Adriana sniffed, wiped her eyes, and then blew her nose. "I'm sorry. One minute, I think I am doing better about missing Antony and the whole mob business is behind me, and then, boom! Something like this." She shook her head, and tears streamed down her cheeks.

Elaine closed the lid on the grill and then sat down with Adriana. "I am sorry, Adriana. But we all need to keep watching for this Camillo character. And if anybody sees him, we should notify the police immediately."

Adriana nodded. She blew her nose again. "Okay. It's okay, Elaine. I know this is for the best."

Elaine hugged Adriana. "I didn't mean to ruin the evening. But Mark thought it best that you all know now in case Camillo comes back to the area."

Bonnie asked, "So he's gone?"

"As far as Mark and his friends at the FBI could tell. He hasn't seen him or Teddy in two days. Hopefully, they are both gone from Sabal Palms forever. Now, how about some dinner? These steaks are almost ready."

It turned out, grilled steaks and an ocean view were great for changing one's mood. A few more bites of dinner were needed for the ladies of Sabal Palms to shift their conversation. Elaine was thankful she had already informed Bonnie about the progress of the search committee. It gave Bonnie a new topic of conversation.

Between bites of her steak and salad, Bonnie announced, "Elaine told me the search committee news."

Mary looked up from her plate, "Oh? What's the news?"

Elaine repeated the same information she had told Bonnie about the telephone conferences and then changed the subject. "Looks like we won't know about the actual candidates until after next week."

"Oh." Mary shook her head. "We sure don't want anybody with bad intentions again. That business last time caused quite a hullaballoo."

Bonnie scooped up the last bite from her plate and uttered, "Uh huh."

"Oh, look," Mary said holding up her phone.

"What?" Bonnie mumbled with her mouth full of food.

"It's a text. It is from my friend at the Texas Antiquities Committee. They are a committee of the Texas Historical Commission."

"What does it say?" Bonnie blurted.

"It says, they rushed the second piece of wood to be examined along with the first one. They have determined it is— Oh! Oh!"

"Oh, spill it!" Bonnie said. "What?"

"Both pieces of wood are dated back to the mid-1500s!"

"My stars," Adriana half-whispered.

"That is pretty incredible!" Elaine added.

"And," Mary continued, "they will continue to examine the pieces in an effort to see if they match other discoveries from— Oh!"

Bonnie reached for Mary's phone. "Want me to read it for you? You seem to be having trouble getting through it!"

"No! Listen, they are trying to determine if it is a match for the three Spanish naos that went aground at Padre. Oh . . . my!"

"There is more?" Elaine asked.

"Yes. If it is a credible discovery, the person who found it will be noted in the discovery information!"

Mary touched Adriana's arm. "See, Adriana! You will get credit for the first piece."

Bonnie rolled her eyes. "I guess Bella gets the credit for the second discovery."

Mary laughed.

"Wait," Bonnie interjected, "what in the world is a nao?"

Mary said, "It is an old three- or four-mast ship. You've seen pictures of them in the Port Isabel Museum."

"Thanks," Bonnie said. "Never knew what they were called.

Elaine said, "Hold on. Adriana found the first piece. Mary secured the analysis. Bella, Bonnie, and I found the second piece. I suggest we all get the credit. It was a team effort, after all."

"Excellent idea," Mary agreed.

Adriana nodded.

"Yes," Bonnie said. "A team effort."

Mary, Bonnie, and Adriana assisted Elaine with the after-dinner cleanup. Mary looked at the pile of paper plates heaped in the trash bin. "What did we ever do before paper plates were invented?"

"We washed a lot of dishes," Bonnie quipped.

Mary stacked her plate and dish together on the counter. "Elaine, we haven't talked about the party yet."

"The party before the shrimp cookoff?"

"Yes."

"Okay, I think we can serve just about anything except shrimp."

Bonnie laughed. "I agree. The next day, all we eat at the festival is shrimp."

"True," Mary said. "Want to have a theme and think up dishes around the theme."

Elaine was curious. "What do you have in mind?"

Mary looked at Adriana's sad demeanor. She tilted her head toward Adriana. Elaine figured Mary might want to try to cheer her up. "How about an Italian night?"

Bonnie picked up on the idea. "Yes! It would be great to have a theme night. Italian gives us lots of options—pizza, pasta, salads."

Elaine noticed Adriana smiled a tiny smile. "Yes, I like the idea."

"It's settled then," Elaine said. "Italian food it is."

Adriana was noticeably quiet the remainder of the evening. She appeared to shuffle through the trips back and forth from the deck to the kitchen and assisted putting a few leftovers in the fridge. She tapped Mary on the arm. "Mary, do you mind calling it an early evening? I feel like going back to my house."

"Of course. Let me grab my dishes to take home, and I'll get my car keys."

Adriana and Mary bid their goodbyes and left to go back into town.

"Elaine, want to go for a walk? The sun is almost set, and it looks like some spectacular clouds out there—the kind you always like to see in the evenings."

"You're right. It is a perfect time for a walk, Bonnie."

The two women and Bella headed north on the shore. Bella ran ahead and returned to the two women several times.

Bonnie examined the sand carefully and turned shells over with her toes.

"Still looking for the whelk shells?"

"Yes. I wonder how long it will take me to find a righthanded lightning whelk shell."

"You are determined to find one. It has been a couple of weeks since you set out on your mission. And you have looked every single time we go walking on the beach."

"It would be such fun to find one for Mary and then see her reaction."

"Bonnie, that is so thoughtful. I thought you just wanted to prove her wrong—that there are righthanded whelks here at the coast."

"Well, I kinda started off that way, but then I got to thinking how surprised she would be and might even display it at the wildlife center."

"That is a nice idea."

"Yeah, sometimes I surprise myself."

Elaine laughed.

"Or maybe I am just getting soft in my old age."

"You know what I think?"

"What?"

"It seems to me that after we all went through in Hurricane Jada together, the four of us, along with Trent and Billy, have all grown closer. Maybe that is part of why you want to find the shell for Mary. It is more like finding something for a younger sister."

"Wait a minute! She is *only* a year younger!"

"See? That is a comment an older sister would make."

The two laughed, and Elaine could not seem to stop herself. For some reason, the idea of Bonnie protesting age at . . . well, at a certain age . . . was laughable, even silly. And Bonnie chuckled right along with her.

"Ouch!" Bonnie shrieked and came to a complete standstill.

Bella scampered to Bonnie's side and examined Bonnie's foot.

"Bonnie! What is it?"

"Not sure, but it is sharp." She leaned over and carefully pushed the sand away from her toes. "It's a whelk shell. A left-handed one. It is broken on this side, and wait . . . " She brushed away the sand. "What in the world is this?"

Elaine drew nearer to Bonnie and looked at what was in her hand. "It looks like a thumb drive."

"A what?"

"I use them. It's a small gadget you can put into your computer and save information on, especially if you want to share the information with someone."

"So how does it work?"

"You put this end—wait, it is pretty sandy." Elaine brushed the sand off one end. "See, you put this end right here into the slot of your computer, and it opens a file. You can view it on your computer or save the files or whatever."

"You think whoever lost it is looking for it? And why would they have it out here on the beach?"

"My guess is it probably fell right out of someone's pocket."

"Wonder if it got wet. I mean, I would think it would not be good if it got wet, right?"

"I wouldn't think so."

"Think we can find the owner?"

"It wouldn't hurt to try. Tell you what, I can find out how to make sure there is no water damage. Then, if I put it in my computer, maybe we can find out who the owner is."

"See, this is why I don't mess with computers and electronic gadgets. Just give me a good old-fashioned piece of paper and a pencil."

Elaine laughed. "I will check it out tonight and see. Should we go back? It is getting dark."

"Yes. But wait. Don't you love seeing the ships out there with their lights on over the water? Nice, calm night."

"Yes, it is."

Bella ran around Elaine's feet and seemed anxious to go back to the cottage. "Okay, Bella. Let's go."

Chapter Fourteen

Upon returning to her beach cottage, Elaine took the thumb drive into her kitchen and examined it carefully. "Hmm . . . well, Bella, looks like it has some sand inside this plastic part. Maybe a small brush. Let me think."

Elaine went into her laundry room. "Wait, I know!" Bella followed Elaine from the laundry room to the bedroom. "Here. This is a tiny makeup brush—never been opened."

Bella sat and wagged her little nub.

Elaine took the thumb drive, pulled a small lamp nearer to her on the desk, and switched the three-way bulb on bright. "Let's have a look." She carefully brushed the few remaining grains of sand and examined it more closely. "There. Sand is gone. Now, for a little research."

She turned on her computer and waited for it to open the desktop options and the applications. She entered the words, "What happens when a thumb drive gets wet" in her browser.

The links filled the page with advice on how to dry out the thumb drive. One thing that was repeated on several of the reference pages was to fill a small plastic bag with uncooked rice, put the thumb drive inside, seal the bag, and leave the thumb drive in the bag for twenty-four hours. "Okay, we have a game plan. Come on, Bella. Back to the kitchen."

Elaine prepared the rice in the bag. "In you go." She dropped the thumb drive inside the bag. "And now, we just wait until tomorrow, Bella."

The next morning, Bonnie knocked on Elaine's door before Elaine was ready for their morning walk. Elaine opened the door. "You're here early."

"I couldn't wait. I'm curious about what you found on the thumb drive."

"I don't know yet."

"No?"

"I did find out how to get the water out. And it might not work."

"Well, what's the hold up?"

"I had to put it in a bag of uncooked rice and let it stay there for twenty-four hours."

"Is it for sure going to dry it out?"

"Won't know until later tonight. I'll let you know as soon as I check it out this evening."

"That is frustrating. I was sure you were able to find out by now. Well, ready for a walk?"

"Of course. Let me get my flip-flops on."

Before they could get out the door, the ring tone on Elaine's phone chimed. Mary, in a frantic tone, said, "Elaine, I think we need an intervention."

"What? What do you mean? What's going on?"

"It's Adriana. She stayed upset all evening, and this morning she is not much better. I talked her into going with me to the coffee shop around ten this morning. Can you and Bonnie meet us there?"

"Sure thing. I'll let Bonnie know."

"See you there."

With furrowed eyebrows, Bonnie asked, "What is it?"

"Mary said Adriana is still upset. She wants us to all meet at the coffee shop this morning and try to cheer her up."

"Okay. How about a quick walk first? Gotta get my steps in."

"Let's go."

Elaine and Bonnie headed into town to the coffee shop right on time to meet Adriana and Mary at ten o'clock. Parking the car on the street of the small town, Elaine looked up and down at the parked cars. "Guess Mary and Adriana aren't here yet."

"Looks that way. Want to go inside? I am ready for a coffee. Didn't have time to grab one at the house."

"Of course." Elaine locked the car, and the two women walked into the coffee shop and were met with the overwhelming aroma of freshly roasted coffee beans and brewed coffee.

"Good morning, Elaine and Bonnie. The regular?"

"Yes, thank you," Elaine said.

"Same for me, Alexa," Bonnie replied.

With her coffee in hand, Elaine went to the back table; and Bonnie sauntered right behind her. They took their seats at the same time the bell on the coffee shop jingled.

Bonnie, taking a sip from her coffee, nodded toward the door. "There they are."

Elaine looked at Adriana's face. She didn't remember seeing Adriana looking so glum since the days after her husband, Antony, died. "Poor Adriana. She is having a hard time."

"She looks to be," Bonnie said.

Mary and Adriana placed their orders then came to the table and joined Bonnie and Elaine.

"Good morning, ladies," Elaine said.

"Hi," Mary said. Adriana, without any characteristic hand movements whatsoever, said, "Good morning."

Mary started the conversation, which was a relief to Elaine. She had no idea how to get Adriana going this morning.

"Adriana reminded me this morning that we were all together when she first learned about Frankie the Gun and how much we all helped her through that."

In a quiet voice, Adriana said, "That's right. You girls—well, I don't know what I would have done during those dark days without you three. And, well, since this whole business with Camillo brought back all those bad memories, I thought the only way to get through this again was to ask you all to help me."

Elaine smiled and reached across the table and held Adriana's hand. "Adriana, you just tell us what we can do to help you. Anything at all."

"I was thinking maybe doing something we don't do often. Maybe it would be fun for us to all hop over to the island for lunch. What do you say? Are you all free?"

Bonnie slurped her coffee quickly and said, "I'm in. I'd love to be waited on for a nice meal."

"Me, too," Elaine said.

Mary replied, "I love going over to the island on the spur of the moment. I know! When we finish here at the coffee shop, let's head across the causeway and do a little shopping before lunch."

Elaine was elated with Mary's idea. If she hadn't suggested it, Elaine was going to because she knew Adriana's favorite pastime was shopping. "Okay, any ideas? Are we looking for anything special?"

Adriana's face brightened. "I could use a new blouse—you know, for all our fall activities. Never hurts to freshen up the wardrobe. A girl can't have too many pretty blouses." And there it was; Adriana began waving her hands around with bracelets jingling with every move.

Elaine smiled, watching Adriana perk up. "Sounds good. I wouldn't mind a new lightweight sweater for church and search committee meetings. The church conference room is always chilly."

Bonnie tapped the table. "It's set, then. Want to go over to Ship Shape?"

"Yes," Adriana said. "I know I will find something there I simply can't leave on display."

Alexa called out, "Adriana, your coffee is ready."

"I'll grab that." Adriana hopped up and along the way to get her coffee, she clicked her strappy sandals on the wood floor, waved her arms, and jingled her bracelets.

Mary laughed. "She is already cheering up."

Elaine said, "You know what? I don't think it's the shopping so much that cheers her up."

"Oh?" Bonnie said. "What then?"

"She likes to be around friends, and the idea of shopping got her mind off Camillo. We just had to help her change the subject."

Mary nodded. "I agree. A change of subject is always good."

Adriana sat back in her chair with her fancy coffee drink with the double whip in hand. "What's the subject?"

Elaine thought quickly and said, "I was about to change the subject and tell you all what Bonnie found last night."

"Oh, yes! I almost forgot."

Mary tapped Bonnie's arm, "Okay, don't keep us waiting."

"It's one of those memory things."

Mary laughed. "We can all use a new memory thing, Bonnie."

The table was full of laughter once again.

"No," Bonnie said, still laughing. "One of those computer thingies."

"A what?" Mary asked.

"Oh, you mean a stick with the memory on it for a computer?" Adriana asked.

"Yes, that's it."

"Well, what was on it?" Mary asked.

"Don't know yet," Bonnie said. "Elaine is drying it out."

Adriana asked, "How long does it take to dry one out?"

"If we have any luck with it, it should be dry this evening. If not, we may never know what is on it or who it belongs to."

"Interesting," Adriana said. "A mystery at Sabal Palms."

"A mystery indeed," Bonnie agreed.

Mary finished her coffee and stood up behind her chair. "You girls ready for some shopping?"

"Yes!" Adriana said. "To the causeway! Should we all go in one car?"

"Sure. I'll drive if you like," Elaine replied.

The island offered a variety of shops along the main road, but the women had their minds set on clothing shopping at their favorite boutique. The little clothing store carried clothing made in Hawaii, designer wear from Tommy Bahama, and clothing from Fiji and many other exotic locations. The clothing ranged from swimsuits to church clothing. There was a nice selection of shoes, purses, and beach attire. Elaine knew this would occupy Adriana and the others for at least two hours. She also knew this was exactly the break from reality Adriana needed to get her focus off the mob and the history of how her husband was killed.

"Girls"—Adriana waved her arms all around the store—"let's get started."

Each took turns selecting clothes, holding up individual pieces and asking each other what they thought about the article of clothing, and trying on the approved blouse or dress. Sometimes, a completely silly choice was held up, and the women laughed and shook their heads no. In addition to getting the approval of the best items held up for the others to examine, they also modeled each selection.

"How about this one?" Mary asked, holding up a Hawaiian dress with a turtle print down the side.

"It's you!" Bonnie said. "What do you think of this?" Bonnie held up a baby blue, silk, scoop-neck blouse with tiny pink plumerias stitched around the neck.

Mary replied, "Yes, and that shade of blue is a great color for you."

Elaine found a lightweight, three-quarter sleeve white cardigan that she could wear over her blouses and summer dresses at church.

Adriana held up a carnation pink casual shirt with small, blingy trim around the neck and sleeves. "This is it. I am thinking this would work for your party, Elaine. What do you think?"

Elaine replied, "It is you! Try it on."

The shopping ended after two hours and thirty minutes; and the women, shopping bags and merchandise in hand, piled into the car.

Elaine drove back down the main street of the island to the collection of restaurants.

Elaine asked the others, "Want to eat on the gulf side or the bayside?"

Adriana said, "It doesn't matter to me."

Mary said, "How about we try The Pier? Haven't eaten there in a while."

"Bayside it is," Elaine said.

Bonnie added, "Fun to see the boats coming and going while we eat."

"And the causeway. I like watching the boats go under the bridge," Adriana said.

Elaine drove ten blocks down the main road and turned right. She went another block and steered into the parking lot. "Looks like we beat the lunch crowd."

"Good deal," Bonnie said. "Won't take us as long to get served."

The women locked their loaded shopping bags in the trunk and went inside.

A hostess seated the women by the window overlooking the pier and the marina just to the south.

Mary sat down and looked out the large window. "Great weather today. Lots of boats going out."

"Lots of sailboats. Guess the wind is just right," Bonnie said. "And of course, the tourist boats."

Elaine pointed. "There goes the Pirate Ship—right under the causeway."

The waitress appeared. "Hello, ladies. Are you ready to order?"

Elaine glanced over the menu. "So many choices. Anyone ready?"

Mary began, "I'd like the crab cakes."

"I'll take the grilled flounder with the side salad," Bonnie said.

Adriana looked up from her menu. "Think I will have the surf and turf."

Bonnie blurted out, "Go big or go home."

The women giggled.

"And for you?"

Elaine said, "The stuffed avocado with the shrimp salad."

The women enjoyed a casual lunch with no pressure to rush. Elaine knew their mission had been accomplished. Adriana was back to her cheerful, often-exaggerated self; and the group had enjoyed shopping, dining, and visiting for hours.

Elaine looked at Adriana to evaluate her expression as she asked, "Ladies, ready to travel back across the causeway?"

Adriana smiled and replied, "Yes, but can we make a stop in Port Isabel?"

"Of course. Where do you want to go?"

"I wanted to run into the bookstore."

Mary turned to Adriana. "Looking for something in particular?"

"Not really. I like to go inside and look around. I think the owner, Gayle, mentioned a new magazine coming in on coastal décor. I wanted to pick one up. Never hurts to come up with new ideas for the house."

Mary agreed. "Yep, I like to move things around in the house, try out new ideas."

"Sounds good."

The sun was setting over the shore when Elaine finished eating her sandwich for dinner. Just as she cleared the table, her phone buzzed. It was Bonnie.

"Well, what's on the memory stick?"

"Just about to try it in my computer."

"Text me if you can get it to work."

"Will do."

Elaine looked down at Bella, who patiently waited to see what Elaine would do next. Elaine took the memory stick out of the rice and brushed it off with her finger. Bella watched her every move and never left her side. "Come on, girl. Let's see if this thing works."

She turned on the computer and waited for the screen to light up. Once the operating system was running, she slowly and carefully pushed the drive into the USB port and waited. The screen displayed the picture of the drive with the words, "Sabal Palms project" and the options to open or reject the memory file. Elaine clicked "Open" and waited.

Once the file opened, several file folders were displayed. Her eyes scanned across the titles. "What have we here? An investor?"

"Look at this. 'History of the Spanish fleets.'" She opened the file. Inside were documents of the sunken ships in the Gulf. Some of the ships were more recent vessels, and others dated back to the 1500s. "Wow, three of four Spanish ships sank in the Gulf due to a storm. They sank April 29, 1554, in the stormy seas. Listen to this, Bella; it was estimated the cargo on those three sunken ships would be worth millions of dollars today. Maybe that is what the plan was—to find the sunken cargo."

She closed the file and looked at the next one. "Hmm... 'Needed Funds.' Bella, this is a spreadsheet. Oh, these line items. Wow. Thousands of dollars needed for renting boats, equipment, even diving equipment. Someone wants to go down pretty deep and look for these boats."

Bella sat up in her bed beside Elaine's desk, tilted her head, and seemed to listen to every word.

She continued examining one file after another. The most significant files—the ones that caught her attention—had the titles "Sketches of Presumed Location" and "Treasures of the Spanish Fleet."

"Bella, I wonder if the people who came out and got the pieces of wood that we discovered dropped this memory stick? What do you think?"

But the next row of files changed her mind. "No, this thumb drive didn't belong to someone from the Texas Antiquities Committee. Listen to this file name, Bella. 'Potential Investors.'" She opened the file. Her mouth dropped open. "Look at this list of names! Adriana Manale, Trent Fortune . . . and even Billy Wrangle? I think this thumb drive belonged to Camillo. Let's see if we can find anything on here that identifies him. I think this was his secret plan to get money."

Bella, who had tired listening to Elaine's ramblings, laid down in her bed.

Elaine scanned the other file titles as her mind raced. *If this belonged to Camillo, I should talk to Mark tomorrow.* Then she found it. One of the files toward the end of the list of file titles. It would be the one that would confirm the owner of the file: "Plan to Sell to Investors."

She clicked the file open. And there it was. A simple plan to meet and socialize with the individual people on the list of investors. The file outlined the instructions. At the top of the file was a salutation: "To Teddy." The instructions provided strategies, such as go to the places the locals frequent, like the coffee shop on the main street in town. And at the end, there was a list of people to avoid for fear of being discovered. That list included Mark, the PI, Pastor Sam, and Elaine Smith.

Her stomach was in a knot. She mumbled, "It confirms it was for Teddy. But I still can't see how to confirm if it was Camillo's thumb drive."

She searched the last of the file titles. "Wait just a minute. Camillo would not have his name as a file title. Too obvious. I need to examine the contents of each file. Bella"—she looked at her sleeping dog—"it's going to be a long night."

Her phone buzzed.

Bonnie texted, "Well? What did you find out?"

"Still looking through the files."

"But you got it to work? It dried out?"

"Yes. I was able to open it. It has several big files saved on it."

"Can you tell who it belongs to?"

"Not yet. But I will keep looking. Might take me a while."

"Okay. I'm going to read and then sleep. See you on our walk in the morning?"

"See you then."

Elaine turned her eyes back on the files. Hmm . . . her eyes darted through the titles. *Short-term rental of film equipment. Short-term? Just for appearance, I suppose?* She opened the file and found the names of several companies in Texas. "Listen to this, Bella. A whole list of places like Video Equipment Rental Office, Panavision, Austin City Camera and Video Equipment, and the list goes on, Bella."

Bella didn't even move. She opened one eye and closed it again.

"Yeah, I know, not very exciting. Let me see."

She wondered if there would be any hint of the name Camillo. But Mark said Camillo had several aliases. She looked for any other names besides Teddy. If she found one, she figured Mark would know if it was an Alias Camillo used. *I'll just keep looking. Might have to open each file, even the ones that don't look like they would have any identifying information in them.*

Then she opened a file titled, "Project Estimates and Expenses." She examined the information. "Ah ha!"

She was not able to find the name Camillo. But the expense file included a list of expenses and contact information for the transactions. "Bella, I'll bet he didn't mean to leave this little tidbit on the contact information."

An estimate from a film rental company was attached to an email. There was no name, but there was an email address. The address was a mix of fifteen letters and numbers for the name, and the email domain was simply ".me." She examined it again. *Interesting. I'll bet Mark can track this down.*

She continued looking at the remaining files. The closest thing she found to a name was the unrecognizable email. She thought Mark must have a technology whiz who could track down the sender. Just to be on the safe side, Elaine copied the complete file onto her own computer. She feared at some point this evidence, the actual thumb drive, could be destroyed or stolen. It didn't take long to download it. She completed the download, ejected the memory stick, and placed it on her desk.

"That's enough for tonight, Bella." Elaine looked at the sleeping bundle of fur, who did not move.

Elaine turned off her computer and called it a day.

Chapter Fifteen

Elaine met Bonnie for their usual morning walk. The sky looked a little threatening to the north. Bonnie bounced down her steps out to the sand where Elaine and Bella were waiting.

"Well, I tossed and turned all night wondering about that memory stick! Did you figure anything out?"

"Not yet. But it contains several interesting files."

Bonnie looked at her step counter. "Let's get going before that storm blows in. The wind is turning cooler."

"It does feel cooler. We better pick up the pace; I feel the mist in the air."

"Okay. Double time! I think our walk will be cut short. Let's try a jog for a few minutes."

"Come on, Bella," Elaine said as she, Bonnie, and Bella picked up speed.

Between breaths, Bonnie said, "I think we have about five minutes before it hits. You'd better go back home, and I'll turn around and go home. Let's go into town for coffee, since we can't finish this walk."

"Pick you up in forty-five minutes?"

"Perfect," Bonnie yelled back to Elaine as she went back toward her own cottage.

Elaine and Bella almost made it back to her house before the rain started. "Oh, Bella! That is a cold rain. Come on, girl."

Once inside her cottage, Elaine turned and locked her door. She grabbed a towel and dried Bella. "There. I think you are dried off. Now, I need a hot shower!"

Within a few minutes, Elaine was showered and dressed in some warmer beach clothes. She grabbed a jacket and an umbrella. Glancing at her desk, she decided to take the thumb drive with her for safe-keeping. She wanted to know where it was at all times. She locked up her cottage and went out to her car. She started the car; and for the first time in weeks, she turned on the car windshield wipers and drove to Bonnie's cottage.

Bonnie texted, "Be right out."

Down the stairs, umbrella overhead, Bonnie bounded out to Elaine's car. "Was this even in the forecast?"

"Not that I know of. Glad you put on some warmer clothes. I guess we are going to have fall after all this year."

"So, it seems. Elaine, what are Adriana and Mary up to today?"

"I have no idea. I suppose they are both home. We didn't discuss any further plans the other day."

"Oh, what *did* you find out last night on the thumb drive?"

"I will tell you everything I found once we get inside the coffee shop. Here is a parking spot right by the door. Let's get coffee, and I'll give you all the details. And I think I could use some breakfast."

"Me, too. Alexa has those yummy egg bites. Great for my diet—no sugar and low carbs."

"Let's get inside."

With coffees in hand, Elaine and Bonnie took their usual seats by the window.

Bonnie glanced outside upon the empty street. "Nobody is out this morning in this weather. Hope the rain lets up."

"Me, too. But if not, it is a great day to drink coffee and write."

"I suppose. Now, spill it all. Every last detail. You said the file was interesting."

"Yes, it looks like there might be something the Camillo character put together."

"You think Camillo dropped it on the beach?"

"Here is the thing. There was a file inside, lots of files. But one was titled, 'Instructions,' and it was addressed to Teddy."

"You think Camillo was going to give it to Teddy; but before he could, Teddy left?"

"Maybe. But what I think happened is that Camillo gave it to Teddy, and it was Teddy who dropped it on the beach."

"That makes sense. Maybe that is why he kept walking on the beach. And what were the instructions about?"

"The instructions confirm what we suspected. Teddy was trying to get investors for the film project. There was a file of potential investors."

"Was Adriana on the list?"

"Along with Trent and Billy."

Bonnie gasped. "Trent, Billy, and Adriana? I'm . . . flabbergasted!"

"I was, too. It confirms there was a scam. At least, there was a scheme to ask people for money for their project. But I am puzzled."

"About?"

"I think the scheme might have been to ask investors to donate money for a film project, but the true plan was to use the money to find the Spanish sunken ships of 1554."

"Seriously? Sunken ships?"

"Yes. Three of the four ships went down in the storm that night."

"So, the film project might be just a scam. Bilk the investors out of their dough and use the cash to go diving for sunken treasure? Can't the authorities use this file to arrest Camillo for fraud?"

"Not that easy. I think we need something that ties the file to Camillo. Right now, it looks like the files of any treasure-seekers. And I know there have been plenty of people who chase after these sunken ships on treasure hunts. There is no crime in going diving for sunken ships. But there is nothing on the file that identifies Camillo as the owner of the files or the plans."

"Were there other plans?"

"Oh, the file was unreal. There were plans to rent equipment for the movie, boats, and for the dive."

"So, you're thinking it was all about sunken ships?"

"It looked like it to me."

The two women looked up at the ringing of the bell on the coffee shop door. It was Trent.

Trent ordered his coffee. His eyes scanned the coffee shop and paused at the table where Bonnie and Elaine sat. He nodded hello.

"Elaine, did you tell him to meet us?"

"No. Just good timing."

"Are you going to tell him what you found out?"

"Yes. I want his advice about what to do with the thumb drive. I'd like to turn it over to Mark and see if he can figure out more from the information."

Bonnie motioned to Trent to come to the table.

"Good morning, ladies. You two ventured out in this rain. Isn't it great weather?"

"I like it," Elaine said. "Makes if feel like a fall day."

Bonnie looked as if she would burst if she couldn't tell Trent what they found in the sand under the broken lightning whelk.

Trent zoomed in on Bonnie and asked, "Know anything good?"

"Tell him, Elaine."

"What's going on?"

"The other day, Bonnie and I walked on the beach; and she found something under a lightning whelk shell."

"Oh? What?"

Bonnie replied, "It was a memory thingy—uh, memory stick thing."

"I took the thumb drive to my house, dried it overnight in a bag of rice, and plugged it in after twenty-four hours."

"Did it work?"

"Yes. It was full of files about a movie project and sunken ships in the Gulf."

"Very interesting. Could you tell whose it was? Any names on it?"

"I am not sure we can prove it belonged to Camillo or someone in his scheme to commit fraud, but it did have names on it. It had one file about instructions for Teddy. And then there was a file about potential investors, including Adriana, Billy, and you."

Trent sat back in his chair, silent, and stared at his coffee. "He was going to attempt to scam me, too? He must not know I've dealt with this sort of thing before."

Elaine replied, "The instructional file had your name as one of the potential investors. I couldn't tell if the plan was to ask you for money or if he just listed people in Sabal Palms who might have the means to invest."

Bonnie rolled her eyes. "Of course, this scammer was gonna hit Trent up for money."

Trent swallowed a sip of coffee. "It makes sense if my name was on the list that Camillo, or whoever made the file, wanted to ask me to invest. I do invest in businesses, and he probably did his homework and knew I have invested in business interests in Sabal Palms and elsewhere."

Elaine said, "The only problem is I couldn't identify Camillo in the file. I only found one email address."

"An email address for Camillo?"

"I couldn't determine that. The email address was a scrambled line of letters and numbers, and the domain was"—Elaine made air quotes with her fingers—"'.me.'"

"One of those kinds of addresses. I see."

With a puzzled look on her face, Bonnie asked, "What kind of address?"

Trent replied, "Anyone or any business can register for a new email account under that domain called '.me.' That doesn't mean it can't be investigated. I think this might be a matter for Mark. He knows people in the field of forensic computer technology. They can track it down. Might provide evidence for a future arrest."

"Really?"

"See, Elaine? That thumb drive thing can help us! Tell him the rest—you know about the ships."

"There was quite a lot of information in the file about the Spanish sunken ships of 1554 in the storm."

Trent said, "I read about those ships. There is an exhibit in the Port Isabel Museum. I read somewhere that there were over a thousand golf coins missing and lost out at sea."

Bonnie said, "Guess I am going to have to visit that museum. Haven't been there in years."

"This all sounds very interesting, and we might be able to use it—or, rather, Mark might be able to. Tell you what. I'll text Mark now and see if we can meet. Can you bring the thumb drive to a meeting?"

"Happen to have it with me." Elaine tapped her purse.

"Want to come, too, Bonnie?" Trent asked. "After all, this is your discovery."

"Yes! This is exciting. I feel like I am in a true-life crime movie!"

Trent laughed. "Okay, then. Let's see if he can meet us today."

Trent text Mark and waited for a response. They finished their breakfast and coffee and chatted about the changing weather and the lighting of the Port Isabel Lighthouse for the first time in more than a hundred years.

Trent's phone buzzed. "He wants to know if you want to meet now on the island?"

"Okay with me," Bonnie said.

"I can drive us over," Elaine added.

The rainy day was unexpected but proved to be a great day for going over to the island without confronting vacationers. The streets were empty, and the parking lot at the restaurant overlooking the marina was all but barren. Elaine, Trent, and Bonnie rode together and parked near the front door.

A hostess opened the door and greeted the three guests. "Three for lunch?"

Elaine replied, "Four of us. Just for a coffee. We are meeting someone."

The aroma of freshly grilled fish filled the air. Trent remarked, "It smells delicious. I might have to have an appetizer or something."

Bonnie blurted out, "I will if you will. My egg bites had a short life span."

Elaine laughed and followed the hostess to a table by the window. "This is wonderful. The boats are still going out in the rain, see?"

Trent held the chair out for Elaine and Bonnie then took his seat. "Elaine, the shrimp cookoff is a couple of days away. Got everything already planned out? Need anything?"

Bonnie spoke before Elaine could. "Oh, you know Elaine. Everything planned and ready ahead of time."

Elaine smiled. "Yes. I think our plans of grocery shopping are completed."

"Good to know, but I will bring anything you think of at the last minute. Just give me a call."

"Thank you. Look, Mark is just coming in the front door."

Mark spoke briefly to the hostess and joined the group at the table.

"Hello, Trent, Elaine. And this is?"

"Hi, I'm Bonnie."

Trent elaborated, "Bonnie made the discovery and wanted to come along."

"Nice to meet you. Now, what did you discover?"

A waitress appeared and took the orders of the group.

"Thank you," Mark said to the waitress. The waitress collected the menus and took their order to the kitchen.

"Now, Bonnie, what did you find?"

Elaine took the thumb drive from her purse and gave it to Mark. "This. It was under a whelk shell on the beach."

Mark took the thumb drive and turned it over and over. "Have you tried to read it?"

"Elaine did," Bonnie replied.

"Did it work?"

"Yes," Elaine said.

"I'm surprised it wasn't wet."

"She dried it out," Bonnie noted.

"You did? Use the rice trick?"

"I did. Found out how to do it online."

"Smart. And what did you find on it?"

Elaine explained the various files—the movie project files, the instructions, the plans, and the invoice with the mysterious email address.

"Nothing that obviously said the name Camillo on it?"

"That is correct."

"I see. The address sounds like a possible lead. Is it okay for me to keep this? I'd like to give it to my forensic technology expert. I can send it to him as a compressed encrypted file. He should have some answers in a day or two."

"That would be great," Trent said. "We would like some answers and want to be sure these guys are not going to show up again in Sabal Palms."

"I don't blame you. And if this file of information will help the FBI find this Camillo, they will be excited. They have been trying to track this guy since he left the prison in Louisiana a few weeks ago."

"FBI?" Bonnie asked.

"Yes. My forensic contact has connections with the FBI. This would be a good discovery for them."

Mark ate his lunch; Trent and Bonnie ate appetizers; and Elaine sipped on a cup of coffee.

After the short visit, Mark stood to leave the restaurant. "Trent, I'll be in touch in a few days. Until you hear from me, it would be smart not to talk about this memory drive in public. If anyone connected with this scheme catches wind of it, they might come after it. Would hate for you to have a break-in or worse." Mark nodded, paid the waitress, and left.

Bonnie's eyes widened, and she turned to Elaine. "Guess we should keep this quiet."

"Yes," Elaine said. "The truth will come out soon enough—once we hear back from Mark."

The days passed, and the party at Elaine's for the celebration of the shrimp cookoff was scheduled for this evening. The girls planned to arrive an hour before the others and prepare the food and help Elaine with any last-minute details. They knew it would be a great evening of visiting out on Elaine's deck.

The weather could not have been better. The evening was warm enough for shorts, but the light breeze signaled the fall chill would settle in once the sun lowered below the horizon. The arriving guests brought their own lightweight jackets or sweaters and joined the party outside.

Adriana, along with her overwhelming fragrance and jingling jewelry, joined the others outdoors. "This weather is delightful! It will be wonderful for the shrimp cookoff tomorrow."

"That's what scares me," Bonnie said.

"What are you talking about?" Mary asked.

"If the weather is perfect, we can hang around all day and eat shrimp! We won't be too hot or too cold."

Mary laughed. "Isn't that the point? Isn't that why they have this the first weekend of November every year?"

"I think it is exactly the point," Trent replied. "I know I stayed all day last year. I think I ate food at fifteen different booths. Do you know how much shrimp I ate?"

Bonnie laughed. "As much as I am going to eat tomorrow!"

Mary scanned the group from one end of the deck to the other. "I have a question for everyone," Mary said. "Which booth was your favorite last year?"

The group fell silent.

Bonnie laughed. "No one is answering, Mary."

Trent spoke, "I don't remember."

Adriana waved her arms around. "Girl, I liked them *all*!"

Trent finished another bite of his appetizer and cleared his throat. "Looks like the only thing left is the sunset dinner cruise to mark the end of the fall season."

Adriana looked down and avoided commenting.

Elaine noticed Adriana's face and said, "Don't worry, Adriana. It will be fun, and it is a safe way to see the bayside and gulf at night. We turn around before we get to the gulf, but you can see it from there."

Trent said, "Hold on. I have an idea. And maybe this will make it easier for Adriana, too. If we wait another week or so after Thanksgiving, after all our families go back home, it will be time for the historic lighting of the Port Isabel Lighthouse."

Mary smiled. "That's right! We had planned to see it. What better way to see it than from the water? We will have the best view and avoid the crowds around the lighthouse."

Bonnie replied, "It's the perfect idea, Trent."

Billy chimed in, "I will make sure I'm in town. What is the date?"

Trent answered, "I think it is the first or second week of December. I'll look it up." He took his phone out of his pocket and entered the question. "Ah, it is December 9. What do you say? Should I reserve our spots on the catamaran dinner cruise?"

Elaine nodded. "I think it is a great idea."

"I'm in," Bonnie said.

"Me, too," Mary added. "Now, Adriana, we will all be there. We can see land the whole time. And the food and music will be great."

"Okay. I'll go."

The party continued for another two hours. The guests stood with small plates heaped with appetizers and tiny desserts. Elaine watched the sunset, put her lightweight sweater on, and said a prayer of thanks for her dear friends. The party concluded, and the guests agreed to look for each other the next day at the shrimp cookoff.

A record number of attendees participated in the shrimp cookoff, and there were a record number of booths as well. Elaine and her friends walked from booth to booth tasting each contestants' recipes. At the end of the day, the group decided once again that they had no true favorite dish but liked all the sampled items.

One by one, Elaine said her farewells; and she and Bonnie drove back from Port Isabel to the beach at Sabal Palms.

Bonnie opened her car door and stepped out. She leaned her head in and said, "I guess our next big event will be the lighting of the old lighthouse in a few weeks?"

"Yes. And then, we can begin thinking about Christmas."

"Oh! Don't rush it! It will be here soon enough, and we will have more parties to plan and attend—and the parade and the lightings all around."

"Yes, it will be another whole party season."

Bonnie closed the car door and waved. Elaine waited to be sure Bonnie was safely inside. Since the sightings of Teddy weeks ago, Elaine always made certain Bonnie was home safely.

She drove home that evening, took Bella for a short walk, and prepared for church and her search committee meeting the next day.

At last, she was able to sit at her desk and write. A mix of emotions filled her heart. She was torn between relief and trust knowing that the immediate fear of Teddy and Camillo seemed to be gone and the insecurities of what the future might bring. Would these schemers return? Would the search committee interview the right candidates to take the place of Pastor Sam? Would the rest of the fall season be peaceful and safe?

She hammered away on the old typewriter until 2:00 a.m. She turned off the typewriter and her desk lamp and got ready for bed.

Chapter Sixteen

The next morning went as planned. Elaine, Bonnie, and Bella took their usual walk along the beach, enjoying the pink and purple clouds projecting out from the orange ball of a sun over the horizon. The water was calm, inviting the shore birds to scavenge the shallow water for food and the pelicans to dip into the water for breakfast.

Elaine called Bella. "Let's go back home. Bonnie, want to walk to church? I will need to stay after for the search committee meeting."

"Okay. Weather is great for walking. See you in about an hour."

"Sure thing."

Elaine ate a quick breakfast, fed Bella, showered, and dressed quickly. She patted Bella's little head and locked the cottage. She met Bonnie, and they walked at a good pace to the Church on the Shore.

"I see we are here before Adriana and Mary," Bonnie said.

"We usually are," Elaine confirmed.

Trent and Billy walked in shortly after Elaine and Bonnie.

Trent nodded. "Ladies, good morning."

"Hi Elaine, Bonnie," Billy added.

"Good morning, Trent, Billy," Elaine said.

Before the music began playing, Adriana's clicking shoes and floral aroma announced that she and Mary had arrived. They walked to their usually seats near the front of the church.

"Isn't this a beautiful morning?" Adriana said, arms fluttering about.

"It is," Bonnie said.

Trent's phone buzzed. He read the text and passed his phone around. "Here, Elaine, Bonnie, take a look."

The text was from Mark. "Heard back from forensics expert. Email was a burner email account. No longer functioning. Probably established by Camillo but no way to trace. No evidence of Camillo's whereabouts. FBI continues to hunt."

"I don't understand. I thought for sure the memory stick would help find this Camillo guy," Bonnie whispered with a disgruntled face.

Elaine shrugged her shoulders and in a low voice uttered, "Guess we don't know anything more than we did before you found it."

The music started and the congregation rose to their feet. Pastor Sam walked in and took his place. He sang along with the congregation; and when the first song ended, he took the podium to make the usual weekly announcements.

"Good morning! God is good"

And the congregation said, "All the time!"

"I want to make a few announcements before we begin. First, the search committee will continue their work this morning."

Bonnie huffed under her breath, "That's nothing new."

"Shh . . . " Elaine admonished.

Pastor Sam continued, "And I wanted to let you all know, I am rethinking my decision to leave. Some factors in my situation have changed. I will make the final decision in the next week or so; and if the congregation will be patient, I can make an announcement next week."

A loud applause erupted. Elaine knew this would take the pressure off the committee and the candidates. She knew the committee would be able to find a good candidate, but the best candidate was standing before the congregation at that very moment. Elaine was anxious to hear all the details in the committee meeting.

Pastor Sam gave an amazing sermon, and the entire congregation left smiling. The congregants loved their pastor and did not want him to leave. Each person took their time greeting Pastor Sam at the door as they exited. When Elaine shook his hand, he said, "Elaine, I think the committee was relieved to hear my announcement."

"Yes. You know we don't want you to leave."

Pastor Sam leaned into Elaine and in a low voice said, "I am rethinking the idea of moving. I will meet with you all in a few minutes and explain."

A smile burst across her face.

"Let's keep this between us until our meeting in a few minutes."

Elaine knew that Pastor Sam did not want her to say anything to Bonnie and the others. But now, her curiosity was getting the best of her. She had to stop herself from asking more questions.

Bonnie followed Elaine down the steps. "What was that all about?"

"Not sure. I might find out more in my meeting. I'll talk to you later."

The search committee gathered in the conference room and waited for Pastor Sam. He had told each one not to start the meeting until he had time to speak to the group.

He entered with a smile spread across his face. "Thank you all for agreeing to serve. I know you have screened the candidates and completed the telephone interviews last week. My announcement to the congregation was honest. I am considering all my options, and one option is to stay here."

Elaine's mind jumped ahead.

"Let me go into details about what is happening. Once you leave today, you may tell others in the congregation if you like. You are free to do so. I had a phone call yesterday that made me very happy. As you know, my son lives up in the northern part of the state. His family, his wife, and his children are the reason I had entertained the call from a church in the town where he and his family live. My son called me last night to let me know that he has been interviewed for and offered a position here in Cameron County. If he accepts the position, my reason for moving north will be moving here. He is going to talk with the company a little more and make up his mind. He is leaning toward taking the job."

The search committee simultaneously clapped.

"That is all for today. No need for the committee to get into the search further until I have made a final decision. I will have my secretary call each of you this week and let you know if the committee will continue this work next week or if I will remain. Thank you for your support and patience as my family and I pray about this decision."

Elaine's heart was full and her stress relieved. She knew that Pastor Sam's final decision was not yet made; but for some reason, she believed he would decide to remain here at the Church on the Shore.

She said her goodbyes to the other committee members, and each one agreed that they felt as she did. This would likely be their last meeting to consider finding a replacement for Pastor Sam. She turned and walked back to her cottage. Then her mind shifted to the text message Trent had received from Mark right before the sermon began. There was still no way to know where Camillo and Teddy, or Theodore, were. She prayed they were far away from Sabal Palms and that no one, especially Adriana, would have to be bothered by those characters ever again.

Bonnie was sitting on her deck enjoying the sunshine. She waved for Elaine to stop by when she walked closer to her cottage. "Come on up."

Elaine knew she was free to tell Bonnie the news. "Hey. Getting some sun?"

"Yep. Come on. Spill it. What is going on with Pastor Sam."

"He told us we can spread the news."

"So do it!"

"Hold on. Let me get up there." Elaine walked up the steps to the deck.

"Let's have it already! You sure know how to make a person anxious."

"Okay. Pastor Sam wanted to move north to be with his son and his son's family."

"Knew that already. Tell me the good stuff."

"His son has been interviewed for a position here in Cameron County."

"Get outta here!"

"He hasn't accepted yet but will make his decision this week."

"So, Pastor Sam might just stay here after all?"

"Yes, he said his son is leaning toward accepting the offer."

"That is terrific news! And the committee might not have to meet next week?"

"That's correct."

"Wonderful! You going to call the others and let them know?"

"I can, or you can if you like."

"Hold on." Bonnie took her phone out of her pocket and dialed Mary's number.

Elaine listened to Bonnie explain the news to Mary and then to Adriana. She heard Adriana's scream through the phone.

Bonnie hung up. "I still can't believe it!"

"Me either. But I prayed a prayer of thanks all the way from the church to your cottage."

"Nice to know we might not have to change. I like things just as they are."

"Me, too. Okay, I'd better go tend to Bella. Call me later if you want to get together for dinner or to go to town."

"Will do."

Elaine stepped inside her cottage door and greeted Bella, and then her phone buzzed. *Probably the others wanting to talk about Pastor Sam*, she thought as she looked at her phone.

It was Trent. He sent a group message to everyone. "Meet at the coffee shop tomorrow around 10:00? Need to plan details of sunset dinner cruise."

"Yes," Elaine texted back.

It was only after she read Trent's text that she realized the sunset dinner cruise had slipped her mind. Since her party before the shrimp cookoff, she had not heard anyone else mention the dinner cruise and assumed they, too, were preoccupied with talk of PIs, crimes, fraud, and, of course, the search committee business for Pastor Sam. It would be a terrific way to say goodbye to fall and hello to the Christmas season. The evening temperatures were a few degrees cooler, making it a perfect time to spend a couple of hours out on the water.

The others in the group replied with the word yes or the thumbs up emoji. She was glad to see Billy would be able to join them.

The next morning, Elaine picked Bonnie up after their morning walk. They drove into town. "I can't believe the fall season is nearly over. Just Thanksgiving and our dinner cruise left. Before long, the streets in town will be decorated for Christmas."

"Have you prepared anything for your son's visit over Thanksgiving?"

"Not yet. I will be spending the next couple of weeks getting ready. You know what gets me about Thanksgiving?"

"What is that?"

"I shop for weeks. I check my recipes at least a thousand times . . . well maybe not quite that many times. I get all the ingredients ready. I cook ahead for days making sugar free desserts and everything else healthy. And then, bam! It is eaten in twenty minutes, and then I clean up for two hours!"

Elaine laughed. "That is a good description."

"Now, I'm not certain about this, but I think Jack might be bringing a girl."

"What? Now that is big news, Bonnie! Why didn't you say so before?"

"He has hinted around; but to tell you the truth, I couldn't tell if he was sure she was coming with him."

"Oh, Bonnie, how wonderful! Then maybe in the future, you will be a grandmother."

"Fiddlesticks! I'm not old enough to be a grandmother. Good grief!"

Elaine laughed. One thing Elaine had noticed about Bonnie. As Bonnie got older, she became spunkier; Mary, on the other hand, seemed to be mellowing a little. But they still bickered when they were together. "Well, here we are. Let's see if the others are here yet."

"I see Mary's car. Hey, don't you mention anything about Jack and a girlfriend. Don't want to start any rumors."

"Your secret is safe with me."

The group gathered around the table with their coffees; and Adriana, late as usual, bounced in and ordered her fancy coffee drink.

Bonnie's eyes rolled, and she tilted her head. "There she is."

Mary said, "She texted me a while ago and said she was not ready. She was putting on her makeup."

"Of course she was," Bonnie said, rolling her eyes.

Billy and Trent laughed.

The heels of her strappy sandals clicked all the way to the table. "Good morning, darlings. How is everyone today?"

"Doing well, thanks," Trent said.

"Much better knowing Pastor Sam might stay," Billy said. "I just don't know what this community would do without him."

Mary added, "He has helped many people, and he is very active in the wildlife groups."

Adriana sat her coffee cup down, and a touch of whipped cream remained on her nose.

Bonnie touched her own nose and said, "Psst, Adriana."

"Oh," she wiped the whipped cream off with a napkin. "That is why I should always use a straw. Hold on." She clicked her shoes at a rapid pace back to the stand with the napkins and the straws, picked up a straw, and returned to the table. "Now, go on, sorry."

"We were just talking about Pastor Sam," Mary noted.

"Yes, I am thrilled he might stay. I know you are, Elaine."

"It will be wonderful if he makes that decision. I should be getting a call in a day or so after his son decides if he is moving here."

Adriana touched Elaine's arm. "You must tell us right away."

"No worries. I will."

"Now," Trent began, "I contacted the dinner cruise first thing this morning. They do have enough remaining seats for the whole group on the day of the lighting of the Port Isabel Lighthouse."

Mary said, "Outstanding!"

"You know, I have played for the dinner cruise captain a time or two. I will check and see if he already has the entertainment lined up."

Elaine smiled. "That would be wonderful. What time and where do we show up?"

"The reservation is for 4:00 p.m."

"That seems early," Bonnie said.

"Yes, I thought so, too," Trent continued, "but it takes that long to get everyone checked in, loaded on the boat, and finally leave the dock. The catamaran will depart that day from the dock at Lobo Del Mar."

"That is near the causeway, right?" Elaine asked.

"Yes. I can swing by and pick you up, Billy, and you ladies want to meet us there a few minutes before 4:00?"

"Yes," Mary said. "I can drive us over."

"I'll pick Bonnie up and be at your place around 3:15. That should give us plenty of time to get across the causeway and be there before 4:00."

Adriana held up her coffee cup. "Cheers! I think we have a plan."

The next day, Elaine got the call. Pastor Sam would stay at the Church on the Shore. It was a relief, and Elaine felt a weight had been lifted from her shoulders. She texted the group, and replies poured in.

"Wonderful!" Mary texted.

"Terrific!" from Bonnie.

"My stars!" Adriana responded.

"Thank God!" Billy replied.

"Great news, thanks, Elaine," texted Trent.

With the matter of Pastor Sam resolved, Elaine was able to turn her focus to writing and planning Thanksgiving. The days passed by following the usual routine and were as predictable as the tides. Since the four women and Trent and Billy each had their own family plans over the Thanksgiving week, Elaine did not see anyone for almost ten days. She enjoyed her family time with her son and daughters.

After Thanksgiving passed, the next event was the sunset dinner cruise. But until then, the days were routine. Elaine and Bella walked with Bonnie in the mornings; and every few days, one of the girls would offer a quick dinner get-together. Trent and Billy met them at the coffee shop a couple of times each week. Elaine was at peace. There was a smooth rhythm to her days, and she appreciated the tranquility. She appreciated no surprises. And that is just when the unexpected happens.

Chapter Seventeen

Elaine woke earlier than usual. Even Bella seemed to know today was different than other days. She jumped around in circles, excited to go for her walk before their usual time. The big day had arrived. It was the day of the lighting of the old lighthouse in Port Isabel. Elaine knew she and Bonnie would not meet Mary and Adriana until later in the afternoon, but she was excited already.

She got dressed for her morning walk, and she and Bella left for Bonnie's cottage just as the sun was rising above the horizon. "Let's go get Bonnie."

In just a few minutes, Elaine and Bella were approaching Bonnie's cottage.

"Hey!" Bonnie yelled out from her porch.

Elaine and Bella walked in the sand at a quick pace. "Good morning! You excited about today, also?"

"Yes, I am. I know we don't drive over until a little after three, but I am already eager to get over there. What's not to love? Sailboat dinner cruise and the lighting of the lighthouse in Port Isabel."

"Quite a day."

"I read the flyer about the old lighthouse. Picked it up at the coffee shop."

"Oh?"

"Yes, it is amazing. I did not realize it was built back in 1852 because there were so many shipwrecks out in the water," Bonnie said.

"Hard to believe the ships couldn't see the land and would run aground—"

"Or into each other. And of course, if there were storms out at sea it guided them back in."

"Did the flyer give information about the light itself? What is so special about this particular kind of light?"

"Oh, that is the cool part, Elaine. It is an old type of lens. And the lighthouse hasn't been lit in 177 years!"

"You are a wealth of information this morning. Any other tidbits of knowledge you want to share?"

"I am pretty smart. I surprise myself with all my knowledge." Bonnie laughed. "But yes, how about this fact? I read the lighthouse is seventy-two feet high. It was decommissioned in 1905."

"You will have to share this information tonight when we are on the sailboat," Elaine suggested.

"Speaking of the dinner cruise, do you think Adriana will be okay tonight?"

"She will be fine if we can keep her mind off Antony's death while he was deep sea fishing. You can distract her with your facts about the lighthouse."

"Good idea. When we finish our walk, I will read the information from the brochures and the newspaper. It is quite the talk in the local paper and the tourist brochures."

"Great. If we see she is having a hard time, we will change the subject."

Later that day, Elaine took out her capris and a Hawaiian shirt. She turned to Bella. "What do you think? Does this say dinner cruise when you look at it?"

Bella wagged her tail.

"I'll take that as a yes."

Elaine dressed, fed Bella an early dinner, and put the remote to her car into her purse. "Okay, girl. I will be home later this evening."

Bonnie was waiting on the porch when Elaine pulled into the drive. She hopped down the steps and got into Elaine's car. "Let's go!"

"Nice outfit."

"This is the new shirt I bought the day we took Adriana on our outing."

"It looks great with those capris."

Elaine and Bonnie would ride over to the island with Mary and Adriana. Elaine hoped Adriana would be in good spirits.

Adriana and Mary were waiting by Mary's front door when Elaine parked the car. The look on Adriana's face told it all.

Waving her hands about, Adriana said, "Let's get going, ladies! The sailboat awaits!"

Bonnie glanced at Elaine and mumbled, "She's in good spirits."

The women chattered across the causeway. There was little traffic, and they arrived dockside a few minutes early. Trent's car turned into the parking lot.

Mary nodded toward Trent's car. "There they are."

Billy took his guitar case from the backseat of Trent's car and greeted the group. "Good afternoon, ladies. Are you ready for a sail around the bay?"

"I'm past ready!" Mary said.

Trent motioned toward the boat. "I think they are expecting us. Ladies first."

Bonnie bounded ahead of the others and the group formed a line up the steps of the dock. When they arrived dockside, one of the dinner cruise guides stepped out from the cabin. "Hello. Welcome. This looks like Mr. Fortune's group. Come aboard."

Elaine examined the situation. She stepped aboard and asked, "Do we pay you now?"

The guide explained, "It's taken care of."

Elaine looked at Trent, who replied, "I am hosting this party—my gift since I didn't host a party on the island this year."

"How sweet of you. Are you sure?" Elaine asked.

Trent nodded. "Yes. Step aboard."

Elaine realized this group of six would have the entire catamaran to themselves. What an unexpected pleasure. She didn't mind sharing the cruise with tourists, but being able to have a private party would be more relaxing; and after the past couple of months with the unpredictable events of Teddy and Camillo and the close call of Pastor Sam announcing a departure, which he later canceled, she could use a night of relaxation.

The captain, other crew members, and the chef stepped out from the cabin and took their places around the various parts of the boat. One of the crew members untied the boat from the pier and gave it a push out into the water. The sails were hoisted upward, and the small motor started up to maneuver the sailboat away from the shore and out into the bay.

Elaine watched the crew busily take their stations and work the sails. She was amazed at their size and how each sail caught the slight breeze that pushed the boat further away from land.

The captain introduced himself. "Welcome aboard. I am your captain today. My name is Captain Skip. Looks like good sailing tonight. You all get situated. Take a seat at the bow"—he motioned toward the front—"or head of the boat. As you know, this is an historic day in Port Isabel, and you all will have one of the best seats to view the lighting. I will announce when the lightkeeper will turn the lantern on inside the lighthouse."

The captain put his hand on a man in a white shirt with a white hat on his head and continued the introductions. "This is Chef Tommy. He will be working down in the galley this evening."

Chef Tommy waved and ducked back into the cabin.

The captain continued. "Chef Tommy told me our menu tonight is shrimp kabobs with pineapple for an appetizer, and our main course will be platters of beef and chicken fajitas with all the trimmings."

Elaine followed Mary and Bonnie to a netting area between the two hulls. Elaine pointed forward. "Great view from here."

Billy took his guitar from his case. "Are you ready for a little music?"

"That would be terrific," Elaine said.

Chef Tommy could be heard in the galley preparing the appetizers and dinner. The smells ascended to the passengers on the sailboat.

"Tommy, that smells positively scrumptious!" Adriana exclaimed.

More clattering of cooking utensils rang out. "Be ready soon."

As the group and crew ate Chef Tommy's offerings, Elaine inhaled the beauty of the open gulf that could be seen in the distance past the boat channel. She nudged Bonnie. "Never gets old, does it?"

"Never. I could jump on this sailboat every day of the year, except in stormy weather!"

"Speaking of stormy weather," the guide began, "let me tell you about what the stormy seas churned up and pushed right out here into our little area of the bay and the gulf coastal waters." She told stories about the Gulf Coast and the history of the waters during the exploration by the French and the Spanish explorers. "And those ships and their unknown valued cargo sunk right out there." She pointed. She then recounted the history of the Gulf Coast during the Civil War. She explained the events during World War II. And in no time at all, the boat was sailing all about the bay.

Bonnie nudged Elaine. "Looks like the guide is keeping Adriana's attention. Do you suppose that was the direction—the area of the Spanish sunken ships—that the infamous Camillo wanted to scavenge?"

"Shh . . . don't let Adriana hear you."

Adriana listened to the details of the stories with amazement and gasped when the guide explained the World War II Nazi submarine activity in the Gulf of Mexico.

But Mary's enthusiasm centered on the natural wildlife above and below the water. "Look at those dolphins!" Her eyes were fixed on the water and noticed any ripple of movement.

The group listened to the stories, laughed, visited, ate, and watched the remarkable sunset over the water. But the most anticipated part of the evening would soon take place. In ten minutes, the Port Isabel Lighthouse was about to be lit for the first time in 117 years.

"What is that noise?" Mary asked.

Adriana motioned toward the shore. "Sounds like it is coming from the town of Port Isabel."

Billy stopped strumming his guitar and listened. "I think they are cheering—or maybe . . . is that clapping?"

"Must be about time to light the lighthouse," Trent offered.

The captain said, "May I have everyone's attention please?"

All heads turned to listen.

"It is exactly one minute until the lighting of the lighthouse. Let's pause and take a moment and remember all those lost at sea before the lighthouse was built. We forget that at the time it was first used, it was considered the best technology for guiding the seafaring ships and souls safely back to the coast."

In the blackness, Elaine saw only the stars over the water, a few lights of the ships at sea, and the lighted establishments in the distance on the shore around the bay.

A bright, piercing light shone directly out over the water and swept across, scanning every inch of the water.

All on board gasped in awe.

The captain said, "I have never seen anything that beautiful over the waters here."

The light swept around and across once again.

After several sweeps across the water, Billy began playing his guitar once again and sang his newest song written and dedicated to Elaine. Adriana, Bonnie, Mary, Elaine, and Trent sang along. At the end, they clapped.

Billy strummed another song, and another, as the light beamed across the water and swept around repeatedly. The passengers on board sang the songs, many of which had been played on the radio for two years now. The group clapped after each one.

As Billy began his next song, the group initially began singing along. Bonnie stopped singing. "Elaine," she whispered, "did you hear that?"

"What?"

"Splashing. Right over there."

The light scanned around. "See? Right there."

Elaine looked out and saw a boat. "It's just a boat."

The light went around once more. Frantically, Bonnie tapped Elaine's shoulder. "No, look. Look!"

Elaine searched, and then she saw what Bonnie was talking about. "It's a man . . . Wait! He has a gun to another man's head! Captain! Look!"

"What?"

By now, Billy had stopped playing; and the eyes on board all turned to see what the fuss was about.

Captain Skip reached for his binoculars. He looked briefly. "I'll radio the coast guard. We'll head back away from the range of the gun."

The captain went to the navigation and picked up the radio and pushed a button. "Sector Laguna Madre, Mayday, this is the *Coastal Breeze Catamaran*. Mayday. Armed man on unidentified boat just to the north of our position. Our position . . . " The captain checked his instruments, reported the longitude and latitude into the receiver, then turned to the passengers and added, "We have eleven souls on board, six guests and a crew of five."

"A gun?" Adriana screeched. "A gun?"

Mary scooted nearer to Adriana and put her arm around her. "It's okay, Adriana. We are getting out of here. The captain has it under control."

Adriana made blubbering noises, stopping every now and then to blow her nose with a loud honking noise. Elaine heard her mummering, "A gun, a gun." She prayed Mary would be able to calm Adriana down.

And then, a shot was fired. It rang out across the water, followed by a loud splash of someone entering the water out by the boat.

"ACKKK!" Adriana screamed. "He shot the gun! He shot it!"

The captain pushed the radio button once more and repeated the message. A member of the crew sent up a flare.

Adriana screamed and cried uncontrollably. Mary squeezed her as tightly as she could and attempted to quiet the screaming.

The splashing in the water continued and seemed to grow louder.

Elaine scanned the water and watched. She looked at the boat now with only one man on board. The man on the boat stood and shone a flashlight in the water and appeared to be searching for the person he shot. With no luck, he turned, pulled in some equipment from the water, and went to the motor of the boat. He attempted to start the motor, but it would not turn. It sputtered and then made no noise whatsoever. He yelled indistinguishable words and tried the motor again.

Bonnie touched Elaine's arm. "Listen. Shh . . . Adriana, quiet. Listen."

The splashing got closer to the boat. A whimper of a voice cried out.

"I think I hear something," Elaine said.

Adriana still murmuring in Mary's arms.

Then, it was clear. The voice sputtered a weak, "Help. Help."

"There," Elaine pointed. She vaguely made out light reflections of splashing in the water. The captain pointed a flashlight and then threw a buoy out to splashing.

The captain and crew assisted pulling the rope and towing the person in closer. "Help. Please. Help me."

Elaine wondered if the swimmer was a criminal or a victim or just someone in the wrong place at the wrong time.

The loud whirring of helicopter blades spinning overhead now stirred the water into ripples. The lights from the helicopter surveyed the water. A loud voice boomed, "This is the U.S. Coast Guard."

The captain waved at the coast guard and pointed with his flashlight to the other boat in the bay. The helicopter continued moving toward the other boat. The man holding the gun looked up. "This is the United States Coast Guard. Drop your weapon. Drop your weapon. We have a sight on you. Drop your weapon."

In the distance, Elaine saw a man go to his knees. She squinted and looked at the man, now lit by coast guard bright lights. "Camillo," she whispered.

The crew pulled the buoy next to the boat and assisted the man on board. A dripping man was provided with heavy towels, and he wrapped them around his shoulders.

Captain Skip said, "Are you hurt? Are you shot?"

"No, he missed."

Captain Skip pointed to the deck. "You sit right there until we can figure out what is going on. Don't move."

One of the crew members returned with a sidearm on his belt. He watched the man's every move.

Elaine watched the whole scene.

The man sat, staring down at the deck of the boat, and did not move. Elaine kept her eyes on him. He sat on the deck near the cockpit, and Elaine could only see his silhouette from where she sat on the bow of the boat. But there was something familiar about him. She felt her stomach begin to knot. He turned his head and looked around. His eyes focused on her. "Elaine?"

Chapter Eighteen

Elaine looked closely at the man. He seemed familiar, and then she made the connection. Of course. It was Teddy.

"Yes?" she guardedly asked. She was afraid he recognized her, and she did not want to speak to him.

"I know you. I looked you up. I need to talk to you."

Elaine's stomach was cramping even worse. What could this charlatan possibly want with her? And Adriana, just a few feet away, would be completely undone with his presence on board. She wanted to be kind, but her heart was hard. He represented a threat to her and the whole group on the boat. She didn't trust him.

"Trent," Elaine whispered, "Camillo was the man on the boat out there."

"I'll notify Mark and the authorities. The FBI will want to know the coast guard has him in their custody."

The captain overheard the conversation. "Trent, you know the man in the boat?"

"I know *of* him. He is wanted by the authorities. I don't know much about this guy, Teddy."

Teddy listened and pled. "Wait, Trent. It is not what you think."

Captain Skip said, "I'll let the authorities figure it out. Until then, remain where you are."

The crew member with the sidearm stood by Teddy, who was seated on the deck and wrapped in towels.

Adriana peered over Mary's shoulder every few minutes and studied Teddy. Following each glance, she whimpered again.

The sailboat turned and headed back to the dock. The bright light from the lighthouse at Port Isabel scanned around. Elaine glanced back at the smaller boat and saw the coast guard had Camillo in handcuffs. The coast guard took over the boat. A larger coast guard boat pulled alongside the smaller one and tied it to tow back to the base. Two officers escorted Camillo to the deck of the coast guard boat.

The radio blurted, "Captain Skip. We have the suspect in custody. Do you need help?"

"Negative. Going into port now. Over."

"Over."

The captain then radioed South Padre Police and asked dispatch to send a patrol car to the dock to pick up Teddy.

The sunset dinner cruise had started off just as expected. It had ended in a manner no one would have ever imagined. The sailboat's motor rumbled along through the boat channel and meandered back to the pier where the cruise began. The group remained quiet as if they feared saying a word with the strange Teddy in their presence. The South Padre Island Police were waiting for Teddy at the dock when the dinner cruise catamaran pulled up.

Once the crew assisted each passenger off the boat, the captain shook Trent's hand. "I will see that you are refunded your tickets."

Trent shook his head. "No, no. You spent your time, and we used your fuel and ate that delicious food. More important, you brought us safely back to shore. I wouldn't accept the money, so please, don't refund the cost of the cruise. We will try it again sometime. The events were not in your control."

"Thank you, Trent. Let me know if you need a cruise outing for your businesses, family, or friends again in the future."

"Thank you, Skip."

Billy followed the ladies off the boat, and they said their farewells.

A sense of relief overwhelmed Elaine when she opened the door to Mary's car and settled in the back seat. Bonnie bounced in on the other side. Mary got in the front of her car and started the engine. She looked at Adriana, who wiped her eyes with a tissue.

Mary patted Adriana's hand. "It's okay, Adriana. Tell you what. You girls want to come inside my house for a bit of dessert and coffee? I have decaf."

Bonnie said, "That sounds like a great idea."

Elaine agreed. She believed it would help Adriana to have a bit of time with her friends before she went home alone.

Mary's house felt like Elaine's home away from home. She attributed the feeling to the weeks they had stayed with Mary during Hurricane Jada. She felt safe in Mary's house during the times when the storm was barreling down on her own house. She remembered how Mary's roof had barely been disturbed, while her own had been ripped off in several places and Bonnie's house was almost a total loss.

"Come in, girls. I'll put on a pot of decaf."

"That light was a sight to see," Bonnie said. "It was mindboggling."

Elaine looked at Adriana's head bent down looking at her tissues. "Adriana." Elaine put her hand on Adriana's. "Our sunset dinner cruise was different than we had hoped for. But it is just like life. We have joyful times and sorrow. We all face disappointments and even grief. We have all lost our husbands. I know being out on the water tonight reminded you of past events and how you lost your husband, Antony."

Adriana's eyes, full of emerging tears, were glued on Elaine.

"And we all lost our husbands due to illnesses. It is still hard sometimes to go into a hospital, funeral home, or cemetery without taking me back to those dark days. But we—all of us here—have made it. We rely on God and our faith. I suppose tonight was more difficult for you, Adriana, because of your recent reminders of the mob and your husband's brutal death."

"Yes, I think you are right," Adriana agreed. She sniffed and wiped her eyes.

Mary toddled to the table balancing cups of coffee for each one.

"But look around. We are four strong women. We read the Bible together. We go everywhere together. We cry on each other's shoulders and even visit our husbands' graves together. We trust each other. And we will do anything to help each other. We are a family of our own."

Adriana smiled, got up from her chair, and hugged each woman. "Thank you. Thank you all for helping me. It was hard facing the idea that someone—this Teddy—was up to no good and I was the target this time. I feel better knowing that he and Camillo have been taken in by the authorities."

Bonnie stood, went to the counter, and took a platter of desserts back to the table. "You forgot these, Mary. You aren't having slippage now, are you?"

The group all chuckled.

"Absolutely not!" Mary retorted. "In fact, I have another tray of desserts—sugar-free, of course—in the fridge, smarty-pants."

"Well . . . what's the hold up?" Bonnie demanded.

The women laughed as they sipped their decafs, and everyone ate two desserts.

After more than two hours, Bonnie said, "Elaine, it is getting late. I'm ready to fall into bed."

"You're right. And poor Bella."

"Oh, that pooch! You worry more about her than any of us!"

"That's not true," Elaine protested. "I worry about her just as much as I worry about you."

The women laughed. Elaine asked, "Adriana, will you be okay to go home?"

Adriana waved her hand dismissing Elaine's worry. "Oh, yes. I am looking forward to being home."

"I'll check on you first thing tomorrow," Elaine said.

"I'll be fine, but thank you."

"You certain?" Elaine asked.

"Yes, thanks."

Bonnie stood and walked with Elaine to the door. They said their farewells and went back to their beach cottages.

The next day, Elaine slowly opened her eyes. She squinted and peered out from her bed through her window. It had been an unusually late and eventful night, and she felt every bit of it. She looked out the window. "Bella, we slept in."

Elaine checked her phone. No message yet from Bonnie. She texted her. "Bonnie, just getting up."

"Me too. Having a cup of coffee. Take your time. See you in a few."

"Come on, Bella. We will get a walk in-just be a little bit late."

Bella followed Elaine around the cottage and ate a bit of her food. She looked up at Elaine.

"It's okay. We will go out in just a minute."

Throwing on her walking shorts, Elaine took a few quick gulps of coffee. "Ready, girl?"

Elaine took her time walking down to Bonnie's cottage. Bonnie had yet to appear on her deck. "Looks like she is having a hard time, also. Come on, girl."

Elaine and Bella walked up the wooden steps, and she knocked on Bonnie's door. "Bonnie."

"I'm coming. Hold your horses—and your mutt."

Bonnie swung the door open. "Goodness. What a night, huh?"

"It was different."

"Not what I expected at all. Good grief! Well, you know, hold on, let me lock up." Bonnie turned and locked her door. "Like I was saying, remember Mark saying how these bad pennies always show up again?"

Elaine nodded.

"Anyway, let's get walking." Bonnie checked her step counter. "Okay. It looks like Mark was right. That Teddy guy and Camillo turned back up."

"Yes, but it doesn't make sense."

"It doesn't matter. Those two scallywags got arrested."

The two women walked; and Bella skirted around in the waves, then darted back in and chased the birds.

"Okay, spill it. What do you mean? What doesn't make sense?"

"Why did they just disappear and then reappear again?"

"Who cares, for crying out loud? They left and came up with some scheme and then showed back up again to pull off the heist."

"But how? According to the thumb drive you found, it looked like they needed money to do a dive."

Bonnie stopped and put her hands on Elaine's shoulders. "Just stop. It doesn't matter. They found another source. Maybe that Camillo guy robbed another bank. Who cares? What we should be concerned about now is poor Adriana. I hope she is okay today. We should check on her later and see how she is doing."

"Good idea."

The women walked north on the beach. Bonnie pointed ahead. "At least we don't have to worry about those scoundrels showing up on our beach again."

"I suppose." Elaine felt like her legs were slow and her feet were dragging. "I'm sorry, Bonnie. I am still tired. You?"

"Yes. I think this walking is helping . . . but not very much." Bonnie chuckled.

"And I think another cup of coffee will help me. Have you walked enough steps for this morning?"

Bonnie looked at her counter. "Yes, I'm good. Let's turn around."

Back at home, Elaine put the lock on the door. "Okay, Bella. I'm going to shower and then go check on Adriana."

Bella sauntered over to her bed and laid down.

A short time later, Elaine, showered and dressed, picked up her phone and called Adriana. "Good morning. How are you doing this morning?"

"Doing well, thank you. I was about to run out to the coffee shop and meet Mary. Come on over if you like. Bring Bonnie."

"I'll check with her. We will probably see you there in a few."

Elaine hung up and text Bonnie. "Mary and Adriana going to coffee shop. Want to meet them there?"

"Sure."

"Okay. Pick you up?"

"No, I'll come over."

She gathered her purse and car remote; and as she opened the door, she said, "How did you get here so fas—"

There before her, with his hand in the air as if to knock, stood Teddy.

Elaine was startled. "Oh!"

"Sorry, Elaine. I did not mean to scare you."

"What are you doing here?" She realized she sounded harsh, but the words spilled out as if she had no control over her mouth.

"I am sorry. Elaine, I just want to explain."

"Explain what? We found the thumb drive with all of the instructions—"

"Wait. That is what I wanted to explain. I didn't know it was all a scam. I believed Camillo's whole story. I was down on my luck. I thought I would work one last job for him, and then I would walk away. I had lost my job and wasn't able to find work. Along comes Camillo with these ideas. He wanted to use me just like he wanted to use Adriana and Trent."

"I'm listening."

"When I opened the thumb drive, I got to thinking. Why did he instruct me to *avoid* talking to you and Pastor Sam? If it was a true documentary, wouldn't he want to ask you to help out, too? And Pastor Sam might have had some useful information about the history of this place, the water, and the sunken ships."

"What about your name? Why were you going as Teddy Carter?"

"That was Camillo's idea. He said I needed a new name for my producer image. I went along with him, thinking he knew best how to do this. That was before I looked at his files of instructions and figured it all out."

Elaine paused for a moment. He looked desperate. "Go on. What else do you want to say?"

"I started doing my own homework. I read all about you online. I read how you turned people's lives around during the hurricane when people found your writing."

"People's lives were changed. But it wasn't me. It was all Divine intervention that helped those people."

"I know—the Holy Spirit. I read some of your devotionals that changed peoples' lives. And that is when I decided maybe you could help me to turn my life around."

"Is this also a scam?"

"I understand completely that you don't trust me. But I was going to come clean and walk away from this idea. I didn't want any part of it."

"If you figured out that Camillo's plan was a scam, why were you on the boat with him last night?"

"I had no choice."

"What do you mean?"

"He came for me. I left the area and went back home as soon as I figured out it was a scam. I went back to Louisiana, and he showed up at my place. He knew where I lived. He knew everything about me and how badly I needed a break. He found my house and forced me at gunpoint. He made me get into the car with him. He cuffed me in the car, and I was stuck like that. We drove back down here all night. Then yesterday, we checked into a hotel; and I got to thinking of how to escape. But he always kept the gun with him. He cuffed me to the bed until it was time to go out on the boat. Look, you can check with the police. He even told the coast guard the truth after he was captured last night. He confessed to everything."

"Hold on. This is too much to believe."

"I know you don't want to trust me, but I want to apologize to you—to all of you."

Bonnie came up the steps and knocked on the front door.

Elaine opened the door and invited Bonnie inside.

"What! Elaine are you okay? What is he doing here? Scoundrel!"

"Tell her," Elaine said to Teddy. He repeated the whole story once again.

Bonnie's mouth gaped wide open. She was speechless. She didn't close her mouth for at least ten minutes while Teddy explained the whole story.

"After I apologize to all of you, there is only one more thing I want to do before I leave Sabal Palms."

Bonnie, still shocked, asked, "What? Want to go dive for treasure before you leave?"

"No, nothing like that. You must believe me. I am changed. I know I am forgiven. I accepted Christ and want to change the way I live. I have Elaine to thank for that. I read all about her, and I read her work."

Bonnie looked at Elaine, "Well, it looks like you saved another one."

Elaine shook her head. "No, not me. It is all Him." She pointed up.

Bonnie smiled and said, "Can we trust you now Teddy? Not like last time we thought we knew you."

"I promise. The one thing I want to do now is . . . well, I want to ask Pastor Sam to baptize me."

Elaine said, "I think we can help you with that, right, Bonnie?"

"Sure. Elaine, let's see if Sam is around this morning and can meet us at the coffee shop. Okay with you, Teddy?"

"Yes, thank you. I would like to visit with Pastor Sam. And will the other ladies be there? And Trent?"

"Adriana and Mary are on their way. I'll see if Trent can join us," Elaine said.

The next Sunday, Teddy gave his testimony in front of the entire church. The congregation applauded. It was one of the most memorable Sundays Elaine could remember.

As the congregation filed out of the sanctuary, Teddy stopped Elaine and asked, "What do I do now? Is it okay to celebrate? I feel like shouting off the rooftops!"

Elaine said, "Isn't it wonderful?"

"Never felt anything so good, ever!"

Adriana said, "I think we should gather for lunch."

Mary nodded. "Yes. Let's do."

Once again, the group made plans to bring food, fun, laughter, and love to lunch. Elaine said a prayer of thanks for her relationships, both old and new. She thanked God for her ability to use words to reach people and turn them to Christ. She prayed she would be able to continue to bring people to God for a very long time.

The story made the newspaper and the local television news. The news was picked up by the network news and was broadcast all over the United States. By the time it made it to the national news, it was no longer a story about a heist, a scam, a conspiracy gone bad. The story didn't elaborate about ships that had sunk during a storm. The story didn't mention deep sea dives or even the historic lighthouse. The story was about a woman living in Sabal Palms who continued to save wayward souls. The story was about the little Church on the Shore and how an unlikely baptism took place. And finally, the story was told a nation of people hungry for faith and the belief that all things are possible with Christ.

About the Author

Terry Overton is a retired university professor of educational and school psychology. She has an Ed.D. in special education and a Ph.D. in psychology. Her professional experience includes teaching public school, teaching at the university level, and being a college dean. She has two children, seven grandchildren, and one great-granddaughter. She seeks to answer God's call to share the good news and grow the church by writing Christian books and devotionals. Her books have won the Mom's Choice Award, Christian Indie Award, Firebird Book Awards, American Writing Winner Awards, Bookfest Winner Awards, Pencraft Award, Reader Views Silver Reviewers Award, and International Book Award Finalist. Her writing examines real world events with a Christian worldview. She enjoys writing for young children, middle grade readers, YA fiction, and adult level novels.

For more information about
Terry Overton
and
Sabal Palms and the Stormy Past
please visit:

www.terryovertonbooks.com
www.facebook.com/allthingspossiblewithhim
@terryoverton6

Ambassador International's mission is to magnify the Lord Jesus Christ and promote His Gospel through the written word.

We believe through the publication of Christian literature, Jesus Christ and His Word will be exalted, believers will be strengthened in their walk with Him, and the lost will be directed to Jesus Christ as the only way of salvation.

For more information about
AMBASSADOR INTERNATIONAL
please visit:

www.ambassador-international.com
@AmbassadorIntl
www.facebook.com/AmbassadorIntl

Thank you for reading this book. Please consider leaving us a review on your social media, favorite retailer's website, Goodreads or Bookbub, or our website.

Rob Wilkinson, a Christian man from Northern Ireland and an avid world traveler in his spare time, finds himself traveling alone on the second anniversary of his wife's untimely death. But through a couple of seeming coincidences, he meets and befriends Gabby, a young woman from Germany dealing with heartaches of her own. As their relationship deepens, Rob must draw on his recently-tested faith to help Gabby overcome her own lapsed faith in God and find a new life beyond her pain.

David al-Nassery is a man of renown. Hailing from distant Chaldea, he has made a name for himself in the United Kingdom as a philanthropist and an advocate for the political interests of the Middle East. Yet even as he surrounds himself with allies, enemies from his past await him. When confronted by a figure from his past on a cold, dark night, David is forced to reckon with the decisions he made in Chaldea—choices that cost thousands their lives.

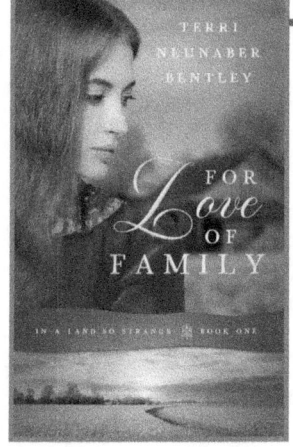

When Lena Neubauer is sent from Germany to America to help her immigrant brother on his farm and with his young children, she never expects what awaits her in antebellum America. With family honor and devotion propelling her across to an unknown world, Lena soon finds herself stepping into this strange world. After tragedy strikes, Lena finds herself finally at the crossroads and must make a decision that will affect her future—and her family's future—forever.

www.ingramcontent.com/pod-product-compliance
Lightning Source LLC
Chambersburg PA
CBHW070104030726
47506CB00002B/590